Feathers in the Wind

Helmut Stefan

BeachHouse Books

Chesterfield Missouri USA

BeachHouse
Books

www.beachhousebooks.com

Copyright

Library of Congress Cataloging-in-Publication Data

Stefan, Helmut, 1942-
    Feathers in the wind / Helmut Stefan. -- BeachHouse Books ed
    p. cm.
    ISBN 978-1-59630-061-3 (alk. paper)
    I. Title.
    PS3619.T444F43 2010
    813'.6--dc22

                                        2010004420

BeachHouse Books

www.beachhousebooks.com

an Imprint of
Science & Humanities Press
PO Box 7151
Chesterfield, MO 63006-7151
(636) 394-4950
www.beachhousebooks.com

To the family:

Ingrid

Heidi and Edward

Peter and Shannon

Proverb:

There are three kinds of people: Those who make things happen, those who watch things happen and those who don't know what's happening.

- American Proverb

Feathers in the Wind

Helmut Stefan

Stories

American Tolstoy

$\mathcal{T}$ he fact that there isn't much to do in this town makes it all the more agreeable to me. I moved here five years ago, and I have never yet been bored.

My name is Leo Fischer. I am an accountant at Burberry and Sons furniture store. The name of the company is a little misleading because old Mr. Burberry died more than twenty years ago, and the oldest son, Victor, got divorced and moved away. So now there is only one son, Samuel, who runs the store. But that is not really true either because he is not in most of the time (he's a drinker), and his wife does the best she can to keep the place going. I do all the invoices, pay the bills and prepare the payroll. The whole operation consists of six people. Business is kind of slow, and there is not really much for me to do. And that's the way I like it. You see, by profession I am an accountant. That pays my bills. But deep down inside, I fancy myself as a writer.

A writer, an author – call it what you will, it sounds great, doesn't it? A writer is a god, a creator, and an omnipotent being. He (or she) can create characters at will; make them happy or sad, heroic or cowardly, noble or evil. They can live lives that he can only dream of; they can speak through him, be like him or what he would like to be. Then again, he can make them the exact opposite of what he stands for. He can build up and he can destroy. He can draw from his past experiences or just imagine things. It is a glorious feeling to create, to philosophize and to preach. Through his characters, the author can say whatever he wants to say. If he is ever questioned, he can always simply reply, "Oh, that is just the fictional character speaking, that isn't really me." And who can argue with that?

You have probably noticed by now that I like to speak, but mostly I speak with myself, through my writings. This is why I like my job. This is why I like this town. Neither expects very much from me, and I can spend my time thinking, dreaming and writing.

During the summer months, I like to go to the river. There, where the little stream takes a rather sharp turn to the right, the Park District created a small park with a playground for children and a short river walk along the river's bank. Here, they have planted a row of willow trees and, about thirty feet apart, three benches have been placed from which there is a pretty view of the slightly more elegant houses on the other side of the river. This is where I like to come and sit, always on the center bench (it gets the best shade), and look across the river. I dream, think and scribble in my notebook. I usually stay until it gets dark, and then, I go for dinner at Bob's Pub.

Although I consider this park to be the prettiest part of town, most people don't really visit it. Once in a while, there is a couple sitting on one of the benches, holding hands and whispering softly to each other. A family might come to one or the other of the benches, and the children may feed the pigeons. But usually I am all alone out there, and that is why I like this place so much.

Well, at least that is the way it used to be. This year, once the weather had gotten warmer, another daily visitor came to this quiet spot. This was an old man. I'd say in his mid seventies. He would come slowly walking down the gravel path, walk past me, and then sit on the farthest bench, the one on my right. He would sit down carefully, stretch out his legs and spread both of his arms over the backrest of the bench. He would sit this way motionlessly and look across the river. Now and then, I would see him close his eyes, and only his heaving chest would indicate that he was a living, breathing man.

After he had walked past me almost daily for about two weeks to take his seat on the far bench, he began to nod his head at me and say "Hallo." I would nod back and say, "Hello, how are you?" He never answered and trudged on toward the next bench. He always wore the same brown corduroy pants and checkered shirt, with the top button always buttoned. Even when the weather was quite warm, he would wear a dark blue jacket. He wore the same ankle-length boots every day, and I could for the life of me not determine their original color.

One day when I saw him approach, I noticed that both of the other benches were occupied. What would he do? He realized the situation when he had already gone past me. He stopped suddenly, still facing forward. Then, he turned around slowly and looked past me at the first bench. Finally, after he had stood there for a few seconds, he walked slowly toward me. I moved a little further to one side to make it clear to him that he was welcome to join me. Just before he reached the bench, he stopped and looked at me with his eyes moving toward the empty space next to me.

"May I?" he said softly.

"Please, do," I answered in the most pleasant voice I could muster.

He sat down slowly, but now, he did not spread out his arms across the backrest. His feet were firmly planted on the ground. He folded his arms across his chest.

"Nice day, isn't it?" I began. I felt that I needed to start the conversation. After this rather bland opening, I was going to leave it up to him to speak as much or as little as he wanted, but I simply could not imagine him to be a very talkative person.

"Yes, it is beautiful," he said slowly, with what I perceived to be an Eastern European accent. I looked down at my notes. Now it was up to him to continue, if he so desired.

We sat quietly next to each other, each one looking out onto the river. Suddenly, I heard him say, "What is that what you do? You write something? What you write every day? Pardon me."

I turned half way toward him. "Oh, this." I said. "Yes, I write something. I'm trying to write a story."

"Have you written many stories?" he asked.

"Yes, I've written quite a few," I answered truthfully. "They are usually very short. I have them at home in my desk."

"Are you a writer?" he continued his questioning.

"No," I said with a chuckle in my voice, "I am an accountant. I only do this for fun and relaxation."

A minute or two had gone by before he continued, "So, what do you write about?"

I thought about that for a moment. "I write," I said, "about people who are in some kind of special situation, and then I give the story a sudden twist at the end that the reader probably did not expect, although throughout the

4

story I drop hints in that direction. A careful reader will know where I'm heading, but I still want there to be an element of surprise, even for him."

He sat there not saying anything. Suddenly he looked up. "My name is Yuri Sewchenkov," he said, and he held out his hand toward me.

I smiled. "I'm Leo Fischer, glad to meet you."

"Your name is Leo?" he asked. "And you write – then you are the American Tolstoy," he continued. I could see his satisfaction with having come up with this connection.

"Don't I wish," is all I could say.

We both looked across the river again and did not say anything. I wrote a few more lines in my notebook – I did not want to force a conversation on him. If he wanted to talk, then he should be the one to take the lead.

"And may I ask," he began politely, "what are you writing about now?"

I usually don't like to discuss my stories until they are finished. Most of the time I don't like to talk about them at all and hardly anyone knows that I write anyway. The people at work do, but they don't ask me about it anymore.

"It is a story about a woman," I told him, "who had a very difficult childhood growing up in the country. Very poor. She's plain looking, not very popular at school. Her parents love her, but they hardly ever show it. After she finishes high school, she moves to the city to start a new life. She is convinced that here everything will be better. After all, with so many people around, she should certainly be able to make some friends, and maybe even find someone special who will love her. This is where I'm at right now. But I don't know what to do next. Should she find happiness, or should she be disappointed here, too? I know everyone likes a happy ending, but that is not always the way things work out, do they?"

The man was silent for a while, and then he said, "Yes, I see you have a problem, but I am sure that you will find the right ending. I wish you luck." He slapped both of his hands on his knees and slowly got up. "I will go now," he said, "but I will see you soon."

He walked away slowly and I followed him with my eyes until he disappeared around the bend in the gravel road.

The next day he was on the bench before I arrived. As I came closer, he stood up and with an elegant motion invited me to sit down.

"Well," he said, "how is the American Tolstoy today? Hard at work?"

"No," I said, "just the usual. Nothing ever changes."

"Maybe that is good," he replied. "If life is good, then it should not change. Unfortunately, everything changes; everything always changes. But now you must write, and I will be quiet."

"That's all right," I said. "I don't mind talking."

"Okay, so tell me, have you found an ending to your story yet, happy or sad?"

"No," I replied. "I still don't know what to do. That is my problem. I never really know what exactly to write about, and when I think I have a story, it falls apart about halfway through. I don't know where to go with it."

He nodded. Then, he asked slowly, "You do not know what to write about? I do not think that should be so difficult." He looked at me, and his eyes were challenging me to refute him.

"That is easy to say," I said, "but just try it. Go ahead and just try to write something that is original, fresh, entertaining and interesting and yet believable and true to life."

He thought about that for a little while.

"Do you see that old lady walking over there across the grass?" he began out of nowhere.

I nodded.

"You should speak with her and ask her about her life." He paused and looked in her direction. Then, he continued, "And do you see that man with the tiny dog? Go speak to him. I am sure that both of them could tell you about their lives, and you would have a wonderful story. Everyone's life story is interesting." He looked at me expectantly.

I thought about that for a minute, and then, I answered, "Sure, everyone has an interesting story to tell. It would at least be interesting to them. But for everyone else? I don't know. And that wouldn't really be literature, would it? That would just be retelling someone's life story. Is that what a writer really wants to do? Where is the imagination? Where is that great idea and powerful ending? The writer should be an artist, and I don't think there is much artistry in simply retelling someone else's story."

He looked down. "I see," he said softly. "You are an artist, and so you must do something artistic. I understand."

We sat there for a little while and talked about the weather and how soon it would be winter and we would have to stay indoors. He said that he hated the cold; he had enough of it in his youth. He grew up in a small village in Russia, he told me, and during the winter there was only one heated room where the family gathered in the long evenings. The bedrooms were not heated. The only warmth for him came from his two brothers who shared the bed with him.

He stood up with a sigh. "Perhaps I will see you tomorrow, but after that, I do not know. The cold is not good for me. Good-bye, my American Tolstoy, and do not worry, your story will come."

I did worry, however. I was hopelessly stuck in my plot. I wanted to continue because I did have a lot of time invested in this story, and if I did it right, this could still turn out okay.

The next day he arrived about fifteen minutes after me. He barely nodded at me and sat down. After a while he began, "Well, my American Tolstoy, have you decided what to do?

I told him that I had not.

He sat quietly for at least five minutes. Then, he turned to me slowly and said, "Do you mind if I tell you a story?" I told him that I did not mind at all. As a matter of fact, I was happy that he wanted to talk to me. It was obvious to me that he did not have too many people to talk to.

"How do you Americans begin?" he started. "Is it once upon a time there was…" he held the last word.

"Yes," I said, "that is how many stories begin. Usually, these are fairy tales."

"So let me tell you this story," he said slowly. He took a deep breath. "Once upon a time there was a boy in Russia..."

"Excuse me," I interrupted, "but does this story have a name? Is there some kind of title to this story?"

He looked down and thought for a while. Then, looking straight across the river, he said, "If you must have a title, then I will call this story The Man Who Killed Four People." He paused, but since I did not say anything, he started over again. "Once upon a time there was a boy in Russia, as happy a boy as he could be in those times. He went to school for eight years, and then he worked in the fields. His life was all right for him, but someday later he hoped to move to the city, learn a real trade, make some money and maybe get to see more of the world. When he was seventeen, he told his father that he would stay one more year. After that, he would take his meager savings and move to the city. The father gave his consent, and the mother cried. Before the year was over, however, the great second war had begun, and the young man had to report to the army. It was in the year of forty-four, the young man and his fellow squad member Vladimir were sent out on patrol one dreary afternoon. It was said that a platoon of German soldiers had been cut off from their battalion, and they had to be found, captured or killed. Vladimir and the young man walked slowly toward the West, as they had been instructed, always seeking cover behind tree trunks as they moved through the forest. Their guns were ready in their hands. Suddenly, they heard a sound in the stillness. They listened. From behind a clump of bushes there came a moan, actually more of a whisper. Vladimir went to the left, the young comrade to the right. As they came around the bushes, they immediately saw the origin of the sounds. There, on the ground with his back against a birch tree, sat a young German soldier. His arms hung limp along his body.

He had no weapons. As he heard the two Russians soldiers approach, he opened his eyes. He did not say anything, but his eyes spoke more clearly than if he had been perfectly fluent in Russian. He was young, very young, and his eyes said, 'Please, don't kill me. Please, don't let me die here.' Vladimir looked at his companion, and both of them, as if some secret message had passed between them, pointed to the bushes and Vladimir whispered, 'Paspieshi! Paspieshi! Let's go! Let's go!' The German tried to get up, but he couldn't. The two Russians slung their rifles over their shoulders, grabbed him under his arms and dragged him into a shallow ravine, which was surrounded by small pine trees. There, they left him and continued on their mission. They had hardly moved fifty meters when suddenly they heard footsteps and subdued voices. They stopped. A few seconds later Lieutenant Kaczynski appeared; he had four men with him. 'Have you seen a German soldier?' he asked gruffly. 'We think he is injured. He has to be here somewhere.'

The two soldiers were both too honest and too afraid of Lieutenant Kaczynski to lie to him. He had a reputation for being the harshest officer in the division.

'We heard some noises over in that direction,' Vladimir said timidly, as he pointed to where they had left the German, 'but we thought those were our men.'

'Stay here,' the lieutenant hissed at them, as he and his men took off toward the pine grove.

Vladimir and his companion stood frozen. What should they do? What could they say? Before they had time to give it any more thought, they heard a shot, then another. Could it be that the German was armed?

And then, Lieutenant Kaczynski and his men were back. He still had his pistol in his hand. 'You,' he shouted hoarsely, 'you did this.' His face was red as a beet. 'We know what happened. You let him go.' And as he raved on, he moved his pistol between Vladimir and the other soldier. 'You are traitors,' he screamed. 'You protect the enemy,' and without any warning, he pulled the trigger twice and Vladimir slumped to the ground without making a sound. Then the lieutenant turned toward the other man and pointed the pistol at his chest. 'You,' he said, 'you run as fast as you can and don't ever let me see you again. But do tell the other men that this is the way we treat traitors here. Tell them, go tell them,' he bellowed, and the young soldier ran as quickly as he could back to the base camp. But he did not, not ever, tell his comrades what had happened there in the woods."

The old man stopped and looked at me. I remained silent. I sensed that he had more to say.

"Yes, you are right," he continued, "the story is not over yet. The young man returned home safely from the war. But there was not much to come home to. Both his mother and father and one of his brothers were dead. The oldest brother was engaged to be married, and that left our young man totally alone. The one thing that continuously went through his mind was, 'I have to get away from here, anywhere but here, and most of all to America. If I could only get to America, that is where I could begin a new life.' And through a friend on a nearby farm, who had relatives in America, he was able to get someone to sponsor him to come to this land." The old man stopped. He looked at me and asked, "Are you tired yet of the story? Am I boring you?"

I assured him that the opposite was true. I was most eager to find out how this story would end. I had also told myself to pay very close attention to what he was saying to see if he would drop any hints whether this story was really about him.

"If I am not boring you, then I shall continue," he said, and he turned to look out across the river again. "The young man came to Cleveland. Here, he found work in a factory that made parts for various machines. He liked his work, and he learned fast. After a few years, he was promoted to be the foreman. His income was not bad. And then, the best thing in his life happened. He met Izabella, a Russian girl who had also come here just a few years ago. They fell in love and soon they married. She also worked in a factory. Their combined income was good. They had a refrigerator, a television, and yes, even an air conditioner in their window. For them, it seemed they had everything they needed, and so it seemed, at least for a while. It did not take Izabella very long to realize that something was troubling her husband. He would sit sometimes for hours without saying a word. At other times, he would become angry without any reason, and he would yell and scream and sometimes even throw things. His wife would ask him many times what was troubling him, but he would only shake his head or say sadly, 'You would not understand.' They both felt that perhaps a child would make a change in their lives, but that was not to be. Gradually, Izabella, so lively and outgoing, also became sad and disappointed, and the two of them lived in the same house, but not really together." He let out a deep sigh. "Shall I continue?" he asked without looking at me.

"Yes, yes, please do." By now he had me totally involved in the story, even though he told it in such a plain and simple way.

"They lived like this for twelve years. Then suddenly, she died. It was probably cancer, but then, the doctors did not know so much about it, or at least they did not say very

12

much. So, now he was all alone again, and he was no longer such a young man. He went to work every day. Sometimes, he would drink with some of the men from the factory, but he did not make many friends. He did not want any friends. When he retired, he sold everything in Cleveland and moved away. Now, he lives in a small town and watches the seasons come and go. And soon he will be gone, too." Now he turned toward me again. "Well, that is my story. What do you think?"

"It is a very good story," I answered, "but there is something I don't understand." He looked straight into my eyes. "You told me," I continued, after it was obvious that he was not going to say anything, "that the title of the story is The Man Who Killed Four People. Even if we assume that the man felt that he was responsible for the death of the German, the death of his fellow soldier Vladimir, and the death of his wife, which I don't think he should …"

"What," he interrupted, "you do not think he should feel responsible? Yes, is that what you feel? That is how it is nowadays. No one is to blame. No one is responsible. Things happen, bad things happen, and no one is to blame, no one is responsible." He was breathing heavily.

We sat quietly for a moment, then I continued, "You told me about three people, but where is the fourth person he supposedly killed, who is the fourth dead person?"

The old man turned to face me. His eyes were fixed on mine. Then he looked down and said softly, "Not all dead people are in the ground. Oh no, there are many of them who walk among the living. They are dead in their hearts and their souls, and the sad part is, that most of them have killed themselves." He looked up again. "You do not have to pull the trigger or stab someone in the heart to kill a person. It is often more what you have not done than what you did that does the damage. And yes, it does not take much to kill yourself."

We both sat there for just a moment, and just when I was about to ask him a question, he slapped his hands on his knees again and stood up. Somehow, he seemed smaller and frailer than I had pictured him before. An ever so gentle smile hushed across his lips.

"It is cold," he said, "and I must go. I do not think that I shall come here any longer, at least not this year. Maybe I will come next spring – who knows. And you, my American Tolstoy, have no fear. The right story will come. And when it is here and here," and he pointed to his head and to his heart, "then you will know that this is the right story for you. This is the one that you must write."

He took a step closer to me and held out his hand, and as we shook hands, he gently patted my arm. I wanted to say something, but he had already let go of my hand and turned away. He walked slowly down the gravel path, and I stood there watching him until he was out of my sight.

I sat down again and tried to collect my thoughts, but all I could do was think about that story. I sat there and looked across the river until it was almost completely dark.

Then I left too, but this time I did not stop at Bob's Pub for dinner. I went straight home. After I had taken off my shoes and jacket, I took my notebook and put it on the writing desk. I pulled out the shredder that I store underneath it, and as I fed one page after another into the crunching, gnawing mouth of that hideous machine, it seemed to me that it was laughing at me – a cruel, bitter, almost obscene laugh – as it spit out strip after strip of unintelligible, meaningless pulp.

The Dinner

here was simply no way around it. I had to go to Miami on December 30 and 31 to meet Mr. Fujima from our Tokyo office.

Not seeing him in person, when he had come all this way from Japan, would have been an unforgivable insult to the head of our Asian Operations. I dreaded telling my wife Iris the news because I was quite sure that she would not be too keen about me having to go out of town on New Year's Eve.

When I told her about my business meeting that evening at the dinner table, she closed her eyes and leaned back in her chair. I watched her closely for a sign of how she was going to take this news. I breathed a sigh of relief when I saw a smile form on her lips. She looked at me and said, "You know, that's not so bad. Actually, that's not bad at all. Paul and Bernice are going to Hawaii over the holidays, and John and Barbara are going to visit his sick mother in Oregon. So, this is what we'll do. Marc and I are simply going to go with you. A few days in the sun will do us all some good. What do you say?"

"What do I say? That's a wonderful idea," I replied enthusiastically. "Why don't we go a day earlier and do some sightseeing. On the 30th you'll just have to occupy yourselves, and on the 31st I'm sure we'll finish early, and then, we can still have a nice afternoon and evening together. We can come home a day or two later."

And that is what we did. Our two-year old son Marc was the most excited of all of us. Although he did not understand where we were going, he did understand that we would fly in an airplane and that later he would be able to play in the sand by a real ocean.

Our first day in Miami was delightful. We spent some time on the beach where Marc loved playing in the sand. Once in a while, he would run up to his ankles into the water. He would then scream with delight when the gentle waves splashed against his knees.

Later, we strolled through the South Beach area. My wife, a great fan of Art Deco architecture, could not get enough of the magnificent buildings, which stand here almost one next to the other. In the evening, we ate at one of the fine restaurants in the Lincoln Road Mall.

I spent the next day with Mr. Fujima and his assistant going over every possible aspect of our business in Asia. As always, Mr. Fujima was extremely well prepared and had all the figures ready for my perusal. I would, of course, share these with the other top people of our company. There was no doubt about it, our company could definitely expand its activities in Asia for at least the next ten years – there was considerable money to be made there.

When Mr. Fujima and I parted that evening, we had covered everything we needed to discuss. He told me that he would retire early this night and leave first thing in the morning.

The next day we enjoyed the city again. There was so much to see and do – and everything under a bright, warm sun.

"This is definitely not Ann Arbor, Michigan," my wife said at least three times that day, and we both giggled like little school children. Marc took everything in with great interest, but the warm sun also tired him out, and we had to carry him quite a lot that day while he slept.

We were back at our hotel at five o'clock, and Iris and I also took a little nap. Two hours later, when we were both wide-awake again, the question about dinner was raised.

"You know, it is New Year's Eve", my wife reminded me, "and I think we should do something special. Let's go to a place where we can have a nice meal and where there is music and dancing. When Marc gets too tired, we can leave. Let's make this night special, a real celebration." Iris looked at me with such enthusiasm that I knew any resistance would be futile.

I went downstairs and asked the concierge whether he knew of a place where we could have a lovely dinner with live music. He made one phone call after another, but he always hung up with a discouraged look on his face, while he shrugged his shoulders. Finally, after what seemed to have been an endless number of calls, he looked at me and gave me the thumbs up sign. He listened intently to the voice at the other end.

"Just a moment," he said. Then, he turned to me. "Tuscany, a real nice place – Italian. They had a cancellation. Two hundred dollars per person, everything included. Yes or no?" I did not think long about it. If I turned this down, we would probably wind up in some second rate restaurant and be back in our hotel room way before midnight. I knew that Iris would be disappointed. To be honest, this is not how either of us wanted to spend New Year's Eve.

"Sure," I told the concierge, "sure, tell them we'll take it. We'll be right there."

Twenty minutes later our taxi stopped in front of a chic looking restaurant on Washington Street. "You're going to like it here," the taxi driver told me as I put the fare plus a generous tip in his hands. "All the big shots come here to eat."

The inside of the restaurant was even more impressive than the outside had suggested. The main dining room was dimly lit – white tablecloths on the tables, heavy leather chairs, and expensive paintings on the walls. In one corner, there was a little stage with a piano where the band was obviously going to set up a little later.

The three of us were led to a table along the right side wall. I was happy to see that we were not that close to the stage, because I do not enjoy having music blast directly into my ears. I like to be able to speak with the people who are with me. I also thought that if Marc got really tired, Iris and I would still be able to enjoy the evening while he slept, and Marc did not like loud music either.

The young woman who had led us to the table pulled out a chair for Iris. Then, she moved over to pull out a chair for me while I waited with Marc on my arm. Before I could sit down, a waiter had approached our table carrying a high chair. I stiffened. This might turn out to be a problem. Marc did not care for high chairs. He usually began to cry and kick with his feet. We mostly wound up having him sit on a chair between us while we fed him from our plates.

18

"I don't know if this is going to work," I told the young lady.

She looked at me apologetically and explained, "Our policy is that if a child sits in a high chair, there is no charge for the child. If, however, the child occupies a regular seat, then the child is served the same meal as the adults and the charge is the same. You have been told, I am sure, that tonight's special menu is two hundred dollars per person."

She looked at me as if to say, 'So, what are you going to do?'

I glanced at Iris, but she only shrugged her shoulders. I had to think fast. Should we simply leave? The expression on Iris's face made it clear to me that she wanted to stay. I now turned with Marc on my arm so that he could see the high chair. The waiter smiled and motioned to Marc that this was indeed a very comfortable seat; he should just try it. Marc turned to me, then back to the high chair. His little nose turned up, and the tiniest furrows appeared on his brow. He turned back toward me and pressed his little fists against my chest. Did this mean yes or no? Was he going to make a scene? I was quite willing to let him sit on a regular chair; the money did not make any difference any longer. I just wanted all of us to have a wonderful New Year's Eve celebration – but for just a second, I could not help but think that a two hundred dollar meal for a two-year old child, who probably would not eat any of it, was an outrage. This bordered on the obscene.

At that very moment, Marc turned away from me again and said, "Da, Da," while he pointed to the high chair. I did not hesitate a second and deposited him gently in the seat. The hostess immediately placed a colorful cone-shaped paper hat on his head. Iris and I did the same, and Marc squealed with laughter as he banged his little hands on the snap-in tray in front of him. I took one of the favors on the table in front of me and blew into it in such a way that the end of it barely touched Marc's nose. He tried over and over again to catch it with his chubby little hands. Then, I let him blow into it, and after every successful uncurling of the paper, he laughed as loud as he could.

The evening turned out to be delightful. The food was excellent, and every time we set our empty wine glasses down, they were immediately refilled with an excellent red wine. The wait staff was most attentive, but not overly intrusive – just the way Iris and I like it.

The little ensemble that began to play after dinner was wonderful. A fairly young lady played the piano; a slightly older man played an accordion; a white-haired gentleman – easily the star of the show – played the mandolin. As the musicians played, they would sing in English, but also in Italian, old favorite songs that everyone knew. Soon, many people sang along. Quite a few people filled the little dance floor. Iris and I, with Marc on my arm, joined in on the dancing, as we laughed and sang and swayed with the music. A very friendly elderly couple at the next table offered to watch Marc for us so that my wife and I could dance by ourselves, too. We took advantage of this offer and danced as happily and romantically as we had not done in a long time.

The time flew by, and before we knew it, it was time for the countdown to the New Year. Marc was wide-awake as we sang Auld Lang Syne and wished each other, and the people around us, a joyous and healthy "Happy New Year."

The evening had been a complete success – as a matter of fact, it was the most beautiful New Year's Eve party we had ever experienced. A generous tip for a friendly wait staff was our sign that we had thoroughly enjoyed ourselves.

Marc fell asleep in the taxi on the way back to the hotel. Iris and I also went to bed immediately after we had returned to our room. In less than a few minutes, we were all sound asleep. I had forgotten what a wonderful exercise dancing could be.

The clock on the nightstand showed 4:17 when I awoke. I felt Marc on my right and heard his little whistling noises as he breathed deeply. Iris was not on the other side of the bed. I saw just a hint of light coming from the washroom door, and then I fell back asleep again.

I woke up again at 7:24. A glimmer of light shone through the curtains. I closed my eyes and tried to go back to sleep, but I knew very well that I would not succeed. I normally get up a little after five – this was way past my usual get up time. I slowly moved the covers from my body and slipped cautiously out of bed. I hoped that there would be a newspaper outside the door. I would just read in the washroom until Iris and Marc woke up. I opened the door gently, but there was no newspaper. I entered the washroom and turned on the light, after I had carefully closed the door.

My eyes fell immediately on a piece of paper lying right next to the sink. I looked more closely – it was a check. I picked it up. It was neatly filled in with Iris's handwriting – "Pay to the order of World Hunger Relief Fund." The amount was written out in letters – two hundred dollars, and then again numerically - $200.

I held the check in my hands for a long, long time, all the while thinking what a tremendously blessed person I was. There, in the next room, just beyond this thin hotel shower wall, slept the woman who had not only given us the most wonderful child in the world, but who also understood me like no one else ever had or ever will. She had also sensed the awkwardness of the situation in the restaurant – one wave of our little boy's hand, one frown, one scream would have placed him on the regular chair, and we would have paid for the meal for him, a two hundred dollar meal which would have been taken away untouched and dumped into a garbage can.

I tiptoed back into the room and knelt beside Iris's side of the bed. I kissed her tenderly on the cheek and whispered, "I love you."

She gently patted my hand, which rested next to her on the bed, and without opening her eyes, she said softly, "I know. I love you, too."

For Mozart Lovers Only

Mr. Klein is a quiet man. He minds his own business, doesn't bother anyone. He is the assistant manager at a supermarket. Mr. Klein is well liked because he is fair and sensitive to the needs of the employees that he is in charge of. They know that he will listen to them if they have a request for a day off due to some family event; he will always work something out that is to everyone's satisfaction. Mr. Grossman, the manager, has complete confidence in him and lets him make almost all decisions regarding personnel.

Mr. Klein does his job well. He is always on time and stays late when necessary. He never complains about all of the extra work that Mr. Grossman assigns him (work that should actually be done by the manager) and never asks for a raise. He accepts the pay increases as they come along. He keeps his thoughts to himself.

The customers love Mr. Klein. To them, he is the store. He knows the price and location of every item and greets every customer with a friendly nod. Some people feel that he has been there forever, but actually, he has been on the job for only twelve years. Sometimes, he gives a piece of candy to a child, or invites a customer to sample one of the freshly baked bagels. Everyone likes him, but if asked, no one would actually know what to say about him. He is always there. He does a good job. The store without him would simply not be the same.

Mr. Klein does not get excited easily. He does not really care for sports. He does not drink or smoke or travel very much. Once, he drove to the Smokey Mountains during his vacation. He liked the scenery all right, but he was glad when he was back home. Women? Yes, he likes women. He enjoys talking to them and has been on a few dates. The right woman, however, has not come along yet, but Mr. Klein feels that somehow, somewhere, she will be there for him. Until then, he can wait.

Mr. Klein does not draw much attention to himself. At five feet seven inches, he is just a little shorter than most men around him. He has brown eyes, wears his hair closely cropped (the short hair cut actually makes his slightly receding hairline less conspicuous than if he wore his hair longer in an effort to try to conceal the fact that he, just like his father, is going to be prematurely bald). He is neither skinny nor fat, but a slight bulge around the midsection shows that he is entering that age when men have to be careful not to develop that gut that hangs over the belt. He dresses appropriately for every occasion – casual when casual is in order; suit and tie when the event is more formal. He owns three suits – brown, blue and black – and has two matching ties for each suit. He is thirty-three years old.

Mr. Klein's routine does not vary very much. He works six days a week. In the morning, he has a doughnut and a cup of coffee at the store; for lunch, he gets himself a sandwich from the deli counter along with a fruit drink. In the evenings, he stops at the café, which is on his way home. There he has the delicious soup or one of the light entrees that he likes so much. With that, he always has a decaf hazelnut latté. He reads the newspapers, which are always available free of charge, and then walks home the remaining two blocks. After the evening news, he may watch the opening of Leno, sometimes Letterman, and then goes to bed. On Sundays, Mr. Klein goes to church, but not to "his" church. Every Sunday morning, he goes to a different church; he has been to churches of almost all of the Christian denominations, but he has also visited various synagogues and Buddhist temples. Sometimes, he attends services that are held in a foreign language. He loves the sacred music of the Russian Orthodox Church and the organ music and hymns of the various Protestant churches and Catholic Masses complete with soloists, choir and orchestra. He likes the idea that no one knows him in these places. He quietly observes how the parishioners interact with their God.

Mr. Klein does not get enthusiastic about too many things, but he does have one passion. Mr. Klein loves music. This needs to be clarified. He likes Jazz, Blues, Dixieland and early Rock 'n Roll. He cannot stand rap, bagpipe music and Wagner. His great love in music is Mozart – anything by Mozart – but he does, of course, have his favorites. He will also listen to Bach, Handel, Haydn, Beethoven and Schubert. But these are only the moons that circle his sun – Mozart!

If one were to ask Mr. Klein why he likes Mozart's music so much, he would be hard pressed for an answer. Some time ago, when he got into a conversation with a lady at the café, while Mozart was piped in, she asked him if he liked this music (she was obviously not aware that it was Mozart). He told her that no one has ever composed so many beautiful melodies, that no one was such a master of music in every field – symphonies, quartets, operas, concertos – Mozart was just great at everything. He died before he reached his thirty-sixth birthday, and look what he left us. Köchel lists 626 compositions, but there were undoubtedly more. As a child, he played before kings and queens, emperors and empresses and the pope. He was knighted at the age of fourteen. Mr. Klein's eyes shone as he spoke to the woman and in the meantime his latté had gotten cold. "And if you listen carefully to the music, you will..."

The woman got up. "I see you are quite a fan of this Mozart fellow," she interjected. "Well, enjoy." And with these words, she put on her coat and tied a scarf over her head. She managed half a smile and then was gone. Mr. Klein was not sorry to see her go. The most beautiful part of the music was just about to start.

It was in January 2006 that the charming young hostess at the café sat down at Mr. Klein's table one evening and said, "I think you will be happy to hear this, Mr. Klein." He looked at her expectantly. "Later this month, we are beginning our year long concert series as a tribute to Mozart and..."

Before she could continue, Mr. Klein interrupted her, "In honor of the 250th anniversary of Mozart's birth. Why, that is a wonderful idea. So, what are you going to do?"

The young lady had waited patiently, "Right," she said with a smile on her face, "once a month, every third Tuesday, to be exact, we will have a chamber ensemble play here in the evening. It will always be the same string trio, but they will be joined by other musicians, perhaps a flutist, or clarinetist or oboist. The music will be mostly Mozart, but once in a while there might be music by one of his contemporaries. Doesn't that sound great?" Her face was beaming with enthusiasm. Before Mr. Klein could say anything, she went on, "And that's not all. We are also planning afternoon performances, duets and perhaps trios, but also mostly Mozart's music."

Mr. Klein's face shone. "That is just wonderful, just wonderful. Finally, a bit of class in this cultural wasteland. Thank you, thank you, thank you. So, when is the first concert?"

"Well, since this is January," she said coyly, "you tell me when we should have the first performance." She looked at him in a way that indicated that she knew that he knew the right answer.

"Of course," he said, "on the 27th, his birthday."

She smiled at him, "Right, we thought that since we are an affiliate of the famous Viennese chain of coffee houses, this is the least we can do. Shall I reserve you a table close to where the musicians will sit?"

"Yes, please," he answered eagerly, "You know, for me it is very important to see the musicians as they play. That makes the music twice as enjoyable. I love to watch how they interact with each other." He reached across the table and patted her hand. "Thank you, thank you, you have just made my day."

On January 27, Mr. Klein arrives at the café at 6:30 in the evening. The performance will begin at eight. The hostess greets him as soon as he enters, (he notices that she is dressed especially elegantly this night) and leads him to the second table from the corner that has been cleared for the musicians, whose five chairs are lined up in a row.

"Is this all right?" she asks.

"This is perfect," he replies, as he sits down and looks around the tastefully decorated café. There are a few people in the back of the room – they have obviously not come for the music. The small tables in front, close to the musicians, are still all unoccupied. Mr. Klein looks at the menu, although he knows quite well already what he will order. He will begin with the goulash, and then have the Kaiserschmarren (apple-filled pancakes, sprinkled with powdered sugar, and plum jam on the side) for dessert, with that, of course, a decaf hazelnut latté. After the waitress brings him the goulash, the hostess comes by and hands him the program. Mr. Klein opens it hastily. Yes, yes, his head nods in approval:

Prelude and Fugue in F Major for String Trio, K404a, J. S. Bach/W. A. Mozart;

Sonata in B flat Major for Bassoon and Cello, K. 292, W. A. Mozart;

Adagio for English Horn and String Trio, K. 580, W. A. Mozart;

Prelude and Fugue in G Minor for String Trio, K. 404a, W. F. Bach/W. A. Mozart;

Trio No. 10 in D Major from Essercizzii Musici, G. P. Telemann;

Quartet for Oboe and Strings in F Major, K.370 W. A. Mozart.

This is going to be just wonderful. A few of these pieces Mr. Klein does not know, but the Quartet for Oboe and Strings is one of his all time favorites.

The café begins to fill up slowly, and Mr. Klein enjoys his meal. An elderly gentleman is brought to sit on the other side of his table. He introduces himself as Professor Klingel. Mr. Klein stands up and shakes his hand. "Good idea, these concerts, is it not?" he asks to be polite.

"Yes, indeed," answers the professor, "but let's see, let's just wait and see."

A waitress comes and asks him, "The usual, Professor?" He only nods.

At this point, Mr. Klein's attention is drawn to the entrance. Three young musicians have entered. The man carries a violin case, one of the young women a cello case, the other a viola case. They all look to be in their twenties. They fling their coats over a chair and take out their instruments. Another young man and woman enter. When they unpack their instruments, it becomes apparent that he will play the bassoon; she is the oboist and English horn player. Soon they are warming up. Mr. Klein enjoys this part of every performance. He just loves to hear how good musicians play scales, arpeggios, chromatic runs from the lowest register of their instruments to the highest. This is when they have fun; they play a few notes from one piece, then another. They might put their instruments down for a moment and say something to the player next to them – and both might laugh. Mr. Klein would love to know what they just said. This evening, he is close enough to them to hear what they are saying, and he loves every minute of this time before the actual concert.

The young waitress has returned and brings the professor his "usual" – a green tea and a piece of pastry that Mr. Klein recognizes as the one labeled 'Esterhazy Torte' inside the glass pastry counter. The hostess, who has been extremely busy seating the customers, now takes her place next to the seated five musicians. She clears her throat several times, and gradually, the chatter and clinking of silverware stops. She thanks everyone for coming and introduces the five musicians, although the program contains a picture and short biographical sketch of each of them. She also explains why the café is having this concert series. Once again, she thanks everyone for being here tonight and wishes all to have a good time. There is polite applause from every corner of the room. The bassoonist and oboist get up and sit down along the wall. The three string players wiggle slightly on their chairs to find the right position; a music stand is adjusted ever so minutely. They raise their instruments and begin with the Prelude and Fugue in F Major for String Trio by J. S. Bach/W. A. Mozart.

Mr. Klein watches intently as the bows touch the strings. A smile fleets across his face. Yes, this is it. This is the real thing. He closes his eyes. He loves how the theme is passed back and forth between the instruments – the harmonies are beautiful, the rhythms perfectly phrased. Mr. Klein knows that one of the reasons why Mozart worked with Bach's music is that his wife Constanze simply loved Bach's fugues and begged her husband to write such music for her. And he did. She obviously was not such a silly dumb girl as they made her look in that Amadeus movie. Mr. Klein looks up. The professor is looking at him and winks his eye. He obviously approves, too.

After this piece, received with enthusiastic applause, comes the Sonata for Bassoon and Cello. The two musicians play as if they were one. The music is enchanting. But then, during the Andante, precisely at the most expressive section, Mr. Klein's head jerks to his left. There it is again, this time louder. Behind the counter, Mr. Klein sees a tall, dark-haired man stacking plates and cups, three at a time, on long shelves. When the man is finished, he walks away. Mr. Klein turns his attention back to the music. The Rondo is delightful, and Mr. Klein applauds louder than usual when the piece is finished. The other music is played without a hitch. Once in a while there is a little chatter from the tables in the back, and now and then a patron is a little too loud when placing his order. Mr. Klein is willing to put up with that; after all, they are in a café, and that is part of the atmosphere.

Now comes the piece that Mr. Klein wanted to hear most of all, the Quartet for Oboe and Strings. This is one of the many Mozart compositions that he has at home on CD. He listens to this Quartet at least once a week. The music begins. Mr. Klein closes his eyes. Oh yes, this is wonderful. The ensemble plays magnificently. Now, he watches once again. The lady oboist, who had laughed so heartily before the concert began, is all business now. Her head, neck and shoulders sway with the music. She casts a quick glance over to the violinist, and all four musicians execute the ritard perfectly, a little chromatic run by the oboe, and then the strings are back at exactly the right tempo, with the cello part rising just a little above the others. Perfect! Just perfect! These young musicians are playing Mozart's music as well as the famous musicians on his CD, and the fact that they are sitting here right in front of him, no more than ten feet away, makes this performance more enjoyable than any recording he has ever heard before.

The first movement, the Allegro, comes off perfectly. Mr. Klein is ready to enjoy the Adagio. And it begins – and it is beautiful. But then, about two minutes into the movement, it happens again. Suddenly, there is a clatter of porcelain hitting against porcelain. Mr. Klein turns again toward the counter – and yes, it is him again – the tall mustached man, who is now furiously stacking cup upon cup into the cupboard. He is obviously oblivious to the music.

'Swine, nothing but a swine,' thinks Mr. Klein, as he tries to ignore him. Fortunately, the cups are soon stacked and the 'swine' disappears. When the piece comes to its cheerful ending, Mr. Klein jumps to his feet like many of the other patrons. All five musicians bow. They smile. They certainly look as if they feel that they just had a very successful performance – and they have every right to feel that way. This is chamber music making at its finest: close, intimate, brilliantly performed. Mr. Klein says good night to the professor, waves to the hostess and stuffs a twenty-dollar bill into the glass bowl that stands by the exit – and as he walks home, there is a special bounce to his steps.

The next concert is scheduled for Tuesday, the 21st of February. All Mr. Klein knows is that this time the clarinet is to be featured. He is really looking forward to this performance, because deep down inside, he hopes that the Clarinet Quintet will be on the program. This composition ranks among his top five of Mozart's music.

He arrives early, and while he is eating, the hostess brings him the program once again. He looks inside and nods. Yes, this is fine – a Quartet for Clarinet and Strings by Mozart; a Duo for Clarinet and Cello by Beethoven; a Duo for Violin and Viola by Mozart; and a Quartet for Clarinet and Strings by Hummel. The professor soon joins him. They exchange a few comments of how wonderful the last performance had been. The café begins to fill and the musicians arrive. This time there is a new young lady among them. She is the clarinetist.

The music is wonderful again. Mr. Klein is in his element. The Mozart piece is magnificent, just as expected. The Beethoven composition, for clarinet and cello, is quite unusual, but the Rondo Allegretto is so bouncy – something one would not expect from Beethoven. Then comes the Duo for Violin and Viola. The violinist explains that this work was written by Mozart for his friend Michael Haydn, who had been commissioned to write such a piece, but then had fallen ill, and was in danger of losing the pay for this work.

Mozart did it for him in a few days. Mr. Klein knows this already, because he reads almost everything that has been, and still is, published about Mozart.

The Allegro comes off beautifully, and the first few measures of the Adagio are an absolute delight. Mr. Klein is ready to close his eyes and float away in the music, but there it is again. Are those plates? Are those cups? Is it silverware? It makes no difference. The moment is ruined. Mr. Klein turns around. Yes, it's him again, the 'Swine'. In his mind, he calls him 'The Swine', and he pronounces it 'THEE SWINE'. The man, THE SWINE, is as reckless as ever as he literally throws the plates and cups on the shelves. Mr. Klein tries to give him a menacing look, but the swine does not seem to notice. Mr. Klein leans back in his chair and tries to enjoy the rest of the music. Yes, the music is great, but it just isn't the same anymore.

The next concert is exactly one month later, Tuesday, March 21. This time the flute is featured, and Mr. Klein hopes that at least one of the Flute Quartets will be performed. He almost gives out a little yell as his eyes glance over the program. Not only one, but two Quartets are listed – the one in A major, K.298 and the one in D major, K.285. This is the one Mr. Klein likes the most out of all of Mozart's compositions for Flute. Along with that, there will be a Serenade for Flute, Violin and Viola by Beethoven, and a Duo for Flute and Viola by Devienne.

Mr. Klein is happy. This will definitely be an enjoyable evening. The professor arrives. The musicians come a little later. Among them is now a slender, tall lady, the flutist. The string players and the flutist warm up briefly. They are perfectly tuned in no time. The music begins.

The Quartet in A major comes off without a hitch. Wonderful music wonderfully played. Mr. Klein sips his hazelnut latté and puts his cup down ever so gently. The Beethoven begins very nicely. Mr. Klein does not know this piece. He listens intently. The Entrata: Allegro sets the mood. Beethoven is going to have a little fun here. The Menuetto and Allegro molto is Beethoven at his most "unbuttoned." The Andante con variazioni begins. The music is more serious. It is absolutely wonderful. And there it is again – at exactly the wrong time. 'The Swine' is stacking plates. Not so loudly as last time, but Mr. Klein is annoyed, nonetheless. He tries to throw 'The Swine' an angry look, but the stacker of plates is engrossed in doing his job. He does not notice Mr. Klein at all. Fortunately, he is done quite soon, and the room becomes comparatively quiet again.

The Duo for Flute and Viola by Devienne is next. It is a charming two-movement piece, but 'definitely not Mozart,' Mr. Klein thinks to himself, as the café applauds politely for the flutist and violist.

And now comes the Quartet for Flute and Strings in D major, K.285. The young musicians play with enthusiasm and fire. This first movement is truly Mozart at his finest. The interplay between the flute and the strings is extraordinary. The little bridge passages by the cello are exacted perfectly. Everything is cheerful, bouncy and absolutely charming. This is western art at its highest level. Mr. Klein could not be more pleased.

The second movement is Mr. Klein's favorite piece. It contains a plain, hauntingly beautiful melody by the flute; the string accompaniment is all pizzicato. The effect is overwhelming. Mr. Klein floats with the music, but not for long. Clank, clank, clank, clank. Mr. Klein snaps out of his trance-like state. 'The Swine' is at it again, and, of course, at exactly the wrong time. Now, Mr. Klein is truly annoyed. He does not even look at 'The Swine'. He knows who is responsible for this. Enough is enough! He is going to have a word with that lout, that ignoramus, that 'Swine'. The short Adagio ends just a few seconds after 'The Swine' has finished with the dishes.

The lively and charming Rondeau is next. Mr. Klein loves this movement, but this time he cannot enjoy it. The mood has been ruined. The evening has been ruined. He looks at the professor, but he is engrossed in the music and pays no attention to him. Everyone else around him is listening intently. Mr. Klein wants to get up and leave right now, but that would be impolite. He remains seated, his arms folded across his chest. What a waste of beautiful music, he thinks. What a waste of talent. What a waste of Mozart's genius. He can't wait for the music to end.

After the final chord fades away, he throws a twenty-dollar bill on the table, grabs his coat, and without saying a word to anyone, storms out of the door. As he walks home, he mutters to himself – something about pearls before swine, uncultured bastards, and a few other expletives that he would never say out loud to anyone. At home, he takes a quick shower – no Leno, no Letterman tonight – he knows he is agitated, but all he wants to do is sleep – just sleep – get all of this over with. He actually thinks about not going back to the concerts any more.

Mr. Klein walks home on his usual route after work. He walks right past the café. He does not go in. As he comes to the alley, he sees 'The Swine' throwing garbage bags into a large dumpster behind the café. 'The Swine' sees him too and puts down the bag he has in his hand. They look at each other. Suddenly 'The Swine' speaks, or rather hollers, "Hey you, come here. I want to talk to you."

Mr. Klein walks toward him.

"Tell me," says 'The Swine', "what is your problem? Do you think I don't see you giving me those dirty looks all the time? You think you're something special? Well, I have a job to do, and no wimp like you is going to make a fool out of me."

He steps toward Mr. Klein and the size difference truly becomes evident now. They almost look like David and Goliath.

"You look at me like that again and I'm going to kick your...."

At this point Mr. Klein takes a step forward and kicks 'The Swine' in the groin with all the strength he has. 'The Swine' doubles over, completely unprepared for this attack from the much smaller man. As he stands there, bent forward with both hands over his crotch, Mr. Klein shoots up his knee striking 'The Swine' right in the throat. The big man stumbles backward, but even before he hits the wall, Mr. Klein is upon him and slaps him hard across one cheek, then backhands him across the other. 'The Swine' stumbles back against the dumpster, stands there lifeless for a second, blood streaming out of his nose. Mr. Klein now punches him in the stomach, and as 'The Swine' jerks forward, Mr. Klein gives him a karate chop to the back of the neck. The mustached man falls like a sack of potatoes.

"You are a swine," Mr. Klein presses out between his teeth. The word 'swine' has never been said with more bitterness, disgust and contempt. As he walks away, he deliberately steps on the huge hand, twitching on the cold cement.

36

Mr. Klein jerks up. He is breathing hard and is drenched in sweat. It is dark all around him, but then he reaches out and his hand immediately finds the button on the lamp on his nightstand. Mr. Klein takes a deep breath. A dream, all of that was just a dream! He gets up slowly and walks into the kitchen. He pours himself a glass of milk, sits down at the kitchen table, still breathing heavily. He begins to laugh. At first it is just a chuckle; then, it gets louder, and then, Mr. Klein has to stifle himself not to laugh so loud in the stillness of the night so that he will wake up the old lady next door.

"I really enjoyed that dream," he mutters out loud. "That was a good dream. That was a dream that should come true. That's exactly what that idiot deserves," and Mr. Klein chuckles again, because he remembers that even in his dream he had called him a 'Swine.'

"I will not go back there," he had told himself after the last disastrous concert, but here he is again. The hostess had told him during dinner one evening that the clarinet player would be returning, there would be an additional violinist, and they were going to play the Clarinet Quintet. That settled it right there and then. The Clarinet Quintet is Mr. Klein's all-time favorite piece of music.

He eats early, looks through a few newspapers, and then, as the musicians arrive, he orders his hazelnut decaf latté. The program is absolutely perfect: The String Quartet in D major, K.499, known as the Hoffmeister, and the Clarinet Quintet.

The music begins. Mr. Klein looks around the room. 'The Swine' is busy at the other end of the café. The musicians play beautifully as ever. Mr. Klein enjoys every moment of the performance. The string quartet is one of his favorite instrument groupings. The Allegretto, Menuetto, Adagio and Allegro – the four movements combined form a perfect entity. It could not have been conceived any better. Mr. Klein considers Mozart's music to be a beautifully designed and presented meal – a delicious appetizer that wants you to have more. Then the main meal, which is absolutely satisfying, but never too heavy. The dessert is always included, and you wish you could just partake of this meal forever and ever.

Now comes the Clarinet Quintet. This is it. The clarinetist has taken her seat next to the first violinist. The musicians look at each other for a split second. The bows glide across the strings. Here is the short introduction. The clarinet ascends in eight notes and then comes cascading down in sixteenths. Yes, yes, yes! This is the musical climax for Mr. Klein. He closes his eyes. Oh, yes, that's it! Well-done cello. Yes, strings, smooth. And clarinet, don't be timid; you are the star. Mr. Klein knows every note of this composition, every crescendo and decrescendo, accelerando and ritard. He knows every entrance by each instrument. Mr. Klein is as close to heaven as one can be here on earth. The first movement has just been beautifully completed. There is complete silence in the room. Now comes the movement that Mr. Klein loves above all others – the Larghetto. He quickly looks around the room. Where is 'The Swine'? He cranes his neck and sees him clearing a table all the way in back of the café. The Larghetto begins. Heavenly! Mr. Klein enjoys every second. A smile flicks across his face at the passage, which he considers to be the most beautiful music ever written. The Menuetto follows and it, too, is played to perfection. The entire audience, not only Mr. Klein, is really into this performance. One can hear a pin drop. Now, there is only the Allegretto con variazioni left. This movement ranks number two of Mr. Klein's all time favorites, right after the Larghetto. And why not? This is Mozart at his most inventive, most charming, most genial. What Mozart does here with only a string quartet and one clarinet is absolutely astounding. This roughly nine minute section is the equal of any symphonic movement as far as Mr. Klein is concerned. The chromatically descending notes in the clarinet are a stroke of genius. But what else can you expect – this, after all, is Mozart.

Minute by minute goes by. The audience sits as if in a trance. There is no talking, no laughter, no clanking of dishes. Mr. Klein hardly dares to breathe in the piano part of the piece. And here it is again, the opening theme – and now it is all bouncing, goodnatured fun until the final chord. There is a moment of silence, but then the applause breaks loose. Most people are on their feet. One hears shouts of "Bravo, Bravo, Bravo Mozart. Bravo Musicians". The five players stand and bow again and again. This is the most enthusiastic applause they have received yet. And even after the applause dies down, no one wants to leave. People go up to the musicians and talk to them. Mr. Klein, too, finds his way to the clarinet player and congratulates her on how wonderfully she has just played his favorite piece and how much he enjoyed the performance. He manages to shake the first violinist's hand and says, "Superb, just superb." He goes back to his table; there are just too many people around the musicians.

Mr. Klein pays his bill and on the way out, hugs the hostess and stammers, "Super, just super." He drops two twenties in the glass bowl by the door and leaves.

Mr. Klein hums parts of the variations to himself, as he sways from side to side, on his way home. He jumps over a crack in the sidewalk. On the next block stands the crippled man on the corner, holding out his tin cup. Mr. Klein puts in a five-dollar bill and hurries away before the man can say anything. At home, he quickly showers. He lies down on the sofa. No, he will not turn on the television. That would only destroy the mood he is in. He wants to savor the experience for as long as he can. He hums little sections of each of the four movements. Finally, after he has gone over the last section of the Variazioni for at least the third time, he goes to bed and sleeps like he has not slept for a long time.

It is a Thursday night, two weeks after the last concert. Mr. Klein is in the café. He has just finished his meal (this time topped with a delicious slice of the Linzer torte) and is enjoying his hazelnut decaf latté. He watches as a lady in the back of the room puts on her coat and starts toward the door. Suddenly, she stops in front of his table.

"Pardon me," she begins, "am I right to think that you have been here for all of the Tuesday night concerts?" She stands there and looks slightly embarrassed.

"Yes, you are right," Mr. Klein answers. "I have been here for every one of the concerts."

She pulls back the chair opposite his, throws her coat over the backrest and sits down. "Well, what do you think? I love the music, but I'm certainly no expert. I'd like to know what you think of the ensemble, the programs, and the overall experience. You seem to know a lot about this. I've been watching you," is her reply.

Mr. Klein had not expected this torrent of words. There she is, sitting opposite him. Reddish brown hair, hazel eyes, blue turtle-necked sweater, no rings on any finger – pretty smile.

"I think the concerts are wonderful. The selections are excellent, and the ensemble... I tell you, the ensemble is outstanding. They are so young, yet they play so masterfully, with so much feeling. I'm thoroughly enjoying these little musical evenings... except." He pauses.

She looks at him without saying a word.

"Except sometimes," Mr. Klein continues, "I get annoyed when people make too much noise. And I don't mean the customers. They come here to enjoy the food and coffee, and some of them don't even know that there will be live music on specific evenings. They are insensitive, but I can at least somewhat understand them."

She continues to look right into his face.

"But there is one person here who drives me absolutely mad. He is one of the busboys – the tall one with the mustache. He doesn't seem to care about what is going on here. He plops the dishes and cups down as if he were the only person in the place. The music obviously means nothing to him." Mr. Klein becomes quite agitated simply by talking about the man.

She keeps looking at him, quite willing to let him do the talking.

"Can I tell you something funny?" Mr. Klein continues, after a short pause. Without waiting for a response, he goes on. "He annoyed me somewhat during the first concert. And again at the second – but during the March concert, when they played the Flute Quartet, that's when he drove me crazy. I went home that night so angry that I could hardly sleep, and I told myself that I would not come to any other concerts." He looks at her, but she keeps looking right into his face, with that gentle, beautiful smile on her lips.

"Now the story gets a little silly," he continues, "but I will tell you the rest anyway even if you think I'm nuts." There is no response from her, but he can read the expectation on her face. "Well, that night I dreamed that I met that man, I call him 'The Swine', for obvious reasons, in the alley behind the café and he yelled at me for giving him dirty looks. He even threatened me..."

"Yes?" she asks.

"And then I beat the crap out of him. I kicked him and punched him until he lay there bleeding. And you know, I felt good about it. He deserved it."

She smiles at him. "I didn't take you for such a violent man. What happened then?"

"Now this is the funny part about the whole story," Mr. Klein continues. "Do you remember the last concert, when they played the string quartet and the Clarinet Quintet? Did you notice how quiet it was? It was extraordinary. I kept on waiting for the clatter of plates and cups, but nothing happened. 'The Swine' worked so carefully that it almost seemed as if my beating did some good – the beating I gave him in my dream. Now isn't that weird?"

She looks at him and her smile gets even wider. "That is truly a funny story," she finally says. "And I will tell you why it's a funny story."

Mr. Klein cannot conceal his surprise, because he certainly did not expect a story from her.

"I, too," she begins, "have enjoyed these concerts very much, but since I work late on Tuesdays, I always arrive just before the music starts, and I have to sit in the back. That

42

means the music is softer back there, and the noise is greater. Now, I don't claim to be an expert, but Mozart's music is so beautiful that any noise really interferes. After the first concert I thought that this might just be a one-time occurrence, and I let it go at that. After the second concert, I was quite annoyed, but who am I to complain? If the real Mozart fans didn't say anything, why should I?" She pauses. "But then, after the third concert, the one with the Flute Quartet, I couldn't take it any longer. Once the music had stopped, I went to the busboy, the tall one, and I asked him whether he wasn't aware of the fact that he was quite disruptive with his plates and cups and silverware?"

Mr. Klein cut in, "So what did he say?"

She looks into his eyes and her expression becomes serious. "He said that he was sorry; that he wasn't aware that he was making too much noise. He told me that he was hard of hearing, almost deaf, and that he did not hear the music at all. He hardly hears the dishes. He was so terribly upset that he almost began to cry. He told me again and again that he would be more careful in the future and that he really needed this job. The people here have been so nice to him, not like at some of the other places. He begged me not to say anything to anyone. He would be more careful..." she stopped. "And he was, wasn't he?"

Mr. Klein looks into her beautiful eyes. His face is quite serious. "I don't know what to say," he finally says softly. "The man can't hear the music? He didn't hear any of it? That's sad. That's really sad."

The woman sits up. "This is the first time I've been here when there is no music. The food is really quite good. I think I'll have to come here more often."

"Yes," Mr. Klein agrees enthusiastically, "the food here is outstanding. I eat here every evening, music or no music. I just love this place."

The young lady stands up. "May I ask you a favor?" she asks slightly timidly.

"Of course." Mr. Klein replies gallantly, as he stands up, too.

"I really would like to know more about Mozart, his music, his life. Would you mind terribly much if I joined you for dinner once in a while, and you could tell me all about the man and his music. I would be ever so grateful. By the way, my name is Natalie Brown." She holds out her hand across the table.

"I'm Peter Klein," he answers, "and you can be sure that I would like nothing more than to talk with you about Mozart. And I'll talk and talk and talk and you might just have to tell me to shut up."

"Well, we'll see about that," she answers, as she flings her purse over her shoulder. "What do you say, tomorrow, same time?"

"Delighted," he answers, "you will find me here, right here."

Mr. Klein sits down. He orders another hazelnut latté regular – not decaf. He savors and enjoys his drink. His fingers are drumming the rhythm of the Variazione. The tall busboy appears from the back of the café. He clears the plates and cups off a few tables and carries them to the back. Then, he returns and stands a pile of washed plates onto the rack. He does it carefully and quietly. Mr. Klein drinks his latté in little sips. It tastes different today. It tastes great – even better than before. Mr. Klein does not think about why that should be so. He is happy. He is content. Life is good.

Finally, he gets up and gives the tall mustached man behind the counter a friendly nod. And the man smiles back and waves a timid goodnight to Mr. Klein. Mr. Klein walks out of the door and feels more joy in his heart than if he had just heard a concert of Mozart's most beautiful music played by the very angels of heaven.

Believe It or Not

My wife and I are both avid readers. She likes murder mysteries, from Agatha Christie to Cleo Coyle. She also enjoys the crime scene investigation shows on television and everything that deals with forensics and methods of solving crimes. Most people are totally stunned when they hear this about her because she is the gentlest creature that you could possibly imagine. She puts out food for the squirrels, rabbits and birds that love to congregate in our backyard during the cold Midwest winter months. More than one stray cat has found at least a temporary home in our house. She is one of those people who could not hurt that proverbial fly. But when it comes to crime and mystery stories – the gorier, the better.

I, on the other hand, usually don't like fiction. My feeling is, why would you have to make up stories when there are fantastic stories taking place all around us? Just read the newspapers and watch the news. I want my readings to take me away from the world. I want to follow the lofty thoughts of the great philosophers, artists – men and women who have accomplished something. What made them the way they were? Where did their talent come from? What kind of people were they in everyday life? And so I read about Einstein, Michelangelo, and Leonardo da Vinci. I study their thoughts. How did Shakespeare construct his plays to make them such popular enduring classics? Why did the French Impressionists paint in such a different way? And what drove Van Gogh to madness? Since I love music, I cannot get enough, especially of Beethoven and Mozart – their music and what has been said about them. Thank you, Maynard Solomon.

Reading and listening to music is what the two of us enjoyed doing most after work, on weekends, and during vacations. No matter where we traveled throughout the world – our reading material was always with us. One of my favorite recollections involving reading is sitting in St. Mark's Square reading Thomas Mann's Death in Venice. The cappuccino, the view, the music, the book – unforgettable.

We retired from work a year apart. Our children were grown and out on their own. Our house had been well maintained. Financially, we were okay. What I'm trying to say is that now we had time on our hands. My wife devoted more time to gardening and her needlework – and she read more. I tried to busy myself around the house, but since I'm not all that handy, I sat around more then ever, usually with a book in my hands.

One day, out of the clear blue sky, my wife said to me, "Why don't you go down to the library and find out if there isn't some kind of reading group you could join. You like to discuss the things that you read. Why don't you check it out?"

That thought had never occurred to me. I'm usually not a "group" person, although with people that I know and like, I do like to talk, too much sometimes, my wife tells me.

The next day I went to the library and asked the lady behind the information desk if there were any book groups that met here. "Oh, yes," she replied. "There are two groups.

One meets the first Thursday of the month at 7:00 p.m. They read current fiction, but sometimes they turn to the classics." By the look on my face, she must have gathered that I wasn't too impressed. Somehow, I had imagined that this group consisted of a bunch of old ladies who probably got together primarily to gossip and fill their time.

"Now, the other group," she continued, "the Great Books group, they meet every second Tuesday of the month at 6:30 p.m. They are a much smaller group, but they are really dedicated. I think every one of them is there every time. If you are a serious reader, this would be the right group for you. Are you thinking of joining one of our groups?"

I scratched my head. "I don't know," I said. "The second group sounds quite interesting. Do you think they would mind if I just showed up one evening?"

"Absolutely not," she replied eagerly. "I'm most certain that they would love to have a new member. They are really a very friendly bunch."

"Well, we'll see," I said in the most non-committal voice I could muster. "Second Tuesday of the month at 6:30 p.m.?"

"That's right," she replied. "I think you'll have a good time."

Two weeks later, I attended the first meeting, always telling myself that if I didn't like the people, what they were reading, or the entire atmosphere, I simply wouldn't go again.

When I entered the small meeting room at 6:25, there were five people in the room – three women and two men. I introduced myself and asked whether they would mind if I sat in. They assured me most eagerly that they were happy to see me. The taller of the two men shook my hand,

48

slapped me on the back and said that now, finally, there was going to be some balance here between the sexes. "The women have dominated long enough," he told me with a wink of an eye. I sat down between two of the women, and the others took their places.

The oldest of the three ladies spoke first. "Well, well, well, isn't this just delightful: a new member. Our motto has always been the more the merrier. My name is Shirley Steward, and I'm kind of the unofficial leader of the group, which basically means I make the coffee." She looked at the man next to her inviting him to introduce himself.

"My name is Hank Bauer. Retired. Widower. Lived here for 36 years. Great town. Welcome aboard."

The tall lady at his left was next. "Hi," she said, "I'm Virginia Bloom, married, three children, do the bookkeeping for our business and, of course, love to read."

Now the lady at my other side spoke up. "I'm Carla Dawson. I'm the head librarian here at this library, and I'm so glad that so many people use our library. What would we do without books?" She looked around the table as if she expected an answer.

The other man spoke next. "Howdy, the name's Wilbur Sneedling, used to teach history down at the Junior College – retired two years ago. I do some tutoring at Jennings High School, but mostly I loiter around here. I'm surprised that they haven't thrown me out yet."

Everyone now turned their eyes on me. I obviously had to say something. "As I said before, my name is Ben Williamson. I am a construction engineer, recently retired. My wife and I moved here five years ago. She is a retired schoolteacher. We travel a lot, and we both love to read.

And we're always looking for something to do. So, here I am."

Shirley Steward opened the folder that lay in front of her, took out a piece of paper and slid it across the table to me. "Here's what we're reading this year. We are very democratic about selecting our material. Anyone can make suggestions, and we usually agree to read and discuss what anyone in our group suggests."

I glanced down the list:

The Four Idols, Frances Bacon

Common Sense, Thomas Paine

Quartet, T. S. Eliot

An Enemy of the People, Henrik Ibsen

The Value of Science, Henri Poincare

Democracy in America, Alexis de Tocqueville

The selection for this day was The Relation of Science and Religion by Richard P. Feynman. This was the perfect topic to discuss for someone who hadn't read the material. Feynman raises the question whether a scientist can believe in God, or in Jesus as the Son of God. Can a person be moral and ethical without believing in any religion? Has the revealing of religious mistakes concerning the universe led people to abandon their faith? The discussion was lively, witty and intellectually extremely stimulating. I added that I knew a surgeon who prayed every time before he performed an operation. And this doctor has told me that he knows of other doctors who do the same. I admitted that I saw no conflict between science and religion – they were simply two totally different methods of inquiry.

While the discussion went on, I had a chance to take a closer look at the five people I had met. Shirley Steward seemed to be around sixty with an excellent figure, pretty face with just the right amount of make-up, and she was very well dressed, perhaps a little too well, I thought, this being just a book club meeting. Her eyes definitely displayed intelligence, curiosity and just a hint of mischief.

Hank Bauer was a tall and lanky man, perhaps around seventy. He was almost completely bald, and the little hair he had was trimmed very short. There was something sad about him.

Carla Dawson, was tall and slender, almost skinny. She had a rather large nose and an unusually large mouth. To me, she seemed the personification of the "schoolmarm" – efficient, level headed, always on task. She wore a large diamond ring on her left hand and an equally impressive emerald ring on her right hand.

Virginia Bloom, also rather tall and let's say, full bodied, had a look of kindness about her. She struck me as a person who would always be willing to help someone in need. She could, however, not be simply dismissed as a "hausfrau." Her comments were insightful and revealed that she had read a great deal and was obviously very intelligent. She ended every comment or question with a broad smile on her good-natured face.

Wilbur Sneedling was short and stocky, quick to laugh, very funny and always tried to see the humor in everything, but he also showed very quickly that he was a serious thinker and that he had enjoyed a very well rounded education.

I had no doubt that I would enjoy being a member of this group, and the coffee, personally served by Shirley Steward, was exceptionally good.

When the discussion came to an end and Shirley Steward said that at the next meeting we would discuss Quartet by T. S. Eliot, Carla spoke up: "No, no, remember Shirley, that next month we are doing something different?"

"Oh my, yes," Shirley replied somewhat sheepishly as she gently slapped her cheek. "I had completely forgotten. Let me explain," she said as she looked at me. "My sister, Anne, who lives in Minnesota, also belongs to a reading group like ours, and she told me that some time ago they decided not to read a book but that each member would tell a story of his own. And guess what? It turned out to be such a success that they are going to do this once every year, and we decided to do it, too. So next month is our 'storytelling' month. She did the quotation marks with her fingers. "Here are the guidelines. Your story can be fact or fiction. Everyone is allowed to ask you questions, that you can answer or not, and you don't have to say whether the story is true or not. What do you think?"

"That sure is a novel idea," I answered, "and I think it might just yield some pretty interesting results."

"Well, okay then," she said cheerfully, "see you all next month."

At home, I showed my wife the reading list, and she was quite impressed. "Didn't I tell you that you would find something interesting to do?"

"Yes, dear," I said with self-mocking humility, "you're right, you're always right."

During the next few days, I had a hard time concentrating on my reading. The thought of having to come up with a story of my own was always in the back of my mind. Finally, I told my wife about it.

"I don't see why that should be a problem for you," she said, "especially if you can make it up. You've been around, and I think you're pretty good at shooting the bull. You'll come up with something." Sometimes, my wife is brutally honest.

I finally decided that I would tell a true story about myself – the visit to Venice where I enjoyed the view, the music, the coffee and the book so much and where, when the monetary unit of Italy was still the lira, I got so confused with all the zeros in the conversion rate that I think I tipped the waiter twelve dollars for a cup of cappuccino. Every time I told this story, I always concluded with, "And I don't regret it one bit. I would do it all over again if I had the opportunity to be there, to take it all in just one more time. Some things are just priceless."

The time for the next meeting came faster than expected. I had carefully worked out all of the details of my story – the trip to Italy, the fascination with Venice, the magnificent view of the Canale Grande, the gondolas, the splendor of the Doge's Palace, the mind-boggling architecture of St. Marks Cathedral, the pigeons, the Campanile (how could that tall and heavy structure stand where it was, like everything else, built on mud?). And then that afternoon – me, on one of the yellow wicker chairs (the wife shopping), the small orchestra playing sweetly in the background, the delicious cappuccino, the setting sun – the bill, the tip – the moment of hesitation – should I call the waiter back? – but, what the hell, let it go, don't spoil the moment, and yes, I still don't regret it.

Shirley – dressed even more elegantly than at the last meeting – was the first one to speak. "I'll come right out and say it," she began, "this is a true story." She looked around the table to make sure we all got the point.

She was just about to begin when there was a knock on the door. Hank, sitting closest to the door, got up and opened the door.

"Yes?" we heard him say, but we could not see who was outside. "Is this where the book group meets?" we heard a voice say. Hank answered in not exactly the most pleasant tone. "Well," the voice continued, "if it's not too much trouble, do you think I could maybe join you?"

Shirley got up and opened the door wide. In stepped a man, perhaps in his late forties, early fifties. He wore faded jeans and a T-shirt with cut off sleeves. His arms were tattooed. His face was burnt from the sun, and it seemed that he had not shaved for several days. His piercing blue eyes quickly surveyed the room. He bowed politely and said with a deep, pleasant voice, "My name is Ted. I am, what you might call, a traveling man. I like to read, and whenever I stop in a town for the night, I go to the library or a bookstore and find out if there is a reading group. I love to see what people are reading. Today, I was lucky. Hope you don't mind." He walked over to the empty chair at the end of the table and sat down. He folded his hands over his chest and looked around the room. Shirley took out one of our reading lists and slid it across the table toward him. He nodded slowly as he glanced at the list.

Shirley spoke up and told him that today we were not discussing the reading selection for the day and that instead we would each tell a story. Ted looked up and said with a smile, "I like that, I like that very much."

Shirley cleared her throat. "I guess I'm up, so here it goes. As I told you before, this is a true story that my sister told me. You see, my sister knows this immigrant woman from Germany. It was this woman who told her that after she had been in the United States for a while, she received a

54

letter from her sister who had stayed behind in Germany with her husband and three children. This was just a few years after World War II had ended and things were really bad in Germany – everything was destroyed; there was hardly anything to eat. Even worse, her husband had just been killed in a work related accident. So here was this poor woman with three mouths to feed. Her sister in America decided to send her package; after all, everything could be had here, and it was cheap. So she bought dry milk, canned meats, biscuits and plenty of candy and chocolates for the children. When she took the package to the post office, she was asked whether this was a commercial package or a gift. She told the man that this was a gift package, whereupon the postal official told her that she had to write the word 'gift' in bold letters on all six sides of the package. And that's just what she did.

"She received a reply from her sister a few weeks later. The sister wrote, 'Dear sister, thank you so much for the beautiful package with all of the wonderful goodies inside. At first, we were afraid to try any of it, but then the children could not restrain themselves any longer, and we all ate one of the chocolate bars. It sure was good. Then, we tried the other things. Everything was wonderful. But tell me, dear sister, why did you frighten us so much with the package?'" Shirley stopped and looked around the room. "Well, that's my story. It is true."

We all sat there somewhat perplexed. Only Bill had a crooked smile on his face. "You see," he said as he looked at each of us, "the sister had good cause to be concerned about the contents of the package, because 'gift' is the German word for..." He looked around the room again, and when his eyes stopped on Ted, we saw him mouth the word 'poison'. Bill nodded, "Go ahead. Tell them, Ted."

"The word means 'poison'," Ted now said aloud.

Carla Dawson, the librarian/schoolmarm, took a deep breath. "Can you imagine getting a package with food from your sister, but on all sides of the package it says 'poison, poison, poison'? That's a great story, Shirley. Thanks for sharing it with us."

There was a momentary silence in the room. Virginia just kept shaking her head. "Wow, the word 'poison' on the package and food inside, that's something. That's scary."

Bill Sneedling cleared his throat, "I guess it's my turn," he began. "I started my teaching career teaching in junior high school. One time, when I wanted to teach my students to be careful about threatening people, I told them a story that I had read while I was a student in grammar school. I thought it made the point so perfectly that I had never forgotten it. Just a few minutes before I had heard a student out in the hall say that he was going to kick the other guy's ass but good. I really did not know what it was all about, but it reminded me of the story, and so I decided to tell it to my seventh graders. The story goes like this. Back in the olden days when there were still knights riding around Europe, there was one particularly mean knight who pillaged, burned and killed just for the fun of it. Everyone feared him. Now, one day he rode into a town, and since he had been out in the wild for some days, he decided to get a shave at the barbershop that was just coming into sight. He swung open the door and bellowed, 'I want a shave.' With that, he threw down his heavy outer coat and pulled a moneybag from his belt. He looked around the room. 'I have an offer for any one of you chicken-livered city slickers barbershop pansies.' My kids liked it when I talked like this. The three barbers and the apprentice stood there frozen in their tracks. 'I have an offer' he repeated, as he cast an evil eye at all of them. 'Give me a shave, and this bag full of money is yours.' I always told my students that by today's standard, it probably contained twenty thousand dollars. Well, the barbers looked at each other. The deal sounded too good to be true. And so it was. Before any of them could say anything, the knight continued, 'That's right, this bag full of money is yours if you give me a shave – just one condition. If you cut me – even the slightest nick – I will cut your throat,' and with that he pulled the huge dagger from the scabbard, which hung from his belt. He looked around the room again. 'Well, cowards,' he said contemptuously, 'what will it be? Riches, or would you rather go on living your miserable pitiful lives?'

"Nobody stirred. The knight took one step toward the owner of the barbershop, a man with many years of experience. 'You,' he said, 'you're a good barber, aren't you? C'mon, shave me and be rich.' The barber trembled. Yes, he was experienced. He was a good barber. And just because he was an experienced, good barber, he knew the dangers involved in this seemingly so simple task. He knew that no matter how careful he was, the slightest movement by the knight; a pimple, which was hidden under the knight's greasy beard; an old scar: all of this could bring about a small cut – and he was not about to risk his life, no matter for how much money.

"'No,' he said, timidly, 'perhaps I am too old for this.'

The knight sneered at him, 'Coward,' and then he turned toward the next man, also an experienced barber.

"'You,' he snarled, 'you look like a man with confidence. Here, this bag is yours, but one drop of blood and I'll kill you. What do you say, my man?' He obviously enjoyed this challenge.

"This man, too, backed out of the offer because just like the owner of the shop, he knew that no matter how skillful he was, the knight could turn it in such a way that he would have a reason to kill him.

"This left the third barber, a qualified barber, but with considerably less experience. He, too, declined.

"The knight grunted. 'Just as I thought, cowards all of you, nothing but cowards. Go on then, live like swine. I'll get a shave somewhere else.'

"He was about to pick up his coat and sword when he heard a soft voice say, 'I'll do it.' The three barbers and the knight looked to the corner of the room where the apprentice stood with a broom in his hand. 'I'll do it', he repeated, his voice a bit stronger. The barbershop owner was about to say something when the knight spoke up: 'Let him be,' he said, 'let him be; he's young, but he's not a child. He wants to be a man, so let him be a man.' The three barbers looked at the boy incredulously. The boy had started his apprenticeship only a few months ago. His duty had consisted mostly of sweeping up hair and sharpening razors and scissors, and even that had taken weeks of instruction. He had mostly watched the other barbers at work and only twice had the master barber allowed him to shave a man; each time a young man with a very light beard and flawless skin. This was completely different. This was extremely dangerous. This could get him killed.

"'Well, well, well,' said the knight, 'we have a hero here. A boy wants to play a man's game. Very well, I'm willing to play. But listen here, boy, the money will be yours if you do the job right, but don't be fooled. You may be young, but if you cut me, if I see even one drop of blood – mark my words, boy – I will kill you.'

"The boy looked straight into the knight's eyes and pointed to the nearest empty barber chair.

"The knight sat down holding the dagger in his hand. The boy tied the snow-white sheet around his neck and tilted the chair slightly backwards. He then prepared the lather and brushed it smoothly all over the knight's beard. He took a razor and pulled the strap tight and with smooth strokes sharpened the razor to its absolute sharpest.

"The three barbers stood frozen in place as the boy began the first stroke just below the knight's left ear. The knight had his eyes closed and breathed calmly. The boy wiped the blade on the towel that he had flung across his left shoulder. He then made the next stroke, wiped the blade, and then the next stroke. Now he walked around the knight and started on the other side of his face. Again he worked downward stroke after stroke, always wiping the blade on the towel. At last he came to the most vulnerable part – the area around the Adam's apple. He tilted the knight's head backward even a little further than before, and worked meticulously – short strokes now – ever so gently. After every stroke and wipe, he looked at the gleaming blade before continuing his dangerous work. Finally, after what had seemed an eternity to the other three barbers, he put the razor down, walked to the cabinet and took out a steaming hot towel and placed it on the knight's face. When he had gently padded the hot towel on the knight's cheeks and into his ears and around the neck, he took it off, put the chair in its upright position and handed him a mirror. The knight looked at his reflection, felt his chin here and there and finally said with a grin on his face, 'Boy, you are a man, not like those trembling fools. Here, you have earned this,' and flung the moneybag at him.

"He stood up. 'Boy,' he said, 'you are a lucky fellow. You are just a boy, but believe me, I would have killed you if you had cut me.'

"'No, that is not true,' answered the boy calmly. 'That is not true.'

"The knight looked at him in utter amazement and anger crept into his voice. 'What do you mean, that is not true. Do you question me? I tell you, I would have killed you.'

"A smile spread across the boy's face, 'No.' he said again gently, 'You see, if there would have been even one drop of blood on your face, I would have instantly cut your throat before you would have felt anything,' and with his open hand, he swooshed through the air, 'like so. Instead of you wiping a drop of blood from your face, I would now be cleaning up your blood from this floor.'

"The knight's color drained from his ruddy cheeks. His skin looked ashen gray. In a flash, he realized that all the time the boy was shaving him, it was not the boy's life that was in danger, but his very own.

"The knight placed his dagger back in the scabbard, pulled on his heavy coat, and with his huge sword in his hand, looked across the room at the boy who stood there calmly, now with a broom in his hands. For just a split second, there seemed to be the slightest grin on the knight's face. He turned and walked slowly and with heavy steps out of the barbershop."

Virginia spoke up first, "That story has a message…"

Before she could continue, Bill Sneedling went on, "Just a second, please, this story is not quite over yet."

We all looked at him with expectation. What else was there to say?

"No," he started again, "the story is not quite over. You see, about two weeks later, a quiet, little girl from the back of the room, Susie Finkel, I'll never forget her name, came up to me after class and said, 'Mr. Sneedling, you know that story you told us about the knight and the boy?' 'Yes, sure,' I said, 'I remember. What about it?' 'Well, Mr. Sneedling,' she continued timidly, 'Please don't ever tell that story again. You see, the next three nights after you told that story, I had horrible nightmares – there was always a man in a barber chair, and I saw a blade cut into his throat. There was blood everywhere. For three nights, I saw the same scene so vividly in my dreams that even now I can see that horrible act every time I close my eyes and concentrate on it. But I don't do that anymore.'

"I thanked her for sharing her experience with me. And so, the knight never made that same offer to any barber any longer, and I have never told that story again until today."

All of us were quiet. It was clear to all of us that Bill even now, so many years later, was still deeply affected by this event in his teaching career.

After a short pause, Virginia spoke up again. "Okay, let me go next. This is a very unique story. Tell me when you have heard enough. It goes like this,

"There once was a man

This man had seven sons

The seven sons said to him,

'Father, tell us a story.'

And so the father began,

There once was a man,

This man had seven sons

The seven sons said to him,

'Father, tell us a story.'

And so the father began,

There once was a man

She looked around the table, but none of us spoke up, so she continued,

"This man had seven sons

The seven sons said to him,

'Father, tell us a story.'

And so the father began,

"Oh, Virginia, we get it," Carla said.

Virginia looked around the table, "Sorry, that's all I could come up with."

"That's all right," Shirley said gently, "after Bill's story we could do with a little comedy relief."

She nodded at Hank.

"My story," he began, "is a true story. I know it's true because I experienced it myself. I was there." He looked around the table and cleared his throat. "Okay, here goes. I grew up in a working class neighborhood, right near the stockyards in Chicago. Almost all of the men around us worked there, including my father. He worked six days a week, but strangely, I never knew what he did there. He never talked about it.

"Now, there was a little park in our neighborhood, and this is where my friends and I spent most of our time after school and on weekends. The park was left totally to us kids. We were loud and vulgar, and our games were usually quite rough. A bloody nose was nothing special here. It was basically just us kids, except for one old man who would come to the park every day from the beginning of spring until the weather got too cold in late fall. He would always walk slowly halfway around the park, which was only as big as half a block. He always stopped at the drinking fountain at the other end and took a sip of water. Then, he would walk a few steps further toward the park bench. He would hold on to the backrest and do ten knee bends. He did them slowly, and it seemed that he was in pain while he strained to raise himself up from the squat position. Then, he would sit down on the bench and rest for about fifteen minutes. He would walk around the park again and start the whole procedure once again. He always did this three times. After the third time, he would remain sitting on the bench, his chin lifted up to the sky, his eyes closed. We never found out whether that serene smile on his lips was there permanently or whether he just smiled like that when he sat there on the bench. We, however, were not content just to watch him. When he was resting on the bench after his third round, we would sometimes walk past him, stop suddenly at a safe distance and do deep knee bends. Then, we would push each other and roll around on the grass, or the comedian of the day would do a deep knee bend, moan and groan and pretend that he could not get up. Then, one of us would help him up and we would stumble away, laughing all the time. Sometimes we would stop at the water fountain, fill our cheeks with water and squirt at each other. Once in a while, a squirt would go too far and actually reach the old man. He never indicated that he noticed this, and his serene expression never changed, although we all knew that he must have felt the water.

"This went on for three years. We would take bets as to what would be the first day for the man to appear, and in the fall, we tried to guess what his last day in the park would be. In the spring of the fourth year, however, he did not come back. We thought that he might come later, but he did not. We soon forgot all about him.

"Then, in late summer, two city trucks and a bulldozer appeared in the park. With them came several crews of workmen. First of all, they removed the old swing set, the slide, the teeter-totter and the old sandbox with its rotten wooden boards. Then, we saw the two old basketball poles come down, and the cement-playing surface was torn up. The batter's cage and the player's benches were ripped out. We stood at a distance and watched this taking place. Our amazement grew as we saw a whole new play area go up, with shiny new equipment, and woodchips on the ground. The entire baseball field was redone. A new sandbox for the little children was put in with soft rubber sides so that the little kids could not hurt themselves. New grass was sown in all the grassy areas, new bushes were planted, and new, comfortable benches were installed. By late fall the park was ready. It was absolutely beautiful.

"I asked my father whether he knew how all of this came about. He told me he didn't know, but he would ask his friend Paul, who knew the alderman and precinct captain. A few days later, my father told me that he was told that some old man, who had no family, and who had died last winter, left all of his money to the city with the stipulation that the money be used to make this park a more enjoyable place for children to play. We never did find out whether this man was 'our' old man, but somehow we all figured that it was.

"The next year most of us went off to different high schools, and we didn't go to the park that often anymore. And somehow it didn't seem quite the same anyway."

After a pause, Bill asked, "Did they ever put up a plaque or something identifying the donor?"

"I don't know," Hank replied, "maybe they did. We moved away a year later, and I never went back."

"Don't you want to know if it was really your old man who donated the money?" I asked.

Hank looked very thoughtful as he answered, "I'd like to think it was him, and I'll just as soon leave it at that." We all sat there without saying a word.

Shirley nodded at Carla, "Okay, girl, you're next."

Carla began with a challenge to all of us. "I will not tell you if this story is true or not. You decide; and I will not tell you where I got it from, okay?" There was no answer.

"This is the story of a man who married young. Within a year of his marriage, his wife bore him a beautiful son." Carla proceeded to tell the story, quite elaborately, of how this man lived happily with his wife for ten years. The boy grew up strong and bright. The man worked hard and established a successful business and became quite wealthy; but then it was learned that his wife had leukemia and died three years later. The man did his best to raise the boy on his own, but his business took too much of his time, and so he put the boy in a boarding school. Later, as a young man, the father took his son into his business, and for a while everything seemed to be going well. In a few years, however, it became apparent that this is not what the son wanted. He moved away and hardly maintained any contact with his father. The business grew and the father had become very rich, but somehow he felt that he had failed in life. Gradually the thought overtook him that he should try again and do it differently.

"In his mid-fifties, he married a young woman and had a son with her. Now, he was rich enough so that he could stay at home. He did everything that the childcare experts advised – he carried the baby almost continuously in his arms. The child slept in the same bed with the parents. Whenever the boy cried, he was immediately picked up and comforted. The child was exposed to all the good things in life – he heard and saw the finest artists perform. He saw the greatest masterpieces of art in the most renowned museums of the world. He traveled extensively. Since the father owned luxurious residences throughout the world, the boy learned to speak four different languages. The father and mother were with the child all the time and shared all of his experiences. The boy grew up to be a handsome, artistic, cultured and highly creative young man. When he was eighteen, he went off to an exclusive college for gifted students in Switzerland."

Here she paused. "And then," she continued, "two months after he had gone away to college, the parents received a phone call from the school. The young man had shot himself in the head, but was still alive. After spending a year in the hospital, the parents were allowed to take him home. There, he sits in a chair. He cannot move; he cannot speak. The father has not been seen outside the house since the day they brought their son home."

There was absolute silence in the room. Ted looked at Carla and said softly, "Please, don't take this the wrong way. That is a very touching story, but it is somehow reminiscent of a story I read; as a matter of fact, several stories come to mind – but that surely does not detract from the tragedy of your story."

Virginia, who had three children, let out a deep sigh. "That just goes to show you that you never know whether you are doing the right thing. The human psyche – oh well – all you can do is pray."

Again, silence. Now, everyone looked at me.

"Maybe it's time for comedy relief again," I said. "My story is just a silly little anecdote." I then told them my carefully crafted story about our trip to Venice, St. Mark's

Square, the magnificent view, the splendid buildings, the music and the setting sun with my wonderful cappuccino – my tip with my obvious mistake – my moment of hesitation and then the thought – what the hell – I may never experience this again. I closed with the line, "Want me to tell you the truth? I'd do it again, just like that, I'd do it again."

Virginia and Ben nodded in agreement.

"Yes, live the moment," Bill said, as he gave me a thumbs up.

Ted had his eyes cast down, but suddenly he looked up at me and said thoughtfully, "You are a wise man."

"I'm not so sure," I tried to laugh it off. "Twenty bucks for a cup of coffee?"

We had all told our stories, and I think most of us felt that Virginia should decide what to do next. Suddenly, Ted spoke up, "If you don't mind, I'll tell you another story. I promise it won't be long."

We all mumbled our approval.

Ted looked around the room and spent a few seconds looking at each of us as if he could learn something about us.

"I know a man," he began, "whose childhood was and was not just like it was in the stories that you told. He was not neglected, not raised by doting parents. He did not play childhood pranks on an old man, and he did not shoot himself. Maybe that's his problem. He is the eternal Jew, a Faust, a tin drum player and maybe a little bit of a Johnny Appleseed. People have tried to understand him, but he does not understand himself. He has seen the world, and he likes it everywhere, but no place can hold him for long. He has no friends except the wind, the rain and the sun. Does he have kindred spirits? Yes, he does, but they cannot go with him. They are tied to their time and place. Sometimes he pities them, sometimes he envies them."

He sat back in his chair and his eyes were fixed on the ceiling. A smile – an ever so gentle smile – settled on his face. He seemed almost transfigured. There was absolute stillness in the room. After a long pause – we all felt that he had more to say – he began again, "Sometimes, only very seldom, when he is among others, does he feel the eternal pulse of the universe, the music of the spheres, the oneness that embraces us all. It is at moments like this when he knows that there is meaning to life, that the brotherhood of man does exist, that cogito and sum are but one – yet not all – the divine is manifested in beauty all around us – reach for it, grasp it, hold it, cling tightly to it – but know when to let go – and let go gladly – yes, let go gladly – gladly, joyfully, peacefully."

Slowly his gaze came down from the ceiling. He looked around the table and once again his eyes rested for a few seconds on each of us.

He blinked.

"Well, now," he said cheerfully. "I hope I haven't bored you too much. It was a pleasure, a distinct pleasure. He got up and walked to the door. There he turned around and gently said, "Peace." Then, he was gone.

We sat around the table; no one said a word. Finally, Shirley interrupted the silence in the room and said, "I think we better talk about this next time."

We all got up, said our usual good nights and went home.

It was on a sunny afternoon as I was reading in the hammock in our backyard, when my wife called out to me and told me that Shirley from the reading group was on the phone. As soon as I picked up the receiver, I heard her stammer almost inaudibly, "Ben, you got to come down to the library. Don't ask any questions. I called all the others. Just come down here quickly."

I explained to my wife that I had to go to the library. Something had come up. "Sure, go ahead," she said. "At the library, how exciting." The mocking tone in her voice was unmistakable.

When I entered the library, Shirley was waiting for me at the reception desk. "Come with me," she said, as she led the way to our meeting room. All the others sat in their customary places.

Shirley and I sat down.

Clara, at the head of the table, looked at each of us as she slowly pulled out an envelope from a larger manila folder.

"This came today," she said. "There is a letter here and something else. Let me read the letter first." She unfolded the letter slowly. It read,

Dear Members of the Reading Group, my time with you was one of those moments in my life that renews my faith in mankind. I left your town refreshed and invigorated – I go on joyfully knowing that you are there reading, thinking, laughing, sharing. Oh, if it were so everywhere. Be joyful, be happy – live! Peace to you all! PS. Do with the seeds as you please, but you, Ben, please go to Venice and enjoy it all again – with no regrets.

Then Clara took out the other piece of paper. "Here," she said, "is a check for one hundred thousand dollars. Each of us is to get ten thousand dollars. The other forty thousand goes to the library. That's all it says."

Well, dear Reader, that is my real story. Believe it or not!

Vaya Con Dios

I finally did what all my friends have urged me to do for years – I went on a cruise. Since this was to be my first experience at sea, I booked a one-week cruise on the Golden Princess for a tour of the Mexican Riviera, with stops at Puerto Vallarta, Mazatlan and Cabo San Lucas. I figured a one week cruise to be ideal – if I didn't like it, I wouldn't be trapped aboard a ship for a long time, but if I did like it, there would be enough time to really enjoy it. Some of those three-day or four-day excursions just seemed a little bit too hurried for my taste.

The time of the year was also just right. Chicago can be brutal in the winter, and this year it seemed as if we hadn't had a decent day since mid-October. So, at the beginning of March, with Chicago temperatures hovering around forty degrees, I flew off to Los Angeles for my first big adventure on my own. Yes, on my own, because for the last forty years I did everything together with my husband, Michael; that is, until three years ago when he died of a malignant brain tumor.

The size of the ship was mind-boggling. The pictures in the brochure and on the Internet did not do it justice – 900 feet long and as tall as a fourteen-story building. How could they ever maneuver this monstrosity? That last word is not really a good word to describe the ship. It was actually quite beautiful – sleek, colorful and yes, graceful in its lines.

Check-in went surprisingly quickly given the number of people who were boarding at the same time. Before I knew it, I was up on the Aloha Deck, inside my cabin, which had a balcony. I immediately stepped outside and looked down at the pier. Way below to my left were more people entering the ship, and almost right below me, lift trucks rolled pallet after stacked pallet into the ship's huge belly. Further away, giant arms of loading cranes hoisted container upon container down the gaping holes on the ship's deck or were stacked up to eight high on the front or back part of the ship.

I changed into my comfortable traveling clothes, locked my wallet, return airline ticket and passport in the little safe and went out to explore this new world which lay before me.

I walked up one flight to the Lido Deck. My cabin was on the 12th floor, but now I suddenly found myself on the 14th floor. No 13th floor! Perhaps this was an old sailor's superstition?

Stepping through a double door, I unexpectedly found myself out in the open under a clear blue sky. There was a hint of moisture and salt in the air, and the temperature had to be somewhere around seventy degrees. This was exciting; this was wonderful, and we hadn't even left the port yet!

Since my cabin was in the front part of the ship, I decided to walk the entire length of the deck toward the back – I think they call this "aft", but I'm not sure. After just a few steps, I came to the first swimming pool, and children were already splashing around in the water, their parents lounging on the colorful beach chairs surrounding the pool. Everywhere laughter, squealing, exotic drinks carried by elegantly dressed waiters, and above all of this a blue sky, bright sunshine and a gentle breeze coming off the ocean visible in the distance.

From here, I passed through the buffet area where some people were already eating. I decided to wait until dinner – I had a seven o'clock reservation in the Bernini room, where I would dine with three other people at a table set for four. I was looking forward to meeting my dining companions.

Once I passed through the buffet area, I came out onto another enclosed space, the indoor swimming pool. Here, too, there were several children splashing about in the invitingly looking blue water.

Passing through another set of double doors, I was out in the open again, and from here, I could see the end of the ship. My friends had told me that you simply did not call this kind of huge sea-going vessel a "boat." I walked all the way to the railing. Now, I had an unobstructed view of the harbor. As far as the eye could see, nothing but more ships, cranes, and endless rows of containers of all colors, so that this enormous area of commercial activity could have presented a challenge and invitation to an artist who loved the sea and all activities related to it.

I worked my way back to my cabin passing the art gallery, the casino and the theater. I would leave the rest of the ship's exploration until tomorrow. After all, since the next two days were to be spent at sea, I would have to leave something to do for later; you can only look out at the water for so long.

I noticed something strange about my cabin as soon as I opened the door. No, the room was totally untouched, but its entire location seemed to have shifted. I quickly went to the large double door, opened it and stepped out onto the balcony. Without a horn blast, without any announcements, with no band playing at the pier, the ship was slowly and silently backing away from the long dock. There were no tugboats anywhere. There was something eerie, yet so exciting about the entire scene. Three workers walked along the dock way below me. I waved to them, but they did not respond. Silly me, how could they possibly notice one little old lady waving high above among hundreds of other passengers crowding the balconies and decks to watch the departure of the big ship?

I stood on the balcony until the ship had left the harbor and had cleared the breakwaters that separated the port from the open sea. I went inside, unpacked my suitcase, hung up my clothes and put everything else in its proper place for the week ahead. Then, I laid down for a little rest before dinner.

I got up at six o'clock, showered, put on my evening dress and make-up and went down to the Bernini Dining Room on the Plaza Deck. A pleasant young lady escorted me to my seat in the middle of the dining room. The other three people were already seated. They were a couple from Des Moines, Iowa, and an elderly woman from Albany, New York. I say elderly because I took her to be at least five to ten years older than myself. She was cheerful and very talkative. She wanted to know everything about me right away. She had obviously already grilled the couple. Mr. and Mrs. Browers were quiet and basically only spoke when spoken to. After they had heard my story, they did say that they had owned a hardware store, that they were now retired, their children lived in New Mexico and Florida, and that they really had never been anywhere before in their lives, not counting the trip to St. Louis, where they saw the

Arch and the St. Louis Zoo. This cruise was a gift from their children.

The dinner was wonderful – just like in a real restaurant, except that the service was more attentive than at any restaurant I had ever been to before. The menu listed two soups, two salads and five or six main courses. I was famished, and so I ordered the clam chowder soup, the salad with vinaigrette dressing, and for my main course, I had the braised lamb chops. My three dinner companions also ate heartily, and I couldn't believe my ears when the little old lady, her name was Millie Peterson, ordered a second dessert.

After dinner, I took the elevator back up to the top deck, where I stood along the railing and watched the sun sink slowly into the sea – everything golden and shimmering in the distance. I stood there for a long time, savoring the moment, but a voice inside of me asked me again and again why hadn't we done this before, the two of us, together.

I slept like the proverbial log, but at exactly six o'clock, I sat up in my bed and looked around me. To my surprise, I was not disoriented at all. I got up and immediately went to the double door of the balcony. Still in my pajamas, I stepped outside and took a deep breath. Yep, Janie, I told myself, you're not in Chicago anymore, and I clicked my heels. Oh, I forgot. My name is Jane Bendfelder, and I am the last of the Bendfelders that came to America in the 1880's from Austria. My family had lots of girls but very few boys.

The air was hazy and salty and still quite chilly. I got back inside, showered, did my hair, and added just a touch of make-up. I put on my "sailing" clothes – white capris, a blue blouse, and over that, a white jacket with a delicate red anchor embossed above the left breast. No socks, just my comfortable white and blue sneakers.

As I stepped out into the corridor, I was met with a friendly "Good morning" from a rather handsome young Filipino man who was about to take an armful of towels into the open room across the hallway.

"My name is Armando," he said with a pleasant accent. "I am your cabin steward. I'm sorry that I was not able to introduce myself last night," he said with an apologetic smile.

"That's quite all right," I told him. "I was so busy looking around the ship that I hardly spent any time in the cabin at all."

"Well," he strained to look at the little sign posted at the side of my cabin door, "Well, Ms. Bendfelder," he pronounced the name very carefully, but quite correctly, "if you need anything, anything at all, you let me know and I'll take care of it. No problem. You just let me know."

His smile was sincere, but the thought flashed through my mind, how many times a day does that poor fellow have to say that?

"Sure," I said, "I'll let you know. Thank you." He smiled and wished me a good day.

I found my way back to the buffet. Despite the wonderful dinner last night, I was extremely hungry. Must be the sea air, I thought to myself. And dieting? Forget it, not on a cruise where there is food everywhere. Lucky for me, I'm not really too heavy, but the cholesterol, well, let's just say my doctor would like it to come down a few points.

I saw immediately that there were many empty tables, so I went straight to the buffet. I loaded up my plate with scrambled eggs, bacon, sausages and hash browns. On another plate, I had a croissant, butter, jam and a cup of yogurt. I shook my head as I walked to a table right by the window. As soon as I had put my food down, one of the liveried young ladies approached me and asked me what I would like to drink.

"Whiskey," I said, but before the puzzled looking girl could say anything, I told her, "Coffee, my dear, coffee with just a little cream."

"Very well," she replied with a smile. She walked away briskly and was back within seconds to fill my cup to the rim.

I ate leisurely and watched the sea move past me. When I finished my first plate, I went back for the Belgian waffles, which I drenched with a thick strawberry sauce with big chunks of strawberries in it. When I finished my second cup of coffee, I knew I had to leave the buffet. The temptation was just too great. What if I were to eat like this every day?

I went out onto the deck, but did not stay long. The air was still quite cool with a fairly strong wind. I decided to explore a few of the areas that I had seen on the diagram of the ship.

First, I went to the art gallery. Although the store was still closed, there were quite a few pictures openly displayed on the walls and on the gallery floor. Some I found grotesque, some rather nice, and some were absolutely stunning. Sure enough, the ones I liked the best were also the most expensive. I made a mental note to attend one or two of the art auctions that were to be held later in the week.

Next, I went to see where the bingo game was going to take place later that afternoon and also where the Trivial Pursuit game was going to be held. Who knows, maybe I would stop in and try my luck.

I returned to my cabin. The bed was made and everything was straightened up. Armando had done a good job. I stepped out onto the balcony – still rather cool, but it was clear that this was going to be a bright, sunny day.

The big breakfast and the walk had tired me out so much that I decided to take a little rest. I laid down fully dressed on the bed, and for a few seconds, I mused about what a wonderful trip this was turning out to be.

I awoke two hours later – my, I must have been tired, and kidding myself a little, I blamed the fresh sea air.

I got up, combed my hair and then walked up to the top deck. Now, everything was in full swing. Kids were splashing about in the pool. A few adults sat in the Jacuzzi. Others were lying in their bathing suits on the deck chairs. A reggae band played in the corner of the big open space. Waiters hurried back and forth delivering exotic looking drinks. The pizza and bratwurst stands were already open, and some people either had their late breakfast or early lunch here.

I walked along the Promenade Deck again all the way to the rear of the ship. What a different sight than that of yesterday. Now, there was a wide strip of churned-up water behind the ship, as far as the eye could see. I stepped closer to the railing and looked down for a second, but I had to step back immediately. Far down below, two huge propellers were churning the water with such power that they pushed the giant ship forward with such tremendous force that I would have become sick if I had stayed and looked at that heaving cauldron any longer. But I did go back and took another peek – wow!!!

I walked inside to the Gala Deck to see what the various stores had to offer. This area is the showpiece of the entire ship. The space rises unobstructed for three stories. One can walk up or down on either one of the elegantly curved staircases at each end or ride up in the sleek elevators that move from the bottom to the top of the ship. These are exposed during this part of the ride.

I started at the lowest level where the Bernini Dinning Room, my dining room, was located. Here I also found the Aces card room, La Patisserie, the Captain's Circle Desk, the Princess Fine Arts Gallery and the Lobby Bar, soon to become my favorite hangout, for reasons that will become clear later. I slowly circled the entire area, peeking in here or stopping briefly there to more closely inspect everything that was displayed and ready to be sold to customers with too much time and too much money on their hands.

I walked up the curving staircase and made a complete circle around this deck. Here, I found the Canaletto Dining Room, the Atlantis Casino with its blinking lights on the slot machines tempting the gambler, or curious traveler, to come inside and spend a few bucks. Then there was the Donatello Dining Room. I peeked inside – just as elegant as the Bernini Room. There also was the Players Cigar Bar and the Castaways – a bar decorated tastefully in a seafaring motif. Tables were set up all around the railing, where friendly young ladies were selling colorful scarves, trendy purses, T-shirts with pictures of the various locales along the Mexican Riviera - and jewelry everywhere. Since I consider myself somewhat of an expert in this department, I took a closer look at what was being offered in the various stores and on the tables. There was something for everyone in every price range. I found the values to be quite good and told myself to come back here later to check out these beautiful necklaces, earrings, rings and broaches at a more leisurely pace sometime in the next few days.

On the next level were another bar and a few boutiques. Here, too, was the cute Hearts and Minds Wedding Chapel – very tastefully decorated, obviously ready for the next couple to exchange their vows or to renew them. The Internet Café, a photo gallery and the Sterling Steakhouse were also on this deck. And again – tables upon tables with colorful merchandise arranged around the huge opening in the middle of the ship.

Suddenly, I stopped my inspection of everything that was offered on these decks. From way down below, I heard the gentle strains of guitars, soon joined by male voices singing in beautiful harmony. Mexican music. This I had to see and hear from a closer range. I love Mexican music. I looked over the railing, and far down below, I saw three men with their guitars standing in a tiny roped off section, which served as sort of a stage, playing and singing so beautifully that I was completely enchanted.

I walked down the curved staircases as quickly as I could, the music becoming gradually louder and more distinct. When I arrived at the bottom floor, a small crowd had already gathered in front of the musicians. I found an empty chair from where I could see and hear the musicians very clearly. Seeing artists perform is to me just as important as hearing them. When I can see the passion on their faces, when I see their bodies moving as they express the beauty of the music, then the artistic experience is complete for me.

After a few bows in all directions, the three musicians began their next song. This time it was one of those lively tunes where you just have to tap your foot; a song with lots of "aye, aye, ayeee" yells between the stanzas. These were followed by echoing "aye, aye, ayeee" responses in many different keys from the audience.

As the musicians played and sang, I took a closer look at them. All three were of medium height and of slender built, except for the bass guitar player, who had more meat on him.

The three were dressed all in black. The sleeves of their jackets and the sides of their pants were adorned with beautiful silver embroidery. They wore white shirts with ruffles going down the front of their chests. All wore elaborate, huge red bow ties. Their sombreros, black with silver embroidery, seemed ridiculously large to be worn indoors, but complemented their outfits perfectly. And, of course, they wore high-heeled black boots with silver inlays.

Although they smiled a lot as they sang, one could see that they were serious musicians who wanted to make sure that they gave their best first performance on this cruise for their audience. One song after another came from their instruments and lips - each song more enjoyable than the previous one. This was perfect entertainment for a cruise along the Mexican Riviera.

After the performance, for which the three Mexican musicians received an enthusiastic reception, I wandered to the top deck to get some fresh air. The air was warm, and I saw many people eating pizza, hamburgers, hot dogs and brats around the swimming pool. The brats in particular looked good – just like the ones I would get from the German butcher a few blocks down the street from my house back in Chicago. They were my husband's grilling favorites in the summer. I got myself one with just mustard and diced onions and along with a cold beer – absolute heaven.

I went back to my cabin; a little rest period would be perfect before the bingo game later in the afternoon.

Instead of lying down, I put on my bathing suit and stepped out onto the balcony. I arranged my two chairs in such a way that I could sit back on one of them and rest my feet on the other. I closed my eyes. The warmth felt wonderful on my sun-starved skin. I tried hard not to think of anything at all – but again and again a voice inside me kept saying, "Michael should be here. He would love this. He should be here."

The bingo game was great fun. I figured there were about a hundred players seated around the large room. For twenty dollars, each player received five bingo cards. The caller was really skillful and kept the game moving. We played T's and X's and traditional bingo. After the game was over, several people walked out with very nice monetary prizes. I did not win, but the game had been great fun.

As I walked out on the deck, I heard music again, Mexican music. Yes, there they were, my "Tres Caballeros." That's what I called them, not only because they truly did look like gentlemen; they acted like it, too. After every song, they bowed politely, and when someone requested a song, the leader would nod at the person making the request. He would glance at the other two musicians, and through some sort of unspoken communication, they would begin their song, in perfect unity and harmony. I stood by the railing and watched and listened until they once again bowed deeply, waved at the audience and then walked off, in a very dignified manner until they disappeared through one of the doors leading to the interior of the ship.

After dinner, I took in a show. The star of the show was a somewhat sinister looking older magician, although his assistant was a bouncing tiny, perky young thing. As the show progressed, he became more and more likable, and some of his illusions were truly quite unique. By the time the show was over, I was dead tired. I returned to my cabin exhausted. Tomorrow was going to be an exciting day – our first shore visit – in Puerto Vallarta, Mexico.

I had booked a bus tour that would visit the city of Puerto Vallarta and the surrounding countryside. This would to be a four-hour excursion. At nine o'clock, I boarded the bus with about forty other passengers. Our tour guide was a funny fellow who told us that our bus driver was now the best driver working for this bus company. Their number one driver had died last week; their number two driver was put in jail yesterday for drunk driving, and so Eduardo was now the best number one bus driver they had. Everyone aboard laughed at his wit.

Puerto Vallarta turned out to be a wonderful surprise. The broad promenade along the bay was magnificent. Every few yards, there were interesting statues, fountains and all kinds of works of art. One of the most amazing sand sculptures was the Lord's Supper. Our tour guide explained that the figures of Christ and the twelve disciples were rebuilt every few days. We then stopped at the quaint central plaza, which exuded an Old World charm, except for the Starbucks that stood on one corner and the Hooter's that could be seen in the distance. The church was impressive in its simplicity and quiet grandeur.

Our tour continued along the coast, where we saw huge rock formations in the water that were most picturesque. Our bus turned around and drove back to the ship after we had seen the bay where Richard Burton and Elizabeth Taylor had filmed The Night of the Iguana.

Dinner was wonderful once again, and Millie could not stop talking about the wonderful tour she had taken, the highlight of which was a visit to a Tequila factory where everyone sampled that potent brew that was made there. I think that maybe that was the reason she was even more talkative than the night before – and that was good, because Mr. and Mrs. Browers had very little to say – they did not go ashore due to Mrs. Browers's leg problems that he vaguely alluded to.

After dinner, I went to the casino to try my hand at the slots. At one of the machines, I won forty dollars, but that was quickly eaten away again. After I spent nearly a hundred dollars, I admitted defeat and went to my cabin.

The next day was spent at sea again, and I had made my plans for the day. After breakfast, I would participate in the Trivial Pursuit game, later the art auction, lunch, afternoon coffee with Los Tres Caballeros, and then still before dinner, a look into the library, dinner, and then the variety show in the theater before settling down for the night.

For breakfast, I did not eat quite as much this time, and so I felt just right when I entered the lounge for the Trivial Pursuit game. I am a great fan of Jeopardy, a show that I try not to miss at all costs at home. Michael and I enjoyed watching this show together, and despite having been married for so many years, we were still surprised when one of us would know the answer to some obscure question (or rather the question concerning some little known fact) that we would applaud each other or slap our hands together in a high five.

People were sitting around in groups of four and five on colorful chairs or sofas, and the blond young thing with a

Russian accent escorted me to the far corner of the room, where I was asked to join a husband and wife team and their college age son. It became clear to me right away that they were highly educated people and that they intended to win this game. It was explained to me that the young lady would read off a total of 20 questions. Each group would consult for a short period of time, and a chosen group leader would write down the answer that was ascertained by group consensus. The husband, a distinguished looking gray-haired man, already had the answer sheet in his hand, and there was no doubt about who would be the group leader.

The questions began – at first rather easy, but then progressively more difficult. My three team members came up with the correct answer almost immediately, and they were polite enough to give me a quick glance – I would nod my approval – before our team leader would write down the answer on the answer sheet.

Question number 17 asked, "What is the largest lake in the world?" The lady answered the Great Lakes and was immediately shot a disapproving look by her husband and the son. "Lake," the son hissed, "lake, Mom, not lakes." The mother turned slightly red and whispered, "Of course, of course." The father volunteered Lake Baikal, and the son came up with Lake Superior. They looked at me, but I did not see any confidence in their eyes. "I think," I said, "strange as it may seem, that the correct answer is the Caspian Sea." The father looked at the other two and saw blank stares. "Very well, then," he said, "the Caspian Sea it is."

After all twenty questions had been asked, we exchanged our answer sheet with the one from the group next to us. When it turned out that only I and one other person had answered question number 17 correctly, the young man extended his hand to me and said courteously, "Well done." With eighteen correct answers, our group came in at second place. The boisterous group at the other side of the room had scored nineteen correct answers. When I said good-bye to the group, the father was kind enough to say, "Hope to see you next time." Thank you, Alex Trebek.

I went back on deck. Gorgeous sunshine and a gentle breeze enveloped me. I sat down on a deck chair and looked out on the endless sea. The world is beautiful, I thought. So much to see, do and learn. I closed my eyes and savored the moment, but, but ...

I left my spot in the sun when I realized that the art auction was about to begin. This took place in another lounge room. Tables and chairs were arranged on the various levels leading down toward a stage, in front of which the art dealer – a tall, young, blond man – had his assistants arrange the pictures to be auctioned off on easels, which made them clearly visible to the eighty or ninety people who had gathered here to look at these works of art and to bid on them.

The auction was fast and furious. The dealer would have his assistants put one, two, three, or even more pictures on the easels. He announced an opening bid, the reserve, and then waited for the bidding to begin. A picture was usually sold after three or four bids, all at reasonable prices, I thought. There were, however, also some expensive pictures, but there was not much interest in them, and they were quickly taken away.

Up to that point, nothing had caught my eye, and I was quite willing to walk away without buying anything. But then the young man arranged five pictures by the same artist. They were colorful – mostly landscapes – with lots of flowers, about nineteen by sixteen inches. That size would be perfect for my study – cheerful among my stacks of books, I thought.

The fourth one from the left instantly became my favorite. It showed a field of flowers in which a beautifully dressed girl, about five years old, arranges a colorful bunch of flowers in her hand, which she is just about to hand to her delicate and pretty young mother, kneeling in front of her and holding a dainty parasol above both of them. There is a house visible behind a few trees. The two of them are obviously in their garden enjoying a tender mother-daughter moment.

The bidding started at ten dollars. A rather loud woman in the front had bid on all three pictures that had come up for auction, and she got them at twenty-five dollars each. I had not bid on any of the previous pictures, but I was not going to let her have this particular picture for twenty-five dollars. I wanted that picture!

A third woman joined in on the bidding – thirty, thirty-five, forty, forty-five. The other woman dropped out. The loud mouth said, "Fifty." I countered with "Fifty-five" – there was a slight hesitation on her part. Then I heard, "Sixty." My voice was resolute – "Sixty-five." Silence. And then all of us heard her say, "Okay, let her have it!"

In just a few seconds, a young man handed me a form to fill out and asked me for my credit card. I soon left the auction, my head held high, with a smile on my face.

Later that afternoon, I went to hear Los Tres Caballeros again. I found that the high-backed chairs arranged along the side of the bar were the perfect place from which to take in the performance. With my back to the bar and a latté in my hand – this is where they served the best lattés and cappuccinos on the entire ship – I faced the three musicians, who were now dressed in beautiful tan-colored outfits.

The music was lovely as ever. They sang sad songs about lost love and happy songs about love found. Of course, Cielito Lindo was among the songs, as well as La Cucaracha. People shouted out requests, and the musicians played and sang magnificently. Although I did not look at my watch, I realized that their hour had to be up soon, and suddenly, I was seized by an unexplainable urgency that I, without thinking about it, left my seat and took a few steps toward the leader of the group and asked with a shaky voice, "Could you please play Vaya Con Dios for me?" The musician smiled politely and nodded. I had barely seated myself on the barstool again when I heard the three men play a sweet and touching introduction to the song.

When the three men began to sing, I closed my eyes. They sang in Spanish, but I followed along in English:

"Now the hacienda's dark,

The town is sleeping.

Now the time has come to part,

The time for weeping.

Vaya con dios, my darling,

Vaya con dios, my love."

The three caballeros played a beautiful interlude and continued with the verse about the mission bells and then once again the refrain:

"Vaya con dios, my darling,

Vaya con dios, my love."

Faintly in the background, I heard people singing along, but now I could only concentrate on the words:

"Wherever you may be, I'll be beside you.

88

Although you're many million dreams away,

Each night I'll say a prayer,

A prayer to guide you."

My eyes were filled with tears, but the three musicians played on as sweetly as ever and people all around me joined in on the refrain:

"Vaya con dios, my darling,

Vaya con dios, my love."

By the time the song finished, I had found my composure once again, and with a napkin in my hand, I applauded along with the others. The leader of the group bowed in my direction, looking directly at me, and I threw him a kiss.

My glance went past him and stopped on a lady sitting almost directly opposite me. She had her head buried in her hands, which held a dainty handkerchief. Her entire body shook. She sat there, small and all alone among the people who were now beginning to leave, since the head Caballero had told them, "Adios, amigos, until tomorrow."

I could not take my eyes off the woman, still huddled in her chair, her head bowed and her body now shaking ever so gently. Slowly, she sat up and dabbed at her eyes, and then, she looked at me, unmistakably, directly at me. I met her gaze, but then I lowered my eyes, and when I looked up again, I saw her turn away and walk slowly toward the corridor that ran along almost the entire length of the ship.

I sat on my stool for at least another ten minutes. The sight of that woman, so utterly overcome by grief, had shaken me to the core. What had triggered that reaction? What deep wound within her had not yet healed? What had she suffered? What had she gone through? Her pain and loneliness had seemed so totally overwhelming that there was no sense to try and put into words such feelings which our language is simply not capable to express.

That evening at dinner I did not have much to say. Millie did most of the talking, as usual, and Mr. and Mrs. Browser made a few remarks about how good the food and the service was on the ship. They were truly impressed with everything. I was glad that they were enjoying themselves.

We docked the next day in Mazatlan, where I had also signed up for a tour. Again we were shown a beautiful church, where the color blue predominated the interior and left an indelible impression on me.

Later, we were driven to a sort of amphitheater, where dancers in colorful costumes danced for us. One dance was especially interesting. One of the lady dancers unwrapped a broad red ribbon from around her waist and threw it on the floor. Then, she and her partner danced around it, all the time rearranging the ribbon with their feet. At the end of the dance, she scooped the ribbon up with her foot, and now it was in the form of a cleverly wrought heart. We all applauded heartily.

This act was followed with five Aztec Indians dressed in white and red costumes. For the first act, four of the men climbed on a strange wooden contraption. Two sturdy poles driven into the ground were held together by a strong axle, about seven feet off the ground, on which was fixed a cross formed by two heavy wooden beams with handles on the ends of each one. In just a few seconds, the four men had mounted each one of these beams and by propelling themselves forward made this cross go around in a circle at a dizzying speed. At the lowest point of the turn, the man's body was only inches above the ground. It was explained to us that this was a religious ceremony in which the men circling around and around represented the earth circling around the sun – that made it all clear, but what a way to worship!

Even stranger was the next performance. The leader of the group, who had not been part of the sun-wheel feat, now climbed first up an eighty-foot pole and stood on a small platform the top of which was barely large enough for him to plant his two feet on. The other four men followed quickly and sat each again at the end of two beams that stuck out in all four directions just beneath the small space on which the leader was standing. When the four men were seated, he began to dance on that tiny platform, jumping up and down to the tune of a small flute, which he played himself.

Then, suddenly, without warning, the four men slid off their beams backwards, and it seemed that they would fall to their certain death, but it became clear very quickly that each man had a rope tied to one of his legs, and now the four men began to swing around the center pole in a wide circle with their heads always hanging down. With each completed turn, they would descend ever so gradually until finally, one by one, they freed themselves of the loops around their ankles and then gingerly fell to the ground squarely on their feet. The leader of the group now quickly slid down on one of the ropes hanging down from the top of the pole and joined the four men standing in a row before the spectators. The applause was enthusiastic, and I was sure glad that they had all made it down safe and unharmed.

I returned to the ship just in time for the next performance of the Tres Caballeros. This time they were dressed in black pants, white shirts with red, purple, green, blue and white serapes flung over their left shoulders. The outfit was completed by a large red and white speckled bowtie. No sombreros.

I found my seat on the barstool, ordered a latté and turned around to face the musicians. Just as the three men began their first song, I saw her walk in, the little lady from last time. She went to the same seat and sat down gracefully. A waiter approached her. She said something to him, but it didn't seem as if she ordered anything.

The music was as wonderful as it had been at all the previous performances. I was amazed at how many songs these men knew. I don't think I had heard any song twice except for some of the most popular songs like La Cucaracha, La Paloma and the Mexican Hat Dance that someone from the audience was bound to request.

As the musicians played, I would occasionally glance at her. She sat almost completely motionless, but a slight motion of the head, or a tap of her fingers on the armrest of the lounge chair showed that she was following the music very closely. While others applauded loudly and even whistled at the end of a song, she would just smile ever so sweetly, and her little hands barely touched when she joined in the applause.

After the performance was over, I left my barstool and found myself an empty table by the window in the tastefully decorated seating area behind the bar.

I had barely seated myself when Manuel, the tall waiter who was responsible for this area, appeared and asked if I would like anything to drink. I ordered a Margarita, and Manuel said with a smile, "Good choice. Too much coffee isn't good for you, although I think we serve the best coffee on the entire Pacific Ocean right here."

I nodded, "I think you may just be right."

I looked out the window. The blue sea was gliding past at an impressive speed, but further away everything seemed absolutely peaceful and serene. Way back on the horizon, there was another cruise ship traveling parallel to ours. I closed my eyes.

When I opened them, she was there. She stood next to the armchair behind the little round table in front of me. Her right hand rested on the back of the chair, and she looked at me with a gentle smile on her face. I was so taken aback by her sudden appearance that I couldn't say anything.

"Hi," she said as she looked into my eyes.

"Hi," I answered, still bewildered.

"May I?" she asked, and her eyes looked down at the chair on which her hand rested.

"Please, please do," I was finally able to stammer.

She sat down opposite me, no more than four feet away. Manuel appeared with my Margarita and placed it in front of me.

"Madame?" he asked of my little visitor.

"No, thank you," she answered in a charming voice.

She sat back in her chair, and I took a sip of my drink. Heavenly. I looked at her expectantly.

"I don't know where to begin," she finally started, "but somehow I feel that I simply must speak with you. We obviously have something in common."

I knew what she meant right away, but I was willing to let her keep talking.

"I'm sure you saw my reaction to that song," she continued. "I haven't heard that song in twelve years now, and I had no idea that it would affect me in such a way." She paused.

"I'm very sorry," I said, "if that song hurt you in any way. The strange thing is that I don't really know why I asked them to play it. Somehow, it just came out of me, and I had to hear it."

She listened intently with her eyes always fixed on mine.

Suddenly, she slapped herself gently across the right cheek with her dainty hand. "My, oh my," she said with a smile, "how rude you must take me to be. I haven't even introduced myself. Please excuse me. My name is Barbara Ryan." She reached across the table and I shook her tiny hand.

"I'm Jane Bendfelder from Chicago. And you?" I asked.

"I'm from cold, cold Winnipeg. It's good to get away, isn't it?" she replied.

"Sure is," I agreed.

Her face had become serious again. "If you don't mind," she started cautiously, "I would love to hear your story involving that song; only if you don't mind, of course. But if you don't want to, I'll tell you mine; only if you don't mind, of course." She stopped and a gentle smile fell on her lips. "I'm making a terrible mess of this, aren't I? And I thought I knew just what to say to you and you would understand."

"But I do understand," I interrupted her, "and I do also think that we have something in common. I felt that very strongly when I saw you yesterday."

"Thank you," she whispered.

"Okay," I began. "I'll tell you mine if you tell me yours," was my clumsy attempt to lighten the mood a little.

"Sure, please," she said, "you go ahead, then me."

"My story starts a long time ago," I began. "Michael and I met in college, biology class, I believe. We hit it off immediately. We had no other boyfriends or girlfriends all the way through college. After graduation, we worked for a year and then we married. After another year, we were blessed with the birth of our beautiful little Angelina. She was the joy of our life. Michael was successful in his career, and we had a lovely home."

I stopped. I didn't know how the next part would go, the part of my story that had to come next. I took a deep breath and continued.

"And then she died. Suddenly, at the age of three, she died. Pneumonia, the doctor said."

I felt my eyes moisten and looked out to the sea. Barbara said nothing. She was obviously wise enough to know that silence is the only proper response in situations like these.

I turned back to her. "But life went on, and Michael and I made the most of it. We had a wonderful life together, that is, until he died three years ago. Although we did not have any other children, we always felt that our life was complete, as long as we had each other."

Barbara nodded, and it was clear to me that she fully understood what I meant.

"But now to the song," I went on. "This is really quite strange. I only say this because Michael would be the first to admit it, but he wasn't musical at all, and this is the one song he liked and sang along with. He actually stayed fairly well in tune. It was this song that we danced to on our first date. But only later, many years later, when I gave him a tape that contained this song, did he start a habit that became almost a ritual for us. You see, every time we started any kind of longer journey by car, he would put in the tape, advance it to song number four, and we would both start our trip singing along at the top of our voices. Even after spending a night at a motel somewhere along the highway, we would begin the next stretch of our trip again with this song. So you see, this song means good times to me, traveling and singing, experiencing new worlds by the side of the only man I ever loved."

Barbara had held her eyes lowered during my entire speech. Now, she looked up at me.

"And here you are now, on another wonderful voyage, but..." Her voice trailed off. She sighed, "I know, my dear, I know."

We both sat silently for quite a while. She looked out at the sea, back at me and out to the sea again. It was obvious she was struggling with herself. I'm sure she wanted to tell me her story, but somehow she could not find the right words with which to start.

I looked down and out to the sea, too, and occasionally took a sip from my margarita. She had to do this when she was ready, but there was no doubt in my mind that she wanted to do it.

Finally, she took a lace handkerchief from her purse, dabbed gently at the corners of her eyes, and cleared her throat.

"I, too, loved a man," she began, as she looked straight at me, but she quickly corrected herself as she started over again. "I still love Walter, my husband of 48 years, who was taken from me seven years ago. Oh, yes, I love him as much as I ever loved him when he was with me. He was a good, kind man. No woman could have wanted a better husband. He was my friend, companion, lover and the foundation of my life. We were not blessed with children, but our life was never empty. We laughed and danced. We did crazy spur of the moment things. He would think nothing of driving fifty miles with me on a Sunday afternoon just so that I could enjoy the ice cream that I had said was so good in that town. Oh, yes, we had many friends, but we always knew that in the end, it was the two of us, only the two of us, who really mattered to each other."

She spoke slowly and measured her words carefully. Her pronunciation was clear and precise, and she seemed to delight in forming a lovely phrase. There was serenity on her face that showed that long ago she had made peace with her fate. Although I took her to be close to eighty, the skin on her face was absolutely wrinkle-free. Her eyes were the lightest shade of blue that I had ever seen. The nose was exquisite – in perfect proportion to her face. Her lips, with just the slightest hint of color, parted a little as she spoke, and her chin barely moved. I wondered what made her look so young, when it suddenly hit me. It was her hair. This elderly woman was wearing a haircut that was very in with the young set now, but I had to admit that it suited her perfectly. That took guts – but she pulled it off famously.

"But then he was diagnosed with cancer. One year to live, we were told. About one month before he died, he went through our old record collection and pulled out Vaya Con Dios. He told me that he had learned the words when he was still in high school and that they simply did not leave his mind now that his life was drawing to a close. He told me that the last two things he wanted in life was to see me and to hear that song. He said that he would always be with me, always be beside me, like the song says, and he has been. I know he always has been.

"And so I sat there with him and I sang and I sang, and even when his breathing had stopped and his hand had grown cold in mine, I still sang, 'Vaya con Dios, my darling, vaya con dios, my love.'"

Her voice was calm. She was totally in control.

"But then," she continued, "when those three musicians came to the part that goes, 'Now the dawn is breaking through a gray tomorrow, but the memories we share are there to borrow.'..."

She sat back and closed her eyes. "Oh yes," she whispered, "the memories, the memories."

We both sat quietly for some time. Finally, she opened her eyes. Her face was bright.

"Isn't this something?" she began. "We meet here, thousands of miles from home, all because of that song."

"Yes, that beautiful, beautiful song," I agreed.

The next day I participated in a tour of Cabo San Lucas. I was totally impressed with the magnificent harbor and houses that the super rich of the United States and Canada had built here. The city itself was interesting, too, but I was glad to be back on the ship again. I was tired and took a nap. When I woke up, it was almost time to go to dinner. My three dinner companies were very talkative – the Browers were actually sharing their experiences and even managed a joke or two. I listened more than I talked.

The next morning after breakfast, I sat on a deck chair on the sunny side of the ship and looked out to sea. I tried not to think of anything, but the refrain of the song, "Vaya Con Dios, my darling, vaya con dios, my love," repeated itself over and over again in my mind. I don't know if this is possible, but I heard the melody, that haunting melody, too.

I went inside to the Trivial Pursuit game, but I did not volunteer any answers. To be truthful, I never really heard the questions. The four people in my group must have wondered what I was doing there at all.

I slept until dinner and then decided not to go to the Bernini Dining Room. Instead, I went to the buffet and fixed myself a huge salad, which I picked at with my fork and which I did not finish. I did not feel well. Since we would have to get up early tomorrow to eat our breakfast and then report to our disembarkation stations, I went back to my cabin and went straight to sleep.

I got up early in the morning. All my things were packed; I only needed to put my toiletries in my carry-on bag and go to my designated station. On the way out, I saw Armando. I thanked him for the wonderful job he had done. He waved it off and wished me a good trip home.

When I entered my waiting area, I was most surprised to see Barbara there. She sat by herself and did not see me come in. She was dressed in a stunning dark blue suit with a red scarf around her neck and a white wide-brimmed hat on her short hair – the very picture of elegance.

I tapped her on her arm, and she looked up. When she recognized me, she got up with the speed of a young girl and embraced me. I had not expected such an enthusiastic reception.

We sat down and told each other what we had done since we saw each other last. I told her about the enjoyable excursion to Cabo San Lucas, but I also told her about not feeling so well during the last two days.

"You poor thing," she said, "I'm so sorry to hear that. I'm sure you'll be fine when you get home. Strangely enough, for me, these last two days were the best of the entire trip. Would you believe, last night I went to the big farewell dance, and I really enjoyed myself. The music was great. Everyone danced and had such a good time. I wish that we had a couple more days to go on this trip." She was absolutely radiant.

Our group was called down to the huge holding area were our luggage was stored. I found my suitcase right away and waited until she came along with hers.

When we got outside, we were told that I should go to bus number three, and she should go to bus number eight.

As we approached my bus, I turned to her and said, "Well, I guess this is it." I opened my arms for a good-bye embrace.

She put her arms around me and whispered in my ear, "Vaya con dios, vaya con dios."

"And you, too," I replied, "and you, too!"

She let go of me, took her suitcase and started to walk away. After a few steps, she stopped, turned around and waved. There was a smile on her face, and in her eyes there were no tears.

Tables Turned

*H*e stood almost statue-like behind his display table. His eyes were downcast, looking up only once in a while to whisper a gentle, "Hello," or "Fine, thank you." He had lovingly draped many beautiful, hand-made cross-stitched bread cloth covers on the table in front of him. Among the many choices stitched were, 'We Give Thanks', 'Happy Thanksgiving', 'Baked with Love' and 'Our Daily Bread.' The last one came in several different languages and colors.

On the right-hand side of the table stood a pegboard on which he had displayed many handmade, one-of-a-kind Christmas ornaments. Their core consisted of Styrofoam balls that had been star-quilted with brightly colored Christmas fabric. Many of the centers had been dated in counted cross-stitch, and a few had been personalized with 'Baby's First Christmas', 'Our First Christmas Together', or 'Teacher.'

The opposite pegboard contained delicately hand-made bookmarks and banners of various sizes and colors. Some bookmarks were inscribed with 'Mother', others with 'Friend' or 'Sister.' A good seller was always 'Grandmother.' The banners, too, were inscribed with 'Happy Thanksgiving' or 'Merry Christmas' or 'Welcome Friends.' A little wood pole ran through the top of each banner and attached them to a pegboard. These were adorned with gold or silver cord.

It was obvious that his table was the most attractively displayed one in the parish hall. His wrinkle-free, monochromatic tablecloth hung to the very bottom of his display table, hiding his many boxes beneath it out of sight. Each item for sale had a little price tag attached to it. Everything had been carefully laid out so that it seemed this was the only possible arrangement for all of the beautiful wares that he had to offer for sale.

John had arrived early. It took him less than ten minutes to carry the boxes from his old battered station wagon into the hall to set up table forty-six. He was glad to see that he was assigned the same spot as last year, close to the kitchen. The heavy traffic of hungry shoppers and crafters guaranteed him good exposure to potential customers.

He now stood there in his old washed-out jeans and gray T-shirt with its barely visible sport shoe manufacturer logo on it. Over this attire, he wore a faded, thin, green summer jacket. It had to be obvious to everyone that he was too lightly dressed for the unseasonably cold temperatures outside. The conditions inside the parish hall were not much better.

He stood with his hands tucked under his arms. Once in a while, he would rub them together, blow on them, and briefly shove them into his pockets for warmth. His face was unshaven and his hair disheveled. He was tall and slender with eyes, when they were fully open, a blue that made most women think of lilacs or the sky or the blue of Meissen porcelain. When he smiled, which he did not do often, he displayed a set of pearly-white teeth, which contrasted strongly with his tanned, weather-beaten skin.

The large hall, which also served as the gymnasium for the adjacent grammar school, was beginning to fill up. He sensed that this would be a good day for profits. St. Theresa's had been one of his better shows last year, and he just had that feeling that this year would be even better.

His first customer was a blond, freckle-faced girl. 'Seventh grader,' he thought to himself. She quickly scanned the bookmarks and almost immediately reached for the one with 'Grandmother' on it. She handed him a ten-dollar bill. He reached into his left front pocket and pulled out two singles.

"Thank you," he said gently to her. She just took the bills and quickly disappeared into the crowd. He put the ten-dollar bill into his left rear pocket. That was his system – singles, front left pocket; fives, front right pocket; tens, left rear; twenties, right rear. Fifties, if he ever received any, went into the inside pocket of his light jacket.

He stood up straight. Out of the corner of his eye he saw two women three booths down looking in his direction. He quickly lowered his eyes. In no time, they stood before him. The taller one, the blonde, fingered a Christmas ornament.

"This is just exquisite," she crooned, as she took the blue one off the pegboard. "Isn't this gorgeous?" she said to her slightly smaller brunette companion.

"They are all absolutely marvelous," her friend agreed. She turned to him and asked, "Do you make these?"

"Yes," he answered softly, his eyes still cast down.

"How did you learn to make these?" the blonde now asked.

"My wife showed me..." But before he could finish the sentence, she interrupted.

"And where is your wife?" she inquired.

"She's not with me," he whispered, with a sad-sounding voice.

"Oh," is all she could say, and the brunette looked down, too.

They stood and looked at all of the beautiful hand-made merchandise. Now and then, they would take an ornament off a hook, look at it carefully from all sides, and then either place it back on the hook or lay it on the table for purchase. Even though he kept his eyes lowered, he was aware that while looking at his merchandise, they looked even more often at him.

Occasionally, he would look up and smile at one or the other, or he would say, "Yes, that one is especially pretty, don't you think?"

And one or the other would answer, "Yes, I think so, too!" but she would think, 'This shade of blue matches his eyes.'

The two ladies stayed for quite some time admiring his wares, and when they were finally ready to go, the blonde had purchased eighty-four dollars in ornaments and the brunette's selections totaled thirty-six dollars. His "Thank you" sounded sincere and humble as he handed each her plastic bag with their treasures inside.

Sister Mary and Sister Carol approached his table next. While Sister Carol carefully looked through the display, Sister Mary could not help but speak to him.

"Pardon me," she said, "weren't you here last year, too?"

"Yes," he answered softly.

"I thought so," she continued. "Your workmanship is absolutely incomparable." With that, she took a bookmark off its hook and, holding it with both hands, looked at it lovingly. "The color combination between the background, the cross-stitch and the lace border is outstanding." Her enthusiasm was definitely sincere.

"Thank you," he smiled gently at the two nuns. By now Sister Carol had decided on a bookmark – the one with the tan background and the praying hands. The beige matching lace border made the hands stand out, almost like a painting.

"Do you think Father Robert would like this one?" she asked her companion.

"What a charming idea," replied Sister Mary. "He reads all the time. He'll just love it. And I'll take this bread cloth cover, 'Nasz Codzienny Chleb'. You know he still speaks Polish quite well."

"Yes, I couldn't believe it when I heard him speak to Mr. Pavlowski's nephew when he visited from Poland," replied Sister Carol.

When both pulled out their old-fashioned money purses, he told them that for them these items were free and that he was happy that they liked the things he had made. They, however, would not hear of it. Sister Mary said something about every laborer being worth his wage, as she gently reached for his hand. He watched with satisfaction as both of them counted their dollar bills into his open palm.

"God bless you," said Sister Mary, and Sister Carol crossed herself as they turned and walked away.

Business was very good. By ten-thirty, he had to restock his booth. He pulled out the extra boxes that were stored under the table, and within minutes, every single space and hook had a new item on it, as pretty, if not prettier, than the one it held before. While methodically restocking, he was well aware that the attractive redhead in the bright yellow sweater in the booth across from him had been watching him all morning long. She was there with an elderly woman, probably her mother. They were selling Raggedy Ann and Andy dolls that held a jar of jam or some other preserve in their folded hands. Sales did not look too good for them.

A little while later, while he was handing a customer her plastic bag with a few Christmas ornaments, she suddenly stood before him. She was very pretty, and he took her to be in her mid-twenties.

"I was just wondering," she began, "you being so busy and all. Would you like something to eat?" She looked up at him expectantly, but he just looked at her and didn't say a word. "I mean, I'll gladly get it for you. My mom will watch my booth," she said as she quickly looked over her shoulder.

By now, he had regained his composure. He smiled at her and said, "That wouldn't be a bad idea. A hot dog, just mustard, some fries and a Coke would be nice."

He fished in his pocket for money, but before he could hand it to her, she answered with a girlish, "Okay," and was gone.

He had just finished giving a customer her change when the redhead returned. She handed him a school lunch tray with a hot dog, fries and a coke.

"Please enjoy," is all she said with a charming smile. Before he could even thank her, she was standing next to her mother again, straightening up one of the dolls that had tipped over.

Now, he finally sat down. But just as he was about to take a bite, he noticed the business card that lay on the tray.

He picked it up and looked at it. The card was obviously one of those self-made computer-generated ones. The entire border was made up of little dolls and the card gave her name, Tina Brownstone, Custom-Made Dolls, with her telephone, fax and e-mail information. He looked up and saw that she was watching him. He held up the card and mouthed, "Thank you." She smiled back, blushed, and mouthed, "You're welcome."

By early afternoon, he restocked once more. His merchandise was literally flying off the table. At about three o'clock, the little old lady from the table next to him came over.

"You seem to be doing quite well," she said cheerfully and without envy.

"Yes, I'm having a pretty good day," he answered truthfully.

She looked at his display. "Your things are nice, and so are you. No wonder the ladies like to stop here."

"Thank you," he said modestly.

She went on, "Anytime I make my table fee money, I feel like I've succeeded. I really just make these things to keep myself busy. If it stays like this, I might just break even."

John sensed that she was not so much complaining about not making a profit but rather that she simply wanted someone to talk to.

He looked into her kind face and smiled. He took the prettiest bookmark that he had left, the one with the word 'Friend' cross-stitched in pink letters, and gave it to her. "I want you to have this," he said. "We all need a friend, don't we? Maybe I'll see you at another show. I'll be looking for you."

"That is so sweet of you, young man," she said, deeply touched by his friendly gesture. As the little lady walked back to her table, he was very much aware that Tina Brownstone had been witnessing the whole scene.

The customers kept coming at such a rate that sometimes a line actually formed in front of his table. As he served them in his efficient and friendly manner, he realized that this congregation had an exceptionally large number of attractive women. He was also aware of a fashion trend he had not noticed before – teenage girls with extremely low-cut pants and very short tops, exposing their youthful, tight midsections. They, too, seemed to linger longer than necessary in front of his table. Occasionally, amid their shoving each other around and their silly laughter, one or the other would pick up an item and hand it to him with her hand raised up so that he was forced to look into her face as he took her selection from her. When their eyes met, it was usually she who looked down first and perhaps turned slightly red. Once in a while, however, one of them would meet his gaze straight on, and hold it, as if to say, 'Go ahead and look at me. I'm not the child you think I am.' Then, he would smile at her, and she would read in his face, 'I know, I know, but it can't be.' And she would walk away, perhaps a little sad, yet happy, nevertheless, that she had been able to communicate to him, 'I am a woman,' and he had understood.

The announcement was made at a quarter to five that the craft show would end in fifteen minutes. There were a few more sales, but at five o'clock sharp, John packed everything away and began carrying his now much lighter boxes to the car. When he had taken everything down, cleared off the table and stacked up the last two boxes to be

108

carried out, he noticed that Tina Brownstone wanted to get his attention. He looked at her. She moved her bent right arm quickly back and forth in front of her in an awkward wave, which very clearly communicated to him, 'I want to see you again.' He smiled and waved back to her, picked up the two boxes and walked out. He stopped at a trashcan outside and threw away her business card. 'Bye, bye, Tina Brownstone' is all he thought to himself.

After a forty-five minute drive, he pulled into the driveway of his luxurious two-story suburban home. With his garage door opener, he opened only the left door of his three-car garage. As he pulled in, he noticed with a smile that the Lexus 400 and the Porsche Boxter were shining clean. Within a few seconds, he was in the kitchen and in Diane's arms. He gave her a big, long hug, and then held her at arm's length.

"You look absolutely stunning," he said, and he meant it. "Come, let me see all of you," and with that he gently turned her around and looked admiringly at her curvaceous back, amply revealed by her low-cut gown. "Wherever you're taking me tonight, you'll knock 'em dead." Then, he pulled her toward the kitchen table and emptied his pockets. First, he took out the two fifties from his jacket pocket and placed them at the end of the table. Next to them, he lined up the twenties, followed by the tens, fives and a stack of ones. "Now, you count these, and I'll go and take a shower. Then we can go, okay?"

"Okay," she answered, admiring the stacks, as she began to count, "but remember, don't shave. You're at St. Fabian's tomorrow."

Within a few minutes, he was back at the kitchen table. He looked as if he had just stepped out of a men's fashion magazine. He wore a dark-blue Armani suit and a custom tailored monogrammed white shirt with perfectly matching gold cufflinks. His tie, providing a pleasant contrast from his jacket and shirt, was a lighter shade of blue with tiny exquisite Eiffel Towers embroidered on it – a souvenir from their last trip to Paris.

"Well, my dear," he said cheerfully, "how did we do today?"

"Not bad," she answered, winking her eye. "Nine hundred forty-six dollars, you devilishly handsome genius of a salesman."

"No, no, no," he replied laughingly. "It's all you and your talented hands. So, what's the surprise you have for me?"

"You'll see," she answered, with that tomboyish expression that he loved so much.

Her surprise was dinner at Le Chanson, the most elegant restaurant in the city. While driving into town in her Porsche – she had insisted on driving – he could not take his eyes off her. She was so beautiful when she was serious, and even more beautiful when she smiled. But he loved her most when she laughed out loud, girlishly innocent and not very lady-like at all. Then, at dinner, in Le Chanson's elegantly subdued setting, she looked more breathtaking than ever.

"So tell me once again," she said, suddenly changing from the small talk they had engaged in, "what do you tell the ladies when they ask you where your wife is, since by your wedding ring they can see that you are married?"

"I tell them that you are not with me," he answered roguishly, "and that's good enough for them."

110

"And when they ask you who made all of those things?"

"Well, then I lie just a little. I tell them that you showed me how to make them. And that's not really a lie. You showed me how you make them, right?"

"Right," she answered with a laugh, as they slapped hands.

"And how many women made it very clear to you that they would just love to see you again?"

"Today, there was only one. Her name was Tina Brownstone, and she was quite a looker, too."

"You say only one. I bet there were at least thirty to forty women who had some pretty naughty thoughts going through their heads when they saw you."

"Well, I don't know about that, but I have a surprise for you, too." She looked at him expectantly. "What do you say if in the spring we go to the Greek Islands of Mykonos and Santorini?"

"Really?" She got up quickly and threw her arms around him. A few people looked up, but the two of them did not care.

After she sat down again, he continued, "And in the summer, let's escape the heat and do what we've planned for such a long time." The look on her face revealed that she guessed what he meant and now hoped it would be true. "Yes," he said, "let's do it. A cruise up to Alaska with walks on glaciers and all that stuff. That'll be so relaxing and refreshing."

She did not answer anything, but from her look he knew that he had hit the mark.

Then, at home, he had gently kissed her goodnight, and within minutes, he was sound asleep.

She put her book on the nightstand and turned toward him. He was breathing gently now, and there was a slight grin on his handsome, unshaven face. She smiled, too. "Yes, ladies," she said softly. "He is delicious bait, isn't he? After all, is there anything that we love more than a melancholy, sensitive, creative and helpless man? So, go ahead and nibble, but he's mine, all mine!"

She turned off the light. She cuddled up to his chest, and in the darkness, she found his hand and held it until she, too, drifted off into a night of blissful sleep.

Harry Stevens

*H*arry Stevens brought the car to a gentle stop, and put it into park as he leaned toward his wife for the customary goodbye kiss. Nicole leaned toward him, gave him a quick peck on the lips, opened the car door, and stepped out onto the sidewalk. She leaned into the car, smiled at him, and said, "Have a good day."

"You, too," is all Harry could mumble, before she closed the door with an energetic swing.

Harry watched his better half walk across the sidewalk, surrounded by a few running and screaming seventh graders. Within seconds, she reached the main entrance to the school, turned, and waved one last time while throwing Harry a quick kiss. Then, she disappeared into the loud and bustling corridor of Ashville Academy, an inner city school where she worked as a reading specialist.

Harry returned the wave and sat quietly for a few seconds. He finally put the car in gear and drove slowly into the heavy traffic on Claremont Street.

Ever since Harry Stevens retired a few year ago, his daily routine had been fairly much the same. After dropping Nicole off at work, he would drive home, check the messages on the answering machine, check his email, and then leave again. His destination was always the same – the riverboat gambling casino just a few miles out of town.

Sometimes, Harry's friend Morris would come along. Occasionally, he would meet him there and, at other times, like today, he would go alone. Today was Monday, and Morris never went on Mondays. This was the day he spent with his mother in the nursing home.

Harry pulled the car into the garage and pushed the remote control to close the overhead door. He didn't know why he did this; after all, he would leave in just a few minutes.

Once inside, he went to the bathroom to relieve himself of the morning coffee, washed his hands and then quickly ran up the stairs to his study. Harry and Nicole had converted their daughter's bedroom to a study after she married and moved out. Here, he now had a large desk and a comfortable leather chair. The walls were lined with bookcases, which not only held his favorite reading selections, but also were decorated with framed photos of their many travels. The only exceptions were two portraits. Above Harry's desk hung a charcoal drawing of Abraham Lincoln and on the opposite wall a black and white portrait of Albert Einstein.

Harry never really knew why he had hung these portraits among the other pictures. He was a carpenter by profession, but once, when he was asked about the portraits, he answered, "I guess I'm just a realist with a heart!" And that was probably as good of an explanation as could possibly be given concerning the Lincoln-Einstein connection.

Harry checked for phone and email messages – none, good. If Nicole had wanted to call, she would have done so by now. She would be occupied for the rest of the morning

114

and would not have an opportunity to call him before noon. A slightly mischievous grin crossed his face. Had he not sounded quite convincing when he told Nicole that he didn't want a cell phone? That it was nothing but a hazard and could possibly do him more harm than good, especially while driving?

Harry opened the bottom drawer of his desk and removed a slender calendar and a few note pads. Beneath these were several sports magazines. Between them was a manila envelope. He took it out and opened the metal clasp. He held the envelope at an angle until the bankbook inside slipped out. He flipped it open to the last page and checked the final balance – five thousand seven hundred dollars.

"That should do it," he said aloud. "Still enough to make it."

Harry pushed the thin booklet into his jeans pocket and put the envelope back between the magazines.

Harry Stevens had always considered himself a lucky man. Although he had never gone to college, he had been able to make a good living as a carpenter. He met Nicole, a foreign exchange student, while he worked in the dormitory where she lived. It was love at first sight, and they wasted no time getting married. They honeymooned in Europe, where Harry met Nicole's parents and other relatives. Their marriage had been an especially happy one, blessed with a daughter, Helen, and a son, Paul. Harry and Nicole, like all young people of their generation, struggled to make ends meet. Both had enjoyable careers and had established a pleasant household. Even when Nicole was pregnant and stayed home to raise the children, Harry had no problem providing a good income. Once the children were school age, Nicole went back to work to fulfill her own career desires.

Harry and Nicole knew how to live. They traveled from China to Chile; they crisscrossed the United States many times. One of their favorite places to visit was Las Vegas. The glittering lights, noisy casinos, fabulous shows, food and drink – all this fascinated them. They weren't inclined to gamble at craps, roulette or blackjack. This was too much like real gambling. They enjoyed the slot machines, where they would risk perhaps up to one hundred dollars. Once, Nicole won eight hundred dollars. They couldn't believe their luck. It wasn't a question of money. They weren't poor and didn't mind losing. It was the thrill of winning – the fact that they too could be as lucky as other people. They giggled and laughed like school children when the casino payout person counted out the winnings into their hands.

Then, casinos opened across the country. As a matter of fact, four casinos opened not far from their home. They had visited each one several times and usually won or lost a little money. Either way, they'd go back once in awhile, simply because they enjoyed the atmosphere.

Then Harry Stevens retired. It wasn't that he didn't like his job. He did! The daily grind was getting to him. The horrible traffic on the freeway, which was forever under construction, was an added reason to his retirement decision. Not only that – Harry's back began to hurt him almost every day, and it was getting harder and harder to climb up the ladders at the construction sites.

"Let someone younger do this job. I don't need it anymore," Harry thought to himself. Nicole agreed wholeheartedly with his decision. He was also mentally ready for retirement! This made his 58th birthday celebration even sweeter.

"You deserve to retire," Nicole told him. "It's time you started doing what you enjoy – reading, bicycling and playing golf with your friends. That's what you should be doing. You've worked hard and long enough."

And so Harry retired. Financially, there was no problem. He had an excellent retirement plan working for him, and along with Nicole's salary, they were doing quite well. Unfortunately, Nicole could not retire with Harry. She was a few years younger and maintained the health insurance coverage for both of them.

"Just five more years," Nicole pleaded. "Then I can retire with full benefits and both of us will still be young enough to enjoy many active years together."

They often sat together – Harry, usually with an atlas in his hand – discussing where they would go first. They never tired of this pastime, and their enthusiasm grew with each new destination discovery. Harry's first choice was Venice.

"Just once," he said, "would I like to sit in St. Mark's Square, facing that magnificent cathedral, pigeons all around, a band playing in the background on a stage behind me, sipping a real Italian cappuccino." Harry would laugh and slap his knee. "Then, I think, I'll have seen it all!"

Harry Stevens quickly walked into the bank and stopped at the first open counter. He passed his bankbook, driver's license and withdrawal slip to the teller. Two hundred dollars should be enough to hit a good win, he thought. But then he changed his mind and told the teller to give him a new slip.

"I have to risk more to win big," he muttered to himself. Harry had started out playing fifty dollars a visit at the quarter slots. Once in a while he won, but in the next few days those winnings were quickly gone, and then he had to get more money. He was happy that Nicole never concerned herself with monetary matters. Harry was in charge of all their finances. He invested the money and paid the bills. After he had lost a few thousand dollars, he began playing the dollar slots. Only this way, he reasoned, could he make up the amount that he had lost. Now he would occasionally win a larger sum, but in the long run, he had lost more than he had won.

The drive was the same as always. It seemed as if the car drove itself; it knew the way too well. In any case, Harry remembered nothing of the drive when he pulled into the parking lot.

"Good," he thought, "still quite empty. I should be able to get to my favorite machines right away."

Harry Stevens hurried along the long corridor, which was decorated with Egyptian lions facing the middle walkway. It went through his mind that he had never really wondered why these lions were there and what they had to do with a gambling casino. He walked faster and faster and almost ran over an elderly couple walking too slowly in front of him. He turned left into the actual gambling room and without hesitation hurried down the stairs to the non-smoking area. He glanced down the row of slot machines along the left wall. A smile came across his face. The fourth machine, the Yellow Rose, was free. He inserted a hundred dollar bill and grinned as he followed the numbers on the counter move up to one hundred. He played his usual way. First, he bet one dollar, then two, and then three. He would then repeat this process – one, two, three. If he had no winner after five rounds, he would move to another machine. He was lucky today. After a few plays, he hit an eighty-dollar win on a two-dollar play.

"I should have bet three coins," he scolded himself.

Harry played quickly and smoothly. The way he hit the play button made the wheels spin continuously. Every time he hit a winning combination, a flicker of emotion crossed his tense face, which would quickly fade away with the immediate recognition that this also was nothing but a small win.

When the first one hundred dollars had diminished to twenty, Harry pushed the pay out button and sat silently watching the heavy coins hit the metal bin. He scooped the tokens into one of the omnipresent plastic buckets and moved on to the next machine. The Triple Diamond on the right wall had paid off several times before. He played this machine the same way as before – one coin, two coins, three coins. Again, a few wins, but then, an even greater loss. The first hundred dollars were gone.

The fifty-cent slots were next, where he played two coins at a time. At a dollar a play, he could make the remaining money last for some time, and that basically was the point – the chance that the next spin would bring the big win, or maybe it was the spin after that, or perhaps the tenth or the twentieth spin; and if he stopped after that without a win, then it could have been the twenty-first spin that could have brought him the big jackpot.

When Harry was down to twenty dollars, he left the casino in defeat and drove home. He threw himself on the sofa and closed his eyes. His mind began to wander, but it always returned to the same subject: his losses, how little money was left, and how little time there was left to win it back or face the most devastating moment of his life. How was he going to tell Nicole that their nest egg was gone? That he had lost it, squandered it away – not on women or booze. No, on something much worse – Harry had lost their money to one-arm bandits, to dead, lifeless machines, which took and took and made the rich investors richer and poor people poorer. But he was not one of the poor people who played out of desperation, out of a burning desire to finally be someone, to have something, to be like others with their fancy cars and nice houses. No, he was not one of them. He did not have that desperate dream.

He and Nicole had put fifty thousand dollars in their nest egg for the day of her retirement. They would then call their children and plan Nicole's retirement party. Paul and Helen would each receive a generous gift. He and Nicole would buy themselves a new car and spend the remaining money on an extensive trip. This had been planned so long ago. They had planned all the details so carefully.

Harry sat up. Damn it! He slammed his fist down on his knee. How could this have happened? There were about five thousand dollars left and a month to go before the retirement party. He made up his mind. Next time, he would take two thousand and play the five-dollar slots. Either he would win back a substantial amount, maybe even all of it, or he would just have to face the consequences. It was strange, but he did not fear Nicole's outrage or anger; instead, he dreaded the moment when he had to admit his own weakness, his own failure, the total disappearance of his otherwise so logical thinking. All his adult life, people had looked up to him as a man who had his feet firmly planted on the ground. Harry Stevens was a man of principle, integrity, kindness, goodness and common sense. He was the one who had given so much good advice to young people, to friends and family.

And now this!

The two thousand dollars provided another week's play. Sure, there were some winners, but Harry was betting more now, and the money ran out faster. Harry Stevens did not return to the casino when this money was lost. There were three thousand dollars left in the bankbook. The least he could do was not empty it completely!

Harry's daily routine now changed drastically. He would still drive Nicole to work every morning, but then he had to find other things to do. Sometimes he would mow the lawn two or three times a week. Mr. Mabelka, his neighbor next door, who worked nights, was not happy when Harry decided to do this chore so early in the morning. Harry washed the car at least twice a week whether it needed it or not. He vacuumed and dusted the house almost daily. The already painted garage door did not escape his paintbrush. The hedge along the backyard received another close trim. Harry's mind was occupied with only one thought – when, where and how to tell Nicole what he had done!

He weighed the odds about telling her in the car on the way to work, or on the way home. He discarded this thought, because it would not give Nicole the right opportunity to express herself – it was a coward's way out. He finally decided that it had to be done after supper, when the dishes were cleared away and both of them would sit down in the family room, Nicole with her needlework and he with his atlas in hand. Then, at that calm moment, he would have to tell her. And in his mind he played a thousand variations of how he would begin. He tried to imagine at what point Nicole would stop him and perhaps say, "You mean, it's all gone?" or "You have got to be kidding! Tell me it's a joke!" or worse yet, she would say nothing, stare at him and begin to cry.

The remaining days were endless for Harry, and yet they still seemed to pass too fast. The last week before the party loomed ahead. The children would arrive on Saturday; the party was planned for Sunday. Every day, Harry wanted to clear his conscience with his wife, but he could not bring himself to do it. Now, here was the final Friday. Harry had picked Nicole up from school as usual. She was in excellent spirits – after all, she was done working for life.

Harry had barbecued some chicken breasts and baked potatoes for dinner. Nicole threw a salad together, and now, they sat eating their meal on the pretty flower-filled deck behind their house. After the meal, Harry cleared away the dishes, and now, they sat under the garden umbrella, talking about everything under the sun. Their conversation turned most often to their children and how wonderful it would be to see them again.

It was beginning to get dark, and Harry knew that soon they would go inside. This had to be the right moment, this time between light and dark, this time when he would not be able to see her expression clearly, and maybe not even see the tears.

Harry Stevens cleared his throat and took a tiny sip of lemonade.

"There's something I have to tell you," he began. His voice was trembling, but he pulled himself together and said more firmly, "There's something I need to tell you, Nicole."

Nicole looked at him expectantly, "Yes, Harry, what is it?"

122

Harry continued thoughtfully, "You know the bankbook that we have with the retirement money in it and the money for the kids?"

"Yes?" Nicole responded slowly.

"Well, the money isn't quite there anymore," he confessed to Nicole.

"What do you mean, not quite there anymore?" Nicole's voice was still on an even keel.

"Well, you see, when you went off to work every morning, well, after a while, I didn't know what to do with myself, so I began going to the casino to play the slots..."

"To gamble?" she interrupted him, as she rose to her feet.

"Yes, to gamble," he mumbled sheepishly.

"Tell me, Harry, how much did you lose?" Nicole's voice now revealed definite concern.

"Well," Harry continued slowly, "almost all of it... Let's just say, all of it! We have three thousand dollars left!"

Harry looked at Nicole and saw how she slowly lowered her eyes. This was the moment he had dreaded the most. Would she begin to sob hysterically? Would she throw something at him? Would she yell and scream? He would gladly accept any of these immediate reactions.

Instead, Nicole replied in a very soft voice, "Stay here, Harry, please. Stay here for just a minute. I'll be right back." She walked quickly into the house.

Harry's mind raced. What was she up to? Would she get his old baseball bat? Could she possibly come back with a knife or a gun?

Although he didn't want to, Harry had to smile – baseball bat? Knife? Gun? They didn't even own a gun.

Nicole returned and sat down across from him. "Go get the bank book," she ordered him, as she looked straight into his eyes.

"Why?" he asked meekly.

"Indulge me. Just get the damn bank book," she repeated, her tone much harsher now.

Harry got up slowly and walked into the house, got the bankbook from his desk drawer, returned and sat down again in his chair. Nicole had not moved; she just looked at the bankbook that he held with both hands against his chest. Only the chirping crickets broke the silence.

Nicole stared at him. She then got up and said almost too gently for the situation, "Come here, Harry."

Harry took two steps toward her. Now what? A slap in the face? A knee to the groin? All this, and more, would have been okay with Harry. Any emotional outburst would have been better than this quiet and serene approach. He was willing to accept anything she wanted to dish out.

Nicole crossed the distance between them until she stood directly in front of him. She raised her arms and put them around his neck, pulling him close and kissing him on the cheek. Harry stood motionless, ready for anything. He would take it; he would take anything she could possibly do – he deserved it all!

But a kiss on the cheek? And then Nicole began to laugh. She laughed gently, then harder until her entire body shook with laughter. At first, he thought she was crying, but then it was unmistakable. Nicole was laughing – a real happy, joyous laugh. Harry stood straight as a pole. Nicole finally released him and pushed him gently away.

"Give me the bank book," she ordered

Harry handed it over. She sat down and motioned him to do the same.

Nicole looked at him from across the table and said with a sly smile on her face. "Oh, you silly, silly man. Don't you know that you could never lie to me? Do you think for a moment that I didn't know what you were up to? Don't you think I know you well enough after all these years to know what you would do? Believe me, every morning when you dropped me off at work, I felt so much more sorry for you than you could possibly have felt for me. I knew you were lonely. I knew you needed something to occupy your time. And I knew that you meant no harm. I'm sure you wanted to surprise me with your winnings."

Harry looked at her in amazement. No ranting, no raving – not that this is what she had ever done before, but in this situation, he would have understood.

"And that's not all," she continued. "I was quite willing to let you have your way, but I also didn't want to see our special nest egg dwindle away. So I had to do something – guess what?

Harry had no idea where this was going. "What?" is all he could say.

"You know my friend Sally? The one that you say is slightly loony, you know, the special education teacher at school? Well, she isn't as loony as you think. When I told her that you and I would occasionally play the slots at the casino, she told me that she also gambled, but that she played poker. It seems that it was the only thing her no-good husband taught her to play before they divorced. And believe me, he taught her well. She introduced me to the game and showed me all the tricks. Do you really think that every Wednesday when I would meet the girls for dinner we just sat around and discussed school stuff? Didn't you ever wonder why our educational conventions were held in Las Vegas, Reno or Atlantic City? Sally, Marge, Carol and I would go together, but there were no conventions. We gambled. We played poker. And Wednesday nights we went to the riverboat, the one in Justice, because we know that you and Morris would never show up there. And guess what? I did all right."

Nicole reached into the pocket of her skirt and pulled out a different bankbook. She handed it to Harry. He opened it slowly to the first page with the deposit entries. He glanced down the row of numbers: $300, $500, $250, $700, $550. He turned the page. Page after page had similar entries. On the last page, he saw the final total: $57,300!

Harry took a deep breath, all the while staring at the last figure. He tore his gaze away and looked into Nicole's smiling eyes.

"You see," she said, "two can play this game. The important thing is that in the end everything comes out right."

"But," Harry started to say, and Nicole cut him off.

"This is how I see it. We give the kids each ten thousand dollars. Then we will buy the car you always had your eye on. I've done my homework. Even with this, we'll still have enough for that cruise we've always wanted to take. Now, however, we must first get through this party, and then send everyone happily on their way so we can get started on our golden years. Then, it'll be just you and me, and neither one of us will ever have to do anything by ourselves again."

Harry embraced his wife and held her close in his arms for a long, long moment. He was glad that all around them night had fallen.

The Nightingale (Revisited)

*R*oberto Delgado had not really wanted to go to Berlin, but Juan Perez, his Director of European Operations, had been so persistent in his pleas for him to come and see the metal stamping plant that he finally gave in. Here he was now in the elegant dining room of the exclusive Bellevue Hotel, having his morning coffee and croissants. Juan sat opposite him, telling him one more time that the Bremmer Metal Stamping Plant was a sure thing, that if he, Roberto, didn't buy it, and buy it soon, it would surely be bought up very quickly by someone else who also saw the tremendous potential that this company represented. Sure, the plant was a little run down and some of the machinery needed to be modernized, but that was no big deal. With the new markets opening up in Poland, Russia, the Baltic States, the Czech Republic and all of the other Eastern European countries, this was the place to be. Juan was literally glowing with excitement, and Roberto listened to him because his European operations chief had never been wrong in the investments that he had suggested.

Roberto Delgado looked at his watch, and a smile flew across his face. He had often noticed the look of bewilderment that came over those around him when they saw his watch. He, who could easily afford the most

128

expensive Rolex or Tag Heuer watches, always wore a very inexpensive Swiss Army watch, which he knew quite well did not go at all with his very elegant custom tailor made suits. But he just happened to like it, and so he got himself one. He always got himself what he wanted.

It was five minutes before eight, and Roberto began to wonder whether there really was something to that legendary German punctuality. His interpreter was supposed to be here at eight o'clock, and at the moment, there was no sight of him. He was just about to ask Juan whether he was sure about the time that the interpreter was to arrive when he saw Herr Schnittger, the hotel manager, walk toward his table. By his side was a stunningly beautiful woman.

Roberto Delgado and Juan Perez rose, and Herr Schnittger shook both of their hands while bowing deeply.

"I hope you had a good night and that your breakfast was satisfactory," Herr Schnittger said, in fluent English with a pronounced British accent, and with a conviction that indicated that in his hotel one would not expect anything but an affirmative answer.

Before either of the two men could respond, he turned toward the young lady who had been standing next to him and said, "Gentlemen, may I present Frau Ingrid Zimmermann, your interpreter for the next few days."

Ingrid Zimmermann looked straight into Roberto Delgado's eyes and held out her hand. He took it and squeezed it gently. He was amazed how small and smooth it was. "Roberto Delgado," he said, looking into her greenish-blue eyes, "and this is my associate Juan Perez." Turning to dismiss Herr Schnittger, he said, "Thank you, Herr Schnittger, I think we are in good hands with this charming young lady." As he pulled out a chair for her, he asked

Ingrid Zimmermann, "Won't you please join us? Coffee?" and he pointed to the coffee pot in the center of the table.

"Yes, please," answered Ingrid, and Roberto poured the steaming hot coffee into the extra cup on the table, and placed it in front of her.

"Are you from here, from Berlin?" he asked her.

"Yes," she replied, "I grew up in a small town about thirty kilometers east of here, but this is where I went to high school and where I've worked."

"Croissant?" Roberto lifted the basket toward her.

Ingrid shook her head, "Thank you, but I have already eaten."

"Tell me, Mrs. Zimmer..." Roberto Delgado began again.

"Zimmermann," she corrected him, "and it is Miss Zimmermann," she said with a smile.

"But the Herr Direktor introduced you as Frau Zimmermann. Doesn't that mean Mrs.?" He looked at her with wide-open eyes.

"No, not necessarily," she replied. "You see, when the Americans coined the term Ms., the German feminists also questioned why women should be identified as married or unmarried, when no such designation exists for men. But instead of coming up with a new term like Ms, they simply took the word Frau to mean any woman past, let's say, her teenage years. No, I am definitely not married."

"Why is it, Frau Zimmermann," Roberto now asked, "that you don't speak English with a British accent? Just about everyone I've met in Europe speaks British English."

Ingrid Zimmermann smiled. "You see, I learned English in school, just like everybody else. I take that back. Not everybody learned English. My elementary and high school education took place when there was still a German Democratic Republic, or East Germany, as most of you westerners like to say. The mandatory foreign language at that time was Russian. I, however, was able to attend a Gymnasium, that's what high schools are called here, where I could major in other modern languages, and I chose English and Spanish. My English teachers all tried to teach us their best Oxford English, but I always liked the way American English sounded, you know, Elvis, Humphrey Bogart, John Wayne and all of that. And then, after the wall came down, I studied English for two years at the International Language Academy in New York. I've never been in England."

Roberto Delgado had watched her closely as she was speaking. She sat very straight in her chair and sipped her coffee very elegantly. She had blond, almost white hair, which fell straight down to her shoulders. Her eyebrows were rather dark for her light complexion, but they were natural. Her eyes were striking, and Roberto could not decide whether they were more green or blue. The nose was exquisite – not too girlish cutesy and also not too overpowering. 'Perfect,' Roberto thought, but it was her lips that captivated him the most. They looked absolutely delicious when she spoke, smiled, sipped her coffee, or when she looked at him, with her lips slightly parted, revealing the perfectly shaped white teeth beneath them.

He had expected some old grumpy East German interpreter to help him and Juan communicate with their German counterparts, but this young lady was definitely a pleasant, a very pleasant, surprise.

"Well," he said, when she had finished her coffee, "shall we get going then?"

The Mercedes limousine stood outside. Roberto Delgado motioned the limousine driver to step aside, and he himself held the door open for Ingrid; Juan sat up front.

"Tell me a little about yourself," Roberto said to her, as the limousine gently slid out of the hotel driveway and into the heavy traffic of Unter Den Linden Avenue, and headed northeast toward the town of Eberswalde.

"Well, there really isn't that much to say," she answered as she turned toward him. "I'm twenty-four years old, and I was born in a little town not too far from here. My father was a laborer, and my mother was a cleaning lady in an office building. I have a younger brother, Gerhard, who is studying to become an architect. I told you that I majored in languages and that I spent two years in New York. Now, here I am, working for the last two years for World Language Services."

"And do you like your job?" Roberto asked, and it was apparent to her that he was genuinely interested.

"Oh, yes," Ingrid answered enthusiastically. "There is always something new. Like this, for instance. This is what I enjoy most, instantaneous translation. One person says something, I translate, the other person says something, and I translate back. Now, that's fun. That doesn't get boring, and I've met some very interesting people that way."

"Like who?" asked Roberto.

Ingrid smiled as she remembered. "Well, just about two weeks ago, I translated for an English Lord and Lady who were interested in buying an old castle that was up for sale in Thuringia. They were awfully nice, but maybe just a little bit crazy. I thought they were great."

Roberto Delgado loved her enthusiasm, and so he asked, "Who else?"

Ingrid Zimmermann thought for a little while with her eyes half closed and her finger across her lips. "Mm, oh yes," she began with a giggle, "there was this Australian who hired an interpreter, me, to show him around Berlin. Now that is something that I also love. New York and Berlin are the only two really large cities that I know, and strange as it may seem, they have so much in common. During the day, I showed him all of the must see sights, you know, the Brandenburg Gate, the Parliament Building, the Kaiser Wilhelm Memorial Church and all of those places that every tourist wants to see. And they truly are worth seeing. But then, later, I found out that he was really much more interested in Berlin's nightlife. I had to show him the bars, strip clubs and even some houses of prostitution. I must say, however, that he was a perfect gentleman at all times, although I do think that he went back to some of them the next day without me."

Roberto looked straight ahead as the car began to leave the city and move into the countryside. The road was tree-lined, and off to both sides, little villages were visible in the distance. Ingrid leaned back in her corner of the car and glanced over at Roberto, who seemed to be lost in his thoughts. He was of medium height and weight. His hair was shiny, jet-black and parted on the left side of his head. By the temples, there was the slightest hint of gray. His eyebrows were full and arched rather high. His eyes were surprisingly light, given his rather dark complexion, and showed a liveliness and sparkle that Ingrid immediately realized to be his greatest physical feature. Those eyes, not really Latin eyes, could easily break a woman's heart. The nose was prominent, slightly beaked without being too dominant. His lips were full and kissable, she thought, but what she liked most about them was that they were eager to break out into a smile. The chin was fairly square, but not hard, and there was just a hint of a dimple in the middle of it. He wore a charcoal gray suit, immaculately tailored. His subdued red tie had the slightest repetitive dark red design in it. It seemed as if there were tiny gondolas floating all over it. The dark red cufflinks on his shirtsleeves contrasted beautifully with his white hand tailored shirt. He wore no rings on either hand. As he stretched his arms over his knees, she saw his watch.

She smiled, and at that very moment, he turned towards her and saw her eyes fixed on his watch.

"Do you like it?" Roberto asked, eager to hear her comments about it. In the past, he had observed that he actually learned quite a bit about people who were confronted by having to say something about his watch. He enjoyed watching some of them squirm; he could see their mind racing to say something fresh and interesting, making absolutely sure that he would not be offended. He knew quite well that everyone he met knew that he was a rich man, a very rich man, and what do you say to a very, very rich man who asks you about his fifty-dollar watch?

"I like it," Ingrid Zimmermann answered. "I like it very much."

'Oh, well,' Roberto Delgado thought, 'here was one of those who thought that he had to hear some kind of compliment about how unique his watch was, or how refreshing it was for a man like him to choose practicality over price, or how his strong personality was revealed by his willingness to ignore the fashion trend and make his own statement.'

"So, why do you like it?" Roberto was not going to let it rest at that. He wanted to see and hear her reaction.

134

Her face turned serious, almost sad. "That watch means a lot to me," she answered with lowered eyes.

'This is going to be good,' he thought. This was the most unique opening he had heard yet.

Now, Ingrid looked directly into his eyes. "It means so very much to me," she continued, "because it means so much to my brother. You see, ever since he was a little boy, he had wanted a watch like that. Then, finally for this twelfth birthday, my mother was able to get enough money together to buy him that watch. Even then, as a boy, he knew what kind of sacrifice our mother had made for him, and he has worn it ever since. He told me to make sure that no one would ever buy him another watch, for he was going to wear this one forever." Her eyes were on the verge of tears, but she pulled herself together and continued. "So you see, that is why I like that watch, because I love my brother with all my heart."

Roberto was stunned. This was the first time that the person who had to answer his question did not speak about him, Roberto Delgado, the wealthy businessman from Argentina. This was the first time that everything did not revolve around him, his money, and his feelings. No, the very opposite was true. This involved a poor twelve-year-old East German boy to whom this watch meant everything because it was given to him out of pure love and at a great sacrifice. Roberto had never experienced either of these two.

Roberto looked at Ingrid, and she looked back at him with a slightly sad expression on her face. Her eyes were bold enough to say to him, 'So what do you think about that? That watch makes me think about my brother and has nothing to do with you. Poor man, I didn't hurt your feelings, did I?'

Roberto looked into her eyes and smiled, "You know, there is something about you that I like; yes, that I like very much."

There was just a hint of a blush on her face as she whispered, "Thank you."

The owner of the company and his two top assistants were waiting for them outside the main office door. Introductions were made quickly, and then, Mr. Bremmer ushered them all into his rather spacious but barren looking conference room. One of Mr. Bremmer's assistants guided all of them to a round table at the side of the room. The huge table in the middle was obviously much too imposing and too impersonal for this little group. Mr. Bremmer asked if anyone would like coffee and rolls. Roberto Delgado declined graciously.

The meeting went smoothly and proved to be a very easy job for Ingrid Zimmermann. Mr. Bremmer and both of his assistants spoke English quite well, and only occasionally did they turn to her and ask for a particular word or phrase which they could not express to their satisfaction, or when they were not quite clear about what either Roberto Delgado or Juan Perez had said to them.

A short while later, Mr. Bremmer suggested that they look at the plant itself. The little group walked slowly through endless rows of machinery that were hissing and puffing and pounding at various degrees of loudness and shrillness. At times, Mr. Bremmer stopped and shouted a few words of explanation and, in turn, Juan gave a few quick comments to Roberto in Spanish. The entire plant had a worn out look to it: tall grimy windows with a missing pane here and there and machinery that was old and straining. Even the employees' dining room was dreary and begging for a coat of paint, new tables and chairs, and anything else that might bring a little cheer into the dimly lit room.

As they progressed through the company, it became obvious that everything had been done to make the place look as appealing and positive as possible. Workers would stop working and come forward to explain what it was that they were doing at this point in the production process. They were eager to share information and were obviously proud of what they were doing. It was apparent that they tried to make the best impression, and Ingrid could not help but feel sorry for them. She had heard of factory after factory closing because it was outdated and could not compete with the newer and more efficient equipment that was used in the West. Labor in the Asian countries was also much cheaper, so it was not surprising that companies from the West preferred their own countries or the Far East in which to do their business, instead of investing large sums of money in these outdated plants of the former Soviet satellite countries. Ingrid saw the desperation, mixed with hope, in the faces of her countrymen. She knew that they were fighting for survival.

The little group spent less than an hour in the plant. Roberto assured Mr. Bremmer that by tomorrow afternoon he would let him know whether they would meet again. Handshakes were exchanged all around, and then, the three guests headed back toward the city. On the way, Juan presented his boss in Spanish with all kinds of figures about market expansion in the East, and transportation costs from North and South America to the new capitalistic countries in Eastern Europe. He talked about tons per mile and import and export duties and quite a few other things that Ingrid did not understand. Roberto listened intently, nodding his head now and then while staring out the window at the monotonous and dreary landscape.

While Juan was in the middle of a sentence, Roberto turned to Ingrid and said, "Frau Zimmermann," his pronunciation was flawless, "would you let us enjoy your services a little while longer today by having lunch with Mr. Perez and myself? As you can hear, he talks business and business and nothing but business. There has to be something more pleasant to talk about." He winked his eye at her, and patted Juan on the shoulder.

Ingrid thought for just a moment. She knew that she had to stay as long as she was required, but with the tour of the plant ending so early, she had hoped that her services would no longer be needed and that she would be able to enjoy a quiet afternoon and evening at her apartment.

"Sure," she replied cheerfully, "I'd be glad to."

"But we have one little problem," Roberto said with a smile, "Sr. Perez and I have no idea where to go for lunch in this huge city of yours. Would you be able to make a suggestion?"

Ingrid did not have to think long about this one. "Actually," she said, "there is a place I like very much, and it's right on the way back to your hotel, but I don't know, it's not exactly the most elegant place in town. I'm not sure you would like it."

"That is exactly why we are going to like it," Roberto replied with a nod toward Juan. "We do like to experience a country the way the natives do. You can't do that at the Four Seasons, the Ritz, or at the Bellevue. Isn't that right, Juan?"

Juan nodded. "As Mr. Delgado's man in Europe, I get around a lot, and I have never found the most authentic food in these fancy places."

"Well, then," Roberto said, "tell the driver where to take us, Frau Zimmermann." He emphasized the 'ts' pronunciation of the German 'z'. "We are completely in your hands."

Ingrid gave the driver the name of the restaurant and the directions. She then leaned back into her seat, closed her eyes, and for a moment, thought about her new situation. Here she was, sitting in a very elegant limousine, next to an extremely rich and handsome Argentinean businessman. They were going to lunch together. Because of her work, she had dined in some of the finest restaurants in Berlin – places her poor laborer father, who had died ten years ago of lung cancer, and her recently deceased mother, would have never dreamed of going to. She had lived in New York and had met important people – Lords and Ladies, business executives and even some prominent government officials. She had admired their clothes and jewelry. She was impressed by the opulent hotels where they were staying and by the easy manner in which they spent unbelievable amounts of money. Yet, she did not envy them. Her life was just fine: lots of freedom, good working hours, interesting things to do and just enough money to be able to afford half of the rent for a decent two bedroom apartment, which she shared with Erika, her best friend from elementary school, who had also come to the big city and now worked in a real estate office.

The driver pulled up to a not very impressive storefront restaurant called The Golden Earring. People on the sidewalk stopped and watched as the party left the limousine; they did not recall ever seeing such a car stop here before, much less have its passengers enter this restaurant. This was the Prenzlauer Berg district of Berlin, a working class neighborhood, which formerly had been in the eastern sector. Now, it was gradually becoming a fashionable neighborhood. Artists and students had come here because of the relatively cheap rents, but that was beginning to change.

"Well, how do you like it?" Ingrid asked as they stood on the sidewalk.

Roberto smiled, "I told you, we are in your hands. I really want to see why you like it here so much."

Once they were seated at a corner table, Roberto looked around the large rectangular room. It was hard to tell whether the dinginess was original, or whether the run down, bare-walled look had been created by an imaginative interior designer. Roberto had to admit to himself that there was something appealing about the casual and relaxed atmosphere. A young waitress, dressed in black leotards, black shirt, and army boots, with several earrings pierced through various parts of both ears, handed them a sheet of paper – the menu – and walked away without saying a word. Roberto and Juan looked at the six or seven items listed, and then put the sheets down – nothing on them made any sense to them. Roberto turned toward Ingrid, who had not even bothered to look at the menu, and asked, "What is the specialty of the house?" He actually expected her to be a little stunned by this question, because he could not imagine a place like this to specialize in anything.

"There is only one thing to order in this place. Almost everyone does. I am most anxious to find out what you think it could be." She looked at both of them with a mischievous smile. "I bet you will never guess."

Roberto thought for a second, "Pork," he said. "I'm sure it's pork. I heard Germans eat nothing but pork." Ingrid could not tell whether he was serious or not.

140

"And beer," Juan added. "Beer has to somehow be part of it, although I realize quite well that we are not in Bavaria."

"Well, in a way both of you are wrong and also right. The reason I brought you here was for you to experience something that is typical of Berlin," she replied.

The two men looked at her with expressions that seemed to say, 'Come on, tell us already.'

"Okay, get ready," she replied. "It's pea soup with frankfurters on the side, and with that you drink a glass of raspberry flavored beer, the famous Berliner Weisse."

"Pea soup with frankfurters?" Roberto asked in a slightly condescending voice, but he quickly caught himself and then said cheerfully, "You know, that sounds really interesting, doesn't it, Juan?" The head of Mr. Delgado's European Operations nodded eagerly. He had visited almost every part of Europe, and enjoyed the cuisine of many regions, but this was his first time in Berlin, and this local specialty was totally new to him.

The place was packed, and at almost every table, people had a large bowl of pea soup in front of them, two long frankfurters on the side, and a bowl-shaped glass of beer, either red or green in color. The red, Ingrid explained, had a shot of raspberry juice in it; the green had something else added to the light beer, but she did not know the name of that particular flavor.

The meal proved to be quite satisfactory. The thick pea soup was very tasty, and the frankfurters, with their smoked flavor, were a perfect compliment. The beer, too, not too tart and not too sweet, proved to be a good match for the food.

The two men in their expensive suits and the beautiful young lady were somewhat out of place in this ordinary restaurant, and they noticed that quite a few glances were shot in their direction. They ate slowly and thoroughly enjoyed themselves. Roberto and Juan could not praise the food enough, and the beer also had proven to be a pleasant surprise, so refreshing and light.

When they finished, Roberto asked Ingrid whether she needed to be dropped off somewhere. The limousine was to be at her disposal because he and Juan had planned to just walk around a bit before returning to the hotel to look over some figures. Ingrid declined the offer graciously and explained that she wanted to see a friend, and that she worked only a few steps from home. They shook hands, and as Roberto held her hand in his, he asked, "Same time tomorrow?"

She nodded, "Yes, of course. I've been told that this was to be a two day job."

Ingrid arrived again at the hotel the next morning as the two men were eating their breakfast in the hotel restaurant. Both men rose when they saw her enter through the gigantic French doors. Roberto Delgado could not take his eyes off her as she walked toward them. Today, she wore a simple red dress with white polka dots and a fairly wide white belt around her slim waist. The dress was long enough to be appropriate for a business meeting, and short enough to reveal her shapely legs. She wore white shoes, white earrings and a ring with a very light stone in it. Her lipstick matched the color of her dress perfectly. She looked absolutely stunning, although her entire outfit hardly cost more than one of Roberto's neckties. This time she had coffee and a croissant.

"Where are we off to today?" she asked when they were finished eating.

"Actually, Frau Zimmermann," Roberto replied with a smile, "we are not off to anywhere today. We will stay here, and some people will come to see us."

They went upstairs to Roberto's suite. The living room had an oval shaped table in it with six chairs around it.

"If you'll please have a seat, Frau Zimmermann," Roberto said, as he looked at his watch, "maybe right here." He pulled out the first chair to the left of the head of the table. "I'll sit here, and Mr. Perez will sit to my right." There was a folder on the table in front of all three seats.

Ingrid sat down, but the two men remained standing, speaking softly in Spanish to each other. At exactly nine o'clock, there was a knock on the door. Juan opened it, and a dark haired, heavy-set man entered the room, followed by a very tall bald-headed man. Both carried thick briefcases, which they kept in their hands while they shook hands with Mr. Perez and Mr. Delgado. Ingrid was introduced, and the two men nodded at her from across the table. The short man was Mr. Turetsky, and the tall man's name was Mr. Shirov. They took out stacks of paper from their briefcases and sat down at the other end of the table. There was one empty seat between Ingrid and Mr. Turetsky.

Mr. Turetsky began, "Regarding our meeting on the twenty-fifth of September," his English was quite good but revealed a thick "typically" Russian accent, "we feel that we cannot..."

"Excuse me," Mr. Delgado interrupted without looking up from the paper he had taken from the top of the stack in front of him. "We also cannot go along with this offer. I suggest you rethink your position on this matter and communicate your final proposal to our New York office." He placed the paper face down next to the stack in front of him. Mr. Turetsky looked at Mr. Shirov, who smiled a crooked grin and shrugged his shoulders.

"Very well," Mr. Turetsky continued, "this is how we see matters concerning the Moscow Tire Company..."

He continued to explain what improvements had been made in the plant itself and praised the new management team that had been installed. When he did not know how to say something in English, he would turn to Mr. Shirov and say it to him in Russian, who would then repeat the same thing to Ingrid in German, who would then repeat everything in English to Mr. Delgado and Mr. Perez. As the meeting continued, it became obvious that Mr. Shirov's knowledge of German was not really needed. As soon as Mr. Turetsky would say something in Russian, Ingrid would translate it into English without having to wait for the German.

Mr. Turetsky smiled. "I see we have someone here who was well schooled in our mother tongue. I am impressed."

Roberto was impressed, too. As the meeting went on and shifted from acquisition to selling, from imports and exports to labor relations and management problems, Ingrid provided quick and accurate translations whenever Mr. Turetsky could not explain something in English or when he did not really understand what Roberto or Mr. Perez were saying to him. Whenever the conversation went on without her service being needed, she listened attentively, looking back and forth between the speaker and the listener. Roberto noted with great satisfaction that not once during the nearly two-hour meeting did she seem bored or distracted or disinterested. She acted as if she were a member of the team, but playing for both sides.

At ten forty-five, the two Russians closed their briefcases, shook hands with Roberto and Juan, bowed politely to Ingrid, and left the room. The trio stood up. Roberto walked toward the window and stretched out his arms. Juan went to the telephone and ordered coffee. Ingrid walked back and forth. She, too, needed to stretch her legs. Suddenly, Roberto turned around and walked right up to her.

"Well, what do you think, " he began, "are these people we can deal with or not? What would you do in our place?"

Ingrid was stunned for just a second. She certainly had not expected to have the owner of an international business conglomerate ask her opinion about anything, except perhaps where to eat dinner. For a brief moment, she thought that he was testing her, to see how well she could think on her feet. Her opinion would surely not make any difference one way or another.

"Wow," she said, "talk about putting someone on the spot, but I'll tell you what I think. Both men made a very favorable impression on me, and I do not doubt that they have very good intentions. I have no reason not to believe what they said. On the other hand, I would not sign anything with them until I had all of the figures double and triple checked. With the present currency fluctuation, there is great leeway to over- or undervalue anything. I would personally want to see these places that they are talking about. I would definitely want to talk to their current customers about their experience with these people. You are talking about huge sums of money here, and I would be very cautious before I would commit to anything."

Roberto looked over to Juan Perez and said with a smile, "Well, my man in Europe, do you concur? Do you like these people? Do you trust them?"

"Señorita Zimmermann is very astute," Juan Perez replied. "I had the same impression when we first met them two years ago. I had them thoroughly checked out, and on the whole, they are quite accurate in what they are saying. I will have to check once again about their paper production plant; I do believe that there are some environmental issues involved here that they, of course, did not mention."

Roberto walked over to Juan and patted him on the shoulder. He looked back at Ingrid and said, "Now you see why I keep this man with me here in Europe at all times. It surely is not for his good looks," and he jokingly punched Juan gently on his upper arm. "What do you say, Señor Perez? Shall we do as the young lady says?"

"Absolutely," said Juan, and he meant it.

At eleven o'clock, there was another knock on the door. Juan opened the door, and a middle-aged man in a brown suit and a rather elegant lady, perhaps in her early sixties, entered the room. They were seated where the two Russians had sat before. The man, Manfred Kuhle, was the editor-in-chief of the Leipziger Morgenblatt newspaper, and the lady, Frau Helga Brendt, was the manager of all operations. It seemed as if she were also a part owner.

The negotiations went well. Juan had done his homework, and he knew exactly what the two visitors were talking about. They were interested in obtaining a fifty percent partner who would infuse new money into their operations, and they, in turn, would expand their business into Dresden and Halle, two cities where they felt a new newspaper could do quite well. Once again, Ingrid did not have very much to do, but she followed the conversation very closely. At eleven forty-five, Roberto thanked both of them for coming and told them that Mr. Perez would be in touch with them very soon.

When the two guests had left, he turned to Ingrid and said, "That was a good morning's work, don't you think?

You must be quite tired by now. Juan and I still have a few things to talk about, and then we'll meet again with Mr. Bremmer, and after that, I think it will be time for me to leave. I thank you so much, Frau Zimmermann, for a job well done." He held out his hand to her, and she shook his hand with lowered eyes and an ever so slight curtsy that she had been taught when she was a little girl. She wanted to say something, but could only walk over to Juan, shake his hand and whisper, "Muchas gracias." Then she turned around and left the room.

Ingrid had a quick lunch at a restaurant near her office. Although she had expected to spend the whole day with the two South Americans, she was happy to leave early because she had received a message from her boss the night before that once she was done with her interpretation job, there were quite a few pages of translation work waiting for her at the office. This way she would be able to get a head start.

The translation work was not very difficult. An American manufacturer of men's wear had sent a catalog to a German company. All she had to do now was to translate how the various suits, pants, shirts and jackets were tailored, what material had been used in making them, the colors and sizes that were available and how much they cost in America. She worked methodically at her computer and made good progress in her work, but her mind was not really focused on the matter at hand. She could not explain it, but her thoughts kept wandering back to Roberto. He certainly was not the most handsome man she had ever met, or the wittiest, or most charming. And there was the matter of his age. He acted youthful and was very sharp in his thinking, but he had to be somewhere around fifty. During the meetings, she had listened attentively and watched him carefully. She liked the way he sat back and let Juan do the talking when matters were discussed that he was not that well informed about. He obviously did not need to be the center of attention at all times, but even then, when he was silent, one could feel his presence. One could sense that his mind was working all the time; and when he spoke, it was clear that he had understood everything that had been discussed. He was extremely polite to everyone, including her, the hired translator, and she was truly impressed by the way he had treated Juan. There was no doubt about who the boss was, but Roberto had made it very clear how much he trusted and appreciated his Head of European Operations. He treated him like a respected friend, jovial and familiar, never condescending. She also thought about him as a private man. She had heard from her boss that she was to meet one of the richest men in South America, but there had not been a wedding ring or any other ring on his fingers. Was he single, divorced, widowed? Did he live in a villa in Buenos Aires or New York? Did he have a girlfriend or girlfriends? Were his parents still alive, and did he have any brothers or sisters?

Ingrid opened and closed her eyes rapidly. 'I have to snap out of this,' she thought. 'Nice guy, sure, but how does this concern me? All part of the job, but now I better get this done.'

The telephone rang at four-thirty. She picked it up with her left hand, put the receiver on her shoulder, and tilted her ear down to it. She kept her right hand on the keyboard and her eyes on the text in the catalog, which she had propped up next to the computer. The blinking light on the telephone base indicated that a call from the outside had been transferred to her.

"Ingrid Zimmermann," she said in her normal cheerful voice.

There was some hesitation at the other end of the line.

"Ja, hallo, Frau Zimmermann hier," she continued.

"Yes, hi," the voice said softly. "This is Roberto Delgado." He waited.

"Yes, hello, Mr. Delgado," she said, and it was obvious that she was pleasantly surprised.

"I'm not disturbing you, am I?" asked Roberto.

"No, no, not at all. Just doing a little translation work. Nothing special," was her reply.

"You know, I was thinking," Roberto continued, "here I am in Berlin, and the weather is beautiful, and there is so much to see here."

Ingrid was about to say something, but Roberto continued, "Do I remember correctly that you said that one thing you enjoy doing is showing people your city?" She did not answer his question. He continued, "Would it therefore be possible for you to ask your boss whether I could enjoy your services one more day? You see, Juan is leaving for London later tonight, and I was to leave for New York tomorrow, but that would be wrong, wouldn't it? Shouldn't I know more about this great city?"

Now he waited for a response.

"Of course," she said, "you definitely should know more about this city. I'd love to show it to you. Tell me where and when. I know it's okay with my boss. He had told me to be at your disposal whenever you needed me."

"Please join me for breakfast at the hotel," he said. "Let's say at eight? That gives us the whole day to spend together, you know, to see the city."

It turned out to be a gorgeous day. Ingrid wore a cream colored pantsuit, low heeled matching shoes and the tiniest enamel earrings. She wore no other jewelry except an oval amber pendant set in silver. She had arranged her hair in a ponytail, and this made her look even younger and somewhat tomboyish. She hummed to herself as she walked the two blocks from the subway stop to the hotel. Roberto stood outside and hurried down the steps to meet her on the sidewalk. They shook hands and smiled at each other. It was obvious that this was not a typical business meeting.

As they were about to walk up the steps, Ingrid noted the same black limousine parked a few feet to the side. She looked at Roberto and asked, "This is not yours, is it?"

"Why yes," he answered, "I thought it would be nice to see the city this way. We could stop wherever..."

"Oh no," Ingrid interrupted, "there is only one way to see the city, and that is by double-decker bus. You'll see. Shall I tell the driver his services are not needed?"

Roberto nodded. Anything she wanted was fine with him. After all, this was her city, and she would know what to do.

When Ingrid came back from the limousine, she asked him, "Do you want to do this the right way? The way we do it here?"

"Sure," Roberto answered softly, "and what would that be?"

"Well, first of all, we shouldn't eat breakfast inside this fancy hotel. Not too many people do that. There is a cozy place just a few streets down this way," she pointed to her right. "There we can have a typical Berlin breakfast, and I'll tell you what I've got in mind for you for today."

"Excellent," replied Roberto. He liked her enthusiasm.

The place was small; there were just a few tables and chairs, and they looked like they could have been garden furniture at one time. There was a short counter where you picked your own bagels, buns, croissants, butter, cream cheese and jam. There were also hot boiled eggs available. After they had chosen what they wanted, a young man brought them a pot of coffee.

"Bagels and cream cheese?" Roberto asked somewhat sheepishly, "Where are we, New York or Berlin?"

"You see, that's what I like about this city," Ingrid answered. "I was introduced to that in New York, and I liked it, and it was cheap. Here, I just like it."

"So," Roberto asked after he had taken a sip of coffee, "what have you got in store for me?"

"This is what I thought," she replied. "You must certainly not be dragged from museum to museum and from one church to another. I want you to get an overall feel for the city. You know that until recently there was a big wall that ran right through the city and that during the time of National Socialists, this was where Adolf Hitler's headquarters were located. All of this is important in knowing why the city looks the way it does today. And, of course, not far away is where Fredrick the Great had his palace and where the Potsdam Treaty was signed, and then there was the Berlin Airlift..."

"Stop, stop, stop," Roberto held up his hands in protest and said with a wide smile, "That is way too much history for me at one time. Let's take our time. Make sure you include a nice lunch for us someplace, a delicious coffee and pastry break in the afternoon, and let's have a lovely dinner together, shall we? In between that, let's take a look at the city, okay?"

"Okay," replied Ingrid cheerfully. "Whatever you want."

"And, please, remember," Roberto winked his eye at her, "we're not the youngest anymore."

Ingrid pretended not to have heard the last remark.

Once they were outside, they only walked a few steps to a sign that said U-Bahn or subway. Ingrid bought tickets for both of them. The train arrived in a few minutes, and off they went. Three stops later, they got out and took an escalator up to street level.

"So, here we are," said Ingrid. "This is the Tiergarten, the zoo. We'll start our trip from here and take a tour around the city. After that, I have something else planned for you, okay?"

"Whatever you say," replied Roberto.

Ingrid purchased the tickets for a city tour at a nearby kiosk. They climbed to the top of a yellow double-decker bus. Since it was early in the morning and a weekday, they were the only two people here, except for an elderly couple that sat in the second row.

Ingrid and Roberto went to the third row from the back and sat down. The sun was already quite warm. Roberto took off his jacket and loosened his tie. He stretched his arms out along the backrest, gently brushing against Ingrid's shoulder with his left hand. With his eyes closed and his face raised toward the sun, he said with a sigh, "Ah, this is the life. Sunshine, no papers, no Juan Perez, no Russians, a whole day in a new city, with a delightful guide. It doesn't get much better than this."

Ingrid blushed slightly and looked at her watch.

Four more people came noisily up the steps and sat down in the middle of the bus. Then, suddenly, without warning, the bus began to move. A crackly voice over the loudspeaker system welcomed them to the tour and wished all a good time. As the bus drove through the city, Ingrid usually anticipated what the driver would say. She explained the importance of this or that building or monument, or gave the historical background for the name of a particular street. She pointed out the Brandenburg Gate and the Reichstag building and the Alexanderplatz and Adenauerplatz. They saw the Mendelssohn-Bartholdy-Park, Unter den Linden, Kurfürstendamm and the awe inspiring Kaiser Wilhelm Memorial Church – a church that was almost totally demolished during World War II. Although just about everything in Berlin had been rebuilt or was in the process of being redone, this church, in the middle of Berlin, was left standing as a ruin and reminder to the horrors of war.

Ingrid talked on and on, and it was quite apparent that she enjoyed her role as tour guide. Roberto listened attentively, nodded once in a while or asked a question. He was amazed about himself. On any other such tour, he would have become bored after fifteen minutes. Today, he enjoyed every minute of it.

At noon, they had a light lunch in the restaurant high atop the TV tower. The restaurant made a complete rotation in half an hour, and Roberto was able to see the city spread out before him in all directions without having to leave his seat.

Next, Ingrid had planned a leisurely boat ride through the city. The view, she assured Roberto, would be quite different. He did not know that there were two major rivers running through the city – the Spree and the Havel – and that these were connected to an extensive system of canals and lakes so that the city was connected to Potsdam, Spandau, Charlottenburg and areas beyond this. They rode on a small open roof tour boat and got off close to the Museum Island.

"I know," Ingrid started, "I promised that I would not drag you through all of the museums, but here is something that you must see." She led him into the Pergamonmuseum, the imposing neo-classical structure famous for its reconstruction of fragments of ancient towns, as well as the original friezes from the Pergamon altar. Roberto had to admit that he had never seen anything like this before in all of his extensive travels.

They then walked the short distance across the magnificent Schlossbrücke, which under the Communists was called the Marx-Engels Bridge, to the Berliner Dom, a huge cathedral with an elaborate neo-baroque interior. The church impressed Roberto by its sheer size and massiveness, but he did not find it particularly attractive. Ingrid had waited to hear what he would say, and she agreed completely, because she, too, had never found the building to be very appealing.

"When are we going to sit down and have our coffee?" Roberto asked, once they had re-emerged into the bright sunshine.

"Right now," answered Ingrid. "We'll take a taxi and be there in ten minutes. I think I sense that here we have a man

154

with a sweet tooth, and this will be the right place to satisfy that craving."

Twelve minutes later, the taxi arrived at Café Einstein on Unter den Linden. Roberto saw immediately that Ingrid had been right. Along the farthest wall stood a glass case which displayed the most delicious pastries – it reminded him of that day in Vienna when his host had taken him to Demel's Café. Here he was, once again faced with the dilemma of what to choose.

Roberto leaned toward Ingrid and whispered, "Do you think that people will think me crazy if I choose two pieces?"

Ingrid had to smile. Here was a multimillionaire who worried about ordering two pieces of cake. She could still remember herself as a little girl, her nose pressed to the glass window of the bakery in her little home town, wondering whether her parents would ever be able to buy her a piece of that oh so scrumptious looking delicacy, so near and yet so far.

"Believe me," Ingrid said to him, "you will certainly not be the first person to eat more than one piece."

They sat at a little round table with a marble top and ate their cake and drank their coffee. Roberto could not keep his eyes off of her, although he tried not to make it too obvious. He liked the way she ate her cake, drank her coffee; he liked the way she held the cup and how she would dab the napkin about her pretty lips after every other bite. Ingrid was witty and versatile in her conversation. She had read Cervantes, Carlos Fuentes, Gabriella Mistral and Juan-Luis Borges. She was aware of what was going on in the world of politics; and even when he spoke of soccer, his favorite sport, she was knowledgeable and predicted that a European team, perhaps France or England, would win the

World Cup, and not the highly touted Brazilians or Argentineans. And once again, she had to tell him about her family: her father who had died ten years ago, the struggle her mother had faced in raising the two children, and how she, too, died two years ago, possibly from having worked too much, but also, Ingrid said with a melancholy look, perhaps from a broken heart. She had loved him so very much, and now that the children were grown, maybe she just gave up.

"And now," Ingrid continued after they had finished eating and drinking, "I think we should go for a nice long walk, don't you think?"

"You are right," Roberto answered, "I'm afraid in the last few days I've done quite some harm in this area," and he slapped his open hand against his flat stomach several times.

They now walked very leisurely down the Tiergartenstrasse, a beautiful tree-lined street, and continued to the Zoologischer Garten until finally they saw the stark ruin of the Kaiser Wilhelm Memorial Church once again. Now, they were back in the center of western Berlin. Ingrid led Roberto to a bench, and they sat down.

"Do you think you have seen enough for today?" she asked.

"Oh, my, yes," he answered, with a moan. "I have seen enough of the city, but I'm not willing to let you go yet. Didn't your boss tell you to be at my disposal?"

Ingrid nodded.

"Well then," he continued, "there is only one thing left for us to do. I insist; no, I demand, I'm actually asking you very humbly, if you would be so kind to have dinner with me?" While Roberto spoke, he had crossed his hands in front of his heart and looked at Ingrid in such a theatrically pleading manner that she had to laugh out loud.

"Well, are you insisting, demanding or asking?" she questioned him.

"All three," Roberto said seriously, and Ingrid could tell by his eyes that this rich, powerful and charming man really wanted her to stay.

"Okay," she answered, "since it is such a beautiful evening, I have just the right place for you. I think you want to stay with the typically German food, don't you? Otherwise, we have Spanish, Italian, Greek, Turkish, American and other restaurants here from all corners of the world. If you prefer..."

"No, no," Roberto interrupted, "I want to stay with German food. This is my first time in this country, and I want to experience everything from it. I can eat Greek, Spanish or Italian food anywhere."

Ingrid took him to an inn called Zum Nussbaum in an area called St. Nicholas Quarter, named after the Nikolaikirche, the oldest sacred building in Berlin. The area consists of very narrow streets with many small shops, cafés, bars and restaurants. Roberto liked it here immediately. They sat in the tiny outdoor garden. Ingrid had to explain every item on the menu. She was amazed to find Roberto listening so intently to everything she had to say. He finally settled for the pork knuckle with sauerkraut and a glass of dark beer. Ingrid ordered the filet mignon.

After they had finished eating their main course and waited for the desserts, Ingrid leaned back in her chair and said, "Mr. Delgado, I have told you quite a bit about myself. I hope you will not be offended if I ask you to tell me something about yourself."

Roberto looked at her with a pleased expression. "No, I don't mind at all." He was actually happy that she had enough courage to ask him something personal. He did not want to part from her with this having been strictly a business relationship. "No, not at all," he repeated. He leaned forward, "I guess I have to begin with my grandfather. He started a small cannery just outside of Buenos Aires. He made it grow and acquired a few other small businesses. When he died, my father took over and made our holdings go international. He was a stern man, and I'm afraid my poor mother did not have a very easy life. He provided me with the best tutors until I was fourteen years of age. Then, I was sent to military school until I was eighteen. After that I did my undergraduate work at Berkeley in California and earned an MBA from Harvard. From then on, I worked side by side with my father, and believe me, he worked me hard. I had to do the lowliest jobs in some of our factories; then, he would have me promoted into a minor management position, and then, I would work with the plant director. My father wanted me to understand every aspect of our businesses. At that time, I thought he was unnecessarily cruel to me, but now I thank him. He died when I was thirty-two years old. That was fifteen years ago, and I've led a pretty hectic life ever since. I did not see my mother as often as I should have, and she died five years after my father, while I was away on a business trip." All the time that he had been talking, he had looked up and down and to the sides, but never directly at her. Now he leaned back and looked at her face. "And here I am now, far away from home, having dinner with a beautiful young woman, but quite frankly, I really don't know what I'm doing here, except that Juan told me that there were some good business opportunities in this part of the world. By the way, I now spend most of my time in New York."

They took a tram to his hotel. Ingrid walked with him into the lobby. "Well," she said, "I guess this is it. I hope you had a good time and that you were satisfied with my services."

"I had a wonderful time," he replied, "and I could not imagine anyone doing a better job than you did, but – could I entice you for a nightcap?"

Ingrid smiled, "I'm afraid I have to decline. I know that tomorrow I will have a long day ahead of me, and I am quite tired. I really have to go, but perhaps, who knows, maybe there will be another time."

She held out her hand to him, and as he held it, he quickly leaned forward and gave her a quick, gentle peck on the cheek.

"Yes, Frau Zimmermann," he said softly, still holding her hand, "perhaps another time."

Ingrid turned around and walked toward the door, but then stopped, turned around and walked back toward him. She opened the tiny purse, which she had slung over her shoulder, and took out a business card. As she handed it to him, she stood up straight, clicked her heels together, and gave him a quick military salute. She said very formally, but with a grin that could not be suppressed, "At your service, Señor Delgado, any time, day or night."

Three weeks had passed, and Ingrid had returned to her normal life. During the day, she translated written materials, or she interpreted at business meetings and even guided a busload of Russian businessmen on a tour through Berlin. Her evenings, too, were the same again: dinner out with friends, dancing at a disco on Saturday nights, quiet evenings at home curled up on the sofa reading Octavio

Paz, her new favorite author. Then there would be shopping with Erika and lively discussions with her friends at their favorite café. But Ingrid noticed that she thought about Roberto at the strangest times. She would calculate what time it would now be in New York and try to picture what he might be doing. She was amazed every time she found herself thinking about him – of how he had listened to her when she had explained something about the city and how he had held her hand when they got off the bus. Ingrid fondly remembered how he had asked about her family and how he seemed to have been genuinely concerned about her and her brother. His behavior during business meetings had been so self-assured, but never haughty or aloof. Most of all, she had liked his laugh, the way he would simply laugh out loud no matter where they were or who was with them. She also remembered his eyes and his lips – he was like no other man she had met before. And then, she would close her eyes and smile that melancholy smile which was so pretty on her, and hid so well that indescribable longing in her heart. Then, she would get up from whatever she was doing and say to herself, 'What's wrong with you, you dumb goat? These people come and go and you have a job to do, so snap out of it.' And snap out of it she did; then she would hum a tune, or sing a song by Elvis, or the Beatles, or a melody by Verdi, and once again she would be that cheerful and bright and pretty young lady that everyone around her admired so much.

It was on a Tuesday evening when she returned home that Erika met her at the door. "Guess what I have here for you?" she asked teasingly, as she held a handful of mail out to her. "Please, sit down now, while I find something for you." Ingrid sat down. She knew better than to argue with her roommate, who was always full of pranks and surprises.

160

"First of all," began Erika, "here is something from your credit card company. You don't want that." She put the envelope on the little table next to the sofa. "Here is a statement from your bank. Not very interesting. Here is your fashion magazine, but you can read that later. But here, what have we here?" She held the last envelope in her hand. "Why, here we have a letter from New York, and whom do we know in New York?"

Ingrid was stunned. Yes, she had met some people during her stay in New York, but she had never written to them, and they had never written to her. She quickly took the envelope and scrutinized it. Her name and address were handwritten, but on the top left corner was the imprint IFT Industries and the address. Ingrid ripped the envelope open, careful not to tear up the address. There were two plain white sheets of stationery inside; one was a letter that took up both sides, the other was a sheet that had been cut in half, with Airline Ticket printed on top. She looked at both of them and decided to read the letter first. Erika sat on the chair opposite her, far enough to allow Ingrid privacy, but close enough to be readily available for any comments. Ingrid turned to the backside. It was signed, "Sincerely, Roberto Delgado".

Ingrid began to read to herself: Dear Frau Ingrid Zimmermann, you must surely know by now that I am very, very angry with you. A few days ago, my secretary asked me whether I had not stayed in Berlin for three days. I told her that I had. She then asked why the language service company had only billed me for two. She called your employer and was told that you had taken the third day off and that you must have paid for everything out of your own pocket, since you did not submit any bills for your expenditures. This requires me to take drastic actions. I could come to Berlin and pay you myself for your services and expenditures, but I hate to fly, especially such long distances. I think, however, that there is a much better solution to this dilemma that you have put me in. Enclosed you will find an airline ticket (yes, that is my special ticket), and you come to New York and allow me to reciprocate for all that you have done for me. I know that you have been here before, but much has changed, and I might just know a few places that you did not get to experience. You set the time, and I will request your services for that period from your employer. I do not think you should come for less than one week because there is much that I want to show you (in and out of New York) and there is something very important that I need to discuss with you. You have all of my business information, and here is my home phone number. I salute you, and I am at your service, Frau Zimmermann, any time, day or night.

Ingrid looked at the other sheet. He had made the half sheet of paper look like an airline ticket. He had written: "Frau Ingrid Zimmermann, Round Trip, Berlin-New York, First Class. Any Time. Day or Night". Underneath that, he had drawn, quite nicely actually, a picture of the Statue of Liberty and the Brandenburg Gate and an airplane flying between them.

Ingrid put the two pieces of paper next to her on the couch. "Wow," she said, as she looked at Erika, who had been watching her all along.

"Wow, what?" Erika asked. "Come on, details, please."

"Wow," Ingrid repeated softly. "I don't believe it. It's from him. He wants me to come to New York for a week. He wants to show me around, and there is something important he wants to discuss with me."

She held her cupped hands over her mouth and nostrils and shook her head from side to side. This can't be true, she

162

thought; this just can't be true. A week in New York! She had wanted to go back for so long already, and here now was a free trip.

"Well, what are you going to do?" asked Erika. "You're going, aren't you? You'd be crazy if you didn't."

Ingrid sat motionless and did not say a word. Erika watched her friend and realized that she was trying very hard to keep her emotions in check. Finally, after quite a while, Ingrid looked at her and said, "I guess I've got to go."

Upon his return to New York, Roberto's life had returned to its normal pattern. He was in and out of business meetings; there were always pressing emails, faxes and letters to be answered and important decisions to be made. He went about his business with his usual degree of energy, but Lea, his private secretary, and others close to him noticed that he had become more thoughtful and withdrawn. During business meetings, he would let others do more talking while he sat, with the tips of his forefingers touching his chin, and listened. He nodded or shook his head and simply said, "Go ahead, do it," or "Okay, check it out, please." He, who previously had been involved in all of the details, now let others do more of the work.

Roberto was well aware of this, and he did not mind that Lea or one of his close associates threw him a questioning look, as if to say, "Are you all right? Is something bothering you?" He offered no information, although he knew quite well what was bothering him. Ever since he had returned from Berlin, he could not get that girl, no, young woman, out of his mind. Frau Zimmermann – he smiled. That sounded so formal, and if he had been told that a Frau Zimmermann would be his interpreter, he would have imagined an elderly German woman, with her hair in a bun, old fashioned eyeglasses and a black two-piece outfit that came down to at least the middle of her calves. The part of her nylons that would be visible would have that black line running down the back of them. Isn't that the way they always looked in the movies?

And then he met Frau Ingrid Zimmermann, and she had simply swept him off his feet. She was such a gentle creature, and yet, she had been quite bold in her explanation of why she liked his watch. That had definitely gotten his attention. She was also the first hired help who had ever dared to ask him about his private life. She was so versatile and attentive and genuinely funny that he had enjoyed every minute that he had spent with her. He still could not explain what the devil had come over him when he gave her that little kiss when they said good-bye. That had been so out of character for him, and yet, he was glad that he had done it. If she had been offended, she certainly did not show it. But most of all, he had been taken in by her when she had stood there before him, so girlish, with that childlike salute and her laughing, "At your service, Señor Delgado, any time, day or night." And what did she really mean by this 'at your service, day or night?' Was it something that had just slipped out, or was there a little more to it? Was she perhaps hinting that she was willing to be more than just his interpreter and city guide? He had to remind himself that she was not just a cute girl, but a beautiful, self-assured and absolutely charming young lady of twenty-four who, true enough, still blushed at times, but certainly knew how to come across as a mature and seductive woman.

Two weeks later, Ingrid found herself in New York City. Her boss was happy to see her go because this business relationship could turn out to be quite lucrative. Roberto met her in person at the airport. When he saw her coming out of customs, pulling her suitcase behind her, he thought her more beautiful than ever. Her hair was cut very short, and she wore jeans and a white sweatshirt with a red rose on the front. It was obvious to Roberto that she would look fantastic no matter what she wore.

Her embraced her, and when he held her at arms length, she could see that he was truly happy to see her. "Bienvenido, Frau Zimmermann," he said. "You don't know how happy you have made me because now I will finally be able to sleep at night again. Those guilt feelings have been eating me up, you know. I owe you a day's pay, and all those expenses you had..."

"You don't look too eaten up to me," Ingrid interrupted him, "and I didn't go hungry either. So there is no need for you to lose any sleep." She knew that he was joking, but that is just the way he was and she liked him for it.

On the drive into the city in his dark green Jaguar, Roberto told her how often he had thought about the three days in Berlin, especially the last one. That day, he said, had been the most relaxing and enjoyable day he had experienced in a long time. The city was wonderful, Roberto continued, but the city guide had made all the difference, and he owed it all to that sex starved Australian and the crazy English couple, because if she hadn't mentioned that she enjoyed showing people around, he would have never asked her to show him the city.

He pulled up in front of a small but very exclusive hotel on the Upper East Side. Here, he had reserved a small suite for her on the top floor.

"This is beautiful," she said, as she walked from window to window, savoring her view of Central Park. "But you know, Mr. Delgado, this is not really necessary. Any hotel room would have been just fine."

Roberto stood in the doorway and enjoyed watching her survey the entire place. She threw herself on the bed and rolled around on it. Then, she was in the little kitchen, where she checked the well-stocked refrigerator. Now, she sat on the couch and put her feet on the elegant coffee table, but took them off immediately; again, she had that slightly embarrassed schoolgirl smile on her face that he loved so much.

"You get yourself settled in," he said, "freshen up, and I'll pick you up in two hours and we'll have a nice dinner somewhere, okay?"

"Okay," Ingrid smiled, "I'll be ready."

The restaurant was walking distance from the hotel, a quaint Italian place with pots and pans hanging from the ceiling and the walls. The tables were covered with checkered red and white tablecloths, and on each table, there was the mandatory empty Chianti bottle with a candle stuck in it. The restaurant was meant to look like a typical Italian countryside inn, but Ingrid could tell right away that this was obviously a very exclusive place to eat. When she opened her menu, her initial observation was confirmed by the prices of the rather limited available dishes.

Once they had finished eating and waited for the coffee and dessert, Roberto leaned over and placed his hand over her hand.

"I told you that I have something important to tell you," he said, "and I think this is perhaps the right time to do so."

Ingrid looked at him expectantly.

"Ever since I left Berlin," Roberto continued, "I've been thinking of one thing." He looked up into her eyes. "I've

166

been thinking of how I could benefit from your unique talents, primarily your linguistic talents. Your combination of English, Russian, German and Spanish is absolutely perfect for what I need just now. You see, all of our operations are interconnected. I want our American companies to deal much more directly with our South American firms and become more involved with our expansion into Germany and other Eastern European countries, especially Russia. You don't know what kind of little United Nations I've had to set up in my office to get any kind of communication going. With you by my side, however, all of this could function so smoothly. So, there you have it. I would like to make you my special assistant. You would have your own office next to mine, and a secretary would be assigned to you to do all the emails and faxes that we would prepare. In other words, you would be my liaison with most of the outside world that I deal with."

He looked at her carefully. Her expression had not changed, and he was slightly disappointed. He had hoped that she would have agreed immediately, that there would be a look of disbelief on her face, but she just sat there and said nothing.

"If you're concerned about the salary and a place to live," he continued, "I want to assure you that we will be able to work something out that you will find quite satisfactory. My current assistant, Mr. Williams, will take over our West Coast operations and will vacate an apartment that our company owns, walking distance from the office, and that would be yours then, part of the employment package."

Ingrid looked into Roberto's eyes, and he knew that she knew why he really wanted her to come to New York. His voice and his entire manner, so eager, conveyed very clearly to her that he wanted her, just her, and that all this talk about language skills had been a rather shallow attempt to provide him with some justification for his request.

"Mr. Delgado," she began.

"Roberto," he interrupted, "Roberto, please." He felt in his heart that there was no longer any need for this charade about how important she would be as an employee, but before he could say anything else, she continued.

"Roberto, I am truly flattered by your offer, but before I make a decision, why don't we do this? I'll work with you this week, and on Saturday, the day before I leave, I will tell you what I have decided. I hope you will understand that I have several things to consider before I make my decision."

"Yes, of course, I understand," he answered in a subdued voice, and Ingrid could tell that he was disappointed that she had not jumped at his generous offer. "Why don't you get a good night's sleep, and tomorrow morning," he continued, after a pause, "I'll pick you up for lunch and then I'll take you to the office and introduce you to everyone. In the evening, we'll do whatever you want, and then we'll see about the rest of the week."

When he dropped her off at the hotel, he said to her, "You'll see that you will like it here." Then, after a slightly awkward pause, when he did not know whether he should give her another quick kiss, and she did not know whether he would kiss her or whether she should kiss him, he reached into his jacket pocket and handed her an envelope. "Now, Frau Zimmermann," he continued with a grin, "I will be able to sleep again. This has weighed so heavily on me, but now," he put his right hand on his chest, "that you are here, my heart is lighter."

Although this had been a very long day for Ingrid, she could not fall asleep. There was so much for her to consider. It was obvious to her that Roberto had asked her to come to New York for more then just to work with him, and she felt extremely flattered and proud. Wasn't this what she and all of her girlfriends had dreamed of? The opportunity to travel, to have a secure job with good pay, to be able to do all of the things they always wanted to do. And with Roberto, she would not be selling her soul to the devil to attain all of this. He was a charming, considerate man. To be sure, he was a little older than she or her friends would have imagined their 'companion' to be, but Roberto was not an old man by any means. He acted youthful and playful and did not possess an ounce of that arrogance and pompousness that she detested so much in some of the rich and powerful men she had met. She also asked herself how she would fit in here in New York. Would she make new friends that would come even close to being that to her what Erika and her other friends meant to her? What about her brother? Could she leave him alone in Berlin? Financially, she would be able to help him more, there was no doubt about that, but was that really what mattered most?

It was two in the morning when she picked up the telephone and made three calls to Germany. After that she called the front desk and asked for an eight o'clock wake up call. She went back to bed and within five minutes was sound asleep.

The telephone rang at exactly eight o'clock, and Ingrid literally jumped out of bed. She had until noon to do whatever she wanted. She was ready in just a few minutes, but before she left she picked up the envelope once again that Roberto had given her the night before. It contained five crisp one hundred dollar bills and another five hundred in twenties. "Most generous," she thought, "and very thoughtful." She then read the note again that he had included with the money: Thanks for everything. I am happy you are here. Roberto.

She put the money and the note into her purse and left. Outside the hotel, she took a deep breath. This was just too good to be true – back in New York with a tremendous job offer and maybe… She stopped herself from continuing this line of thought. She walked north on Fifth Avenue, bought a coffee to go, and sat down on the steps of the Metropolitan Museum of Art. She simply loved it here – the museum inside and the atmosphere outside. Yes, she could live here. Then, she got into a bus and went to Bloomingdales. There was really nothing that she wanted to buy, but then, as she walked down the aisles with all the wonderful items on both sides, she could not resist and bought herself a brightly colored silk scarf, outrageously expensive, but why not, she thought.

Once outside, she walked and walked and took in the sights and sounds of this familiar, yet once again so new, city. She sang, sometimes to herself, sometimes out loud, songs about the lullaby of Broadway and something about 42nd Street. She did not know all the words, but she knew the tunes, and she did not mind that sometimes people looked at her as she walked, singing, down the wide sidewalks of New York. She was young, free, and a new phase of her life, a wonderful phase, was about to begin.

"Well, are you hungry?" Roberto greeted her as she walked toward him on the sidewalk in front of the hotel.

"Yes, I'm famished, and I know exactly what I want," responded Ingrid.

170

"Name it," he answered. "I am at your service, remember, any time, day or night," and he bowed deeply.

"I would like nothing more than a real authentic New York hot dog. Maybe two," she replied.

Roberto looked perplexed for just a second, but then he smiled and said, "But, of course, Frau Zimmermann, and I know just the place where we can get the best one in town."

They walked together all the way across to the East River, where Roberto bought two hot dogs from Niko, whom he introduced to Ingrid as the man who made the best hot dog in all of New York City. Niko shook her hand and in a thick Greek accent told her that he was glad to meet her. She was absolutely sure that he had no idea who the man who had brought her here really was. They talked as if they had been friends for the longest time. Roberto and Ingrid ate their hot dog sitting on a park bench while numerous pigeons fluttered around them, hoping to pick up a crumb here or there.

When they finished their meal, Roberto looked at her, "Well?" he asked.

"You're right," she answered, "this is the best hot dog I ever had. I'll have another."

Roberto grinned, "I told you so, didn't I?"

The building in which Roberto's office was located was not as impressive as she had expected, but when they left the elevator on the thirty-third floor and she saw ISI, International Services Incorporated, spelled in six feet tall silver letters, she knew that she was at the heart of a truly global corporation.

As they walked toward Roberto's office, they stopped here or there, and Roberto introduced her to many of his top people. He always gave a brief explanation as to what that person's responsibilities were, and Ingrid was amazed at the scope of the entire operation. She was equally amazed that Roberto was able to remember everyone's name and exact duties. As they continued walking, Ingrid was very well aware of all the heads that turned in their direction and the quick once over that she got from men and women alike. She did not have the time to think about what they might be thinking; she concentrated on everything that Roberto was saying to her.

They finally reached the other end of the floor. This area was divided into three offices. The farthest on the left belonged to Lea Greenfield, Roberto's executive secretary; the one in the middle, the largest, was the office of Herbert Williams, the newly named Director of West Coast Operations; and in the right corner, almost insignificant looking compared to the other two, was Roberto's office. The advantage that this office had, however, was that it had large windows on the left and right sides, so that Roberto, whose desk was placed diagonally between them, only had to look to the left or right to have the most impressive view of the East River or the Upper Midtown area of New York.

"Well, here we are," he said as he motioned to a chair beside his desk before he sat down on his leather chair. But before he said anything else, he jumped out of his chair and continued, "Come here, you have to see this." He took Ingrid to the window on the right, and she had to take in the view of the river and beyond. He took her by the arm and led her to the other side, where the city was spread out before them as far as the eye could see; the skyscrapers of Lower Manhattan were barely visible in the distance.

"What do you think?" he asked her. "Isn't this a sight worth seeing? I look forward to coming to work just to see this. I never get tired of it."

He then walked her over to Lea Greenfield, a tall dark haired woman in her mid fifties, who rose from behind her desk when the two of them entered. Roberto introduced her as the woman in his life who he could not do without, who knew more about what was going on at ISI than he did, and who, if she would ever leave him, would force him to shut down the company and retire.

Lea Greenfield smiled graciously, shook hands with Ingrid and said, "Mr. Delgado has told me how invaluable your services have been in Berlin. I hope you will stay with us for some time."

Ingrid smiled meekly and said, "Thank you," and Roberto noticed that once again how a gentle blush came over her face.

Concluding the introductions, Roberto took Ingrid to Mr. Williams's office. In front of the window stood a huge desk with a black leather chair behind it. The view through the window was almost as good as from Roberto's window. Everything in the room was dark and massive.

"This will be your office for the next few days," Roberto told her as he watched her survey the room. "Of course, if you decide to stay with me, you can have this space redone any way that you wish. I realize that this may not be quite to your taste."

Ingrid looked around the room and did not say anything. She had never been in an office like this before. The sheer size of it was overwhelming, and the furniture must have cost a fortune. The table and chair exuded power and authority, and the cabinets along the walls in dark wood, with occasional glass doors, revealed tasteful vases and other art objects, perfectly illuminated by recessed lighting. Roberto walked toward one cabinet and pulled down the door. In a fairly large space, there stood bottles of the most select brandies and champagnes with rows of sparkling glasses to match.

Ingrid turned to Roberto and burst out, "Wow, this is some office. This should be yours. Why aren't you in here?"

"Because," Roberto answered with a smile, "I like the other one better. This room somehow isn't me. But if you fix it up just right, it could be very much you. If you want to, all of this can go right out the window, and you get yourself exactly what you want."

Ingrid looked around the room once more, and she felt that she was perhaps getting exactly what she wanted.

Roberto and Ingrid spent the afternoon in Roberto's office. He had pulled up two chairs on the other side of his desk so that, as they sat side by side, they were facing his empty black leather chair.

"Just so that you don't think that I brought you here under false pretenses," he began, as he placed a stack of files before her, "take a look at this, and you will see that I desperately need help. And this is just the tip of the iceberg."

They looked through letters and faxes and emails from all over the world. Some of them were replies that had come out of Roberto's office.

"Please look very carefully at these," he told her. "I'm not so sure that our last translators were all that competent, because some of the replies that we received did not really make sense. Here is an example." Roberto opened a folder labeled 'Meier und Schmidt, GmbH.' "Please read what they wrote to us, then read our answer, and then read their reply. Something went wrong somewhere."

Ingrid carefully read the first letter, in German, and then she read the response that had come out of Roberto's office. She saw the problem immediately. The translator had translated the German world 'will' as 'will' in English. The true meaning, however, is 'want to.' She explained the misunderstanding. Roberto listened very attentively.

"You see," he began after she had explained how the wrong translation of one word had brought about such far reaching miscommunication between the two companies, "this is why I need someone by my side that I can totally trust. Now their response to our letter makes more sense. I want to get back to them immediately and let them know where the problem was and that we are still interested in their proposal."

In just a few minutes, Roberto had worked out a very clear statement as to the position that ISI was taking, now that they fully understood the initial letter. He hoped that they could soon meet here in New York. Ingrid had the letter translated a short while later and asked Roberto whether he wanted it emailed to the German company?

"Of course," he answered, "you can do it right here from my office," and he watched with great interest as she speedily typed out the letter on the computer.

"How do you want me to close?" she asked over her shoulder.

"Just Roberto Delgado," he said. "They know who I am."

They then looked through a few other materials and arranged them in order of priority. Roberto had coffee and tiny sandwiches brought into the office. They continued working while they enjoyed the refreshments. By the way they were sitting side by side, Ingrid could feel very clearly that he enjoyed being close to her, although she noticed that he made sure not to touch her in any way or to speak too loudly at her from the close distance between them. As the hours passed, they both felt that they were indeed a perfect team – she immediately understood why this or that was a problem, and he noticed with great satisfaction that she took each one of them very seriously. She worked hard to come up with the right answer, and he was absolutely sure that she always did.

The day passed quickly. At seven o'clock, Lea Greenfield stuck her head into the room and said good night. Roberto looked at his watch.

"Oh my," he exclaimed, "it's way past quitting time. What happened to the time?"

"Isn't there a saying," Ingrid asked jokingly, "time flies when you're having fun?"

"That must be it." Roberto answered, "That must be it."

That evening, Roberto took Ingrid to a Chinese restaurant. She had told him that she had never had such good Chinese food in Germany as she had eaten in New York City. As they were uncovering bowl after bowl of steaming, delicious smelling food, Ingrid suddenly looked at him and said, "I've decided that I will stay with you. I mean, not stay now. I will go back after this week, but if you want me to, I'll come back and work for you."

Roberto lowered the shrimp-filled fork back to his plate. "What," he said with an expression of joy on his face that she had not yet seen before, "you've decided already? Really? You're staying? I mean, coming back?"

"Yes," she said simply. "I made a few phone calls this morning and everything is set."

"If you don't mind my asking," Roberto ventured cautiously, "whom did you have to call to make this decision?"

Ingrid sensed that this question might be related to her involvement with a man, a boyfriend perhaps, someone about whom she was not too sure whether their future together would work out.

"Before I could give you an answer, I had to make sure that three things were taken care of." She could see the expectancy on his face, but he did not say anything.

"First of all," she continued, "I had to make sure that my brother would be all right. He assured me that everything is fine. He is well taken care of, and I shouldn't worry about him. But, of course, I do worry about him, you see, we only have each other, and now, I will be able to help him even more financially."

Ingrid looked into Roberto's eyes and felt his approval.

"Number two," she went on, "I had to make sure that my roommate Erika would be okay with the apartment. I know that she cannot afford it on her own. She told me that there was a girl at her office who is desperate for an apartment and who would be overjoyed if she could move in with her. She told me over and over again not to worry about her and do whatever is best for me. She was so happy for me that she cried."

"My third phone call was the hardest to make," she said softly. She noticed how Roberto stiffened just a little. "I called our neighbor, Mrs. Lemke, and asked her if she wouldn't mind tending to the flowers on my parents' grave. Her husband is buried nearby, and she walks to the cemetery almost every day when the weather is nice. I will be able, don't you think, to go back once in a while and see to things myself. That grave in our little town cemetery is the only real connection that I have to my childhood, and those two people in the ground are the ones who have worked their fingers to the bone so that my brother and I might someday have a better life than they did. I will never, ever forget them."

Ingrid looked down, and Roberto saw that she was fighting back tears that had moistened her eyes. Again, she had totally surprised him. He thought that she might be thinking about a boyfriend, or weighing the financial advantages of coming here or staying there. Nothing like this had been on her mind at all. The only way that she had thought about herself was how her leaving could have a negative effect on others and on the care of her parents' grave out in some little churchyard of a town in the middle of nowhere. Roberto swallowed hard as he looked at her sitting there across the table from him with her eyes cast down. For just a second, he thought of the beautiful monument at his parents' grave in the park-like setting of St. Sebastiano's Cemetery on the outskirts of Buenos Aires. He hadn't been there since his mother's funeral.

Roberto called the waiter and asked for a bottle of their best champagne, but the Chinese restaurant did not have a liquor license and did not sell any champagne. He filled both of their teacups and then, holding his cup in the air, he looked into Ingrid's eyes and said, "To a long and fruitful relationship. You have made me very happy."

Ingrid smiled back as their teacups gently clinked in the dimly lit restaurant.

When Ingrid arrived at work the next morning, Robert was waiting for her at the receptionist's desk. He took her by her arm and led her straight to her office. She stopped at the door. Something was different. Everywhere, on the desk, on the side table, on the open shelves of the long cabinet running alongside the wall – wherever it was possible, there was a bouquet of flowers. She walked around and picked up each vase and smelled the flowers. Each bouquet was different and contained a combination of flowers. Their color coordination and arrangement was masterfully done, and Ingrid could not stop going from one to another while she bubbled over in absolute delight. Roberto stood by the door and enjoyed her childlike enthusiasm. Lea Greenfield came into the office and congratulated her on becoming part of the firm. She wished her all the best, and Ingrid was happy to see that there was no hint of jealousy in her older colleague's face.

"With two such magnificent women by my side," Roberto said with obvious pride, "we can take on the world, and believe me, we will."

The day was spent working. Again, they sat side by side and determined what needed to be done. When Roberto had finished explaining how he wanted to handle various correspondences, Ingrid picked up a stack of the papers and took them to her office. She went around the huge desk and sat down on the black leather armchair. She looked around the room. The flowers looked even more beautiful than before. The glass sparkled and the dark wood gleamed. She closed her eyes and leaned back, her hands folded behind her head. This was too good to be true. She quickly opened here eyes and once again saw the splendor before her. Yes, it was true.

The next business day, Ingrid told Roberto that he should not even think about taking her to all the places he had suggested in the letter. After all, she was coming back, and they would have all the time in the world to do all those things. The important thing now was to get this backlog of work done. She threw herself into it with such vigor that Roberto was not surprised when she told him that she did not want to go out to lunch. Just something brought up from the cafeteria downstairs would be fine. She continued working at her computer while she took a bite of her chicken sandwich without looking up from her work.

Later that week, Roberto took Ingrid out to dinner and dancing at one of New York City's most popular nightspots. The atmosphere inside was a little too loud and wild for Roberto's taste, but he saw how much Ingrid enjoyed swaying to the music, while she clapped her hands. He did his best to keep up with her, although he felt a little silly gyrating to the pulsating beat that blasted down at them from all directions.

It was past midnight when Roberto stopped in front of her hotel. As he walked her to the front door, Ingrid turned and looked him in the eye and said, "I know I turned you down before, but that was then and this is now. Will you come up for a little nightcap?"

They made love that night, and Roberto now knew for sure that she was not that sweet young innocent thing that he thought her to be, and Ingrid experienced, just as she had expected, that Roberto was definitely not a tired, old man.

Things were quite hectic again the next day at the office. Roberto and Ingrid concentrated on their work. When she came into his office with a question, he would act very businesslike, but then he would suddenly wink at her, and she would blush a little – she knew it was childish, but there was something deliciously sweet about their little secret. Later, when he came into her office with a letter that needed an immediate answer in Russian, she winked back at him, and they both laughed at their silliness, and both were very happy.

On Friday, they left work early because Ingrid was to fly home the next day. They took a carriage ride through Central Park, drove by taxi down to Battery Park, from where they took the ferry out to the Statue of Liberty. Ingrid had been here before, but this is what she had wanted to see again, and as she looked into the gigantic lady's face, it seemed to her that she was extending a personal invitation to her to come across the ocean and start a new life for herself here in the new world.

On the ferry ride back, Roberto turned to her and said, "Let's make this a special evening, because everything has been special since you've been here. I want you to miss the city, and to miss me even more, so that you come back as soon as you've got everything settled."

Ingrid's face was filled with joy as she looked toward the skyline, which grew taller with every minute. "I will," she said softly.

They dined at the Four Seasons that night, because Roberto had read in a restaurant guide that the Pool Room was the perfect setting for special occasion dinners. They were almost finished with their dessert when Roberto reached across the table and took Ingrid's left hand in his right hand. When she looked at him, with her fork raised in her right hand, he asked firmly and without warning, "Will you marry me?"

Ingrid was stunned for just a second, but then she was on her feet and threw herself at him, flinging her arms around his neck with such force that she almost knocked his chair over backwards. "Yes, I will," she began softly, and then more loudly, "Yes, I will," as she kissed his right cheek, then his left, and then, holding his head between her hands, she kissed him long and hard on the lips. As she drew back a little, with tear filled eyes, she said softly again, "Yes, I will," one more time. Her words were no longer audible to anyone except Roberto. Cheerful applause came from the tables around them.

A beautiful and relatively small wedding took place in August. Ingrid's side included only her brother and her friend Erika. She had offered to buy an airline ticket for Mrs. Lemke, her neighbor, but she declined to come to New York for health reasons and a fear of flying. Roberto's uncle and aunt had flown in from Argentina. The other guests were employees, including Juan Perez. Lea Greenfield, his executive secretary, had taken charge of the whole affair as if her own son were getting married.

They honeymooned in Paris, Venice, Florence and Rome. These were the places that Ingrid had wanted to see more than any other. The days flew by as if in a dream. Never had Ingrid been so pampered. They stayed in the most luxurious hotels, and ate wherever they liked, sometimes cheap and sometimes extravagantly expensive. Anything that Ingrid saw in any of the thousands of shops could be hers – price was no object to the new and proud husband, but she bought almost nothing.

They returned to New York and to their work in the middle of September. Ingrid kept her office exactly as it was, for it was quite possible that she might not be working there for too long. Roberto had made it very clear to her that he wanted nothing more than to become a father. Ingrid, too, although she was still quite young, felt that a child would be a gift from heaven that would complete their happiness.

During the week, they worked side by side. Ingrid was amazed at the intricacies of Roberto's business dealings and the ease with which he dealt with even the most complex situations. He explained to her why this seemed like a good business venture to pursue and that was something that was not wise to get into. His logic was convincing, and his grasp of the business world was most impressive. The evenings and weekends were spent at home in his luxurious penthouse apartment. Here, too, Roberto told Ingrid to make whatever changes she wanted. The apartment definitely displayed a man's taste, or at least what an interior designer considered to be a man's taste. Roberto had left it all up to a well-known New York company to furnish his place. Although he liked the way the rooms were done, it was quite all right with him to have them decorated differently. In his business life, he made the decisions. In his home life, he was quite happy to let the woman he adored have her way.

Ingrid made only a few minor changes: A new bedspread and pillow covers for the bed, different pillows on the huge couch in the living room and brightly colored towels in the bathrooms. She did not want to make too many changes because Roberto told her that every year he spent the winter months – from October to March – at his place in the Dominican Republic. As much as he loved New York, he explained, he could not get used to the winters, and he did not want to go back to Argentina.

"I really can't explain why that is so," he told her. "I just do not want to go there." Then, he bubbled over telling her how wonderful the house was on the island. It had a swimming pool, and the most wonderful beach was only a ten-minute walk away. There was golfing, which he enjoyed very much, and horseback riding. Wonderful shops and restaurants were in close vicinity. "You will see, you'll love it," he told her while he held both of her hands, his eyes sparkling with enthusiasm and anticipation so that there was no doubt in her mind that she would love it, too.

The "place," which turned out to be an imposing villa, was located in the sprawling and elegant Casa de Campo complex in La Romana on the south coast of the Dominican Republic. On their arrival, Roberto introduced the staff, who had lined up by the main entrance. There were Linda and Rudolfo, the married couple who lived permanently on the grounds in a little house in the garden. Then there was Ernesto, the manager; he was responsible for running this place, the hacienda just outside of Rio San Juan, and the estate in Argentina. Mario, the cook, and Juanita his assistant, were introduced next; they both came in the morning and left in the evening on a bus which was provided especially for employees in the Casa de Campo complex. Finally, there was Pedro, the gardener. He, too, came and went by bus that shuttled workers in and out of the complex at all hours of the day.

Although the villa looked impressive from the outside, it did not truly reveal the splendor that was found within. It was a two-story horseshoe-shaped building finished in white stucco with a red tile roof. A kidney-shaped swimming pool with a slide that came down from a waterfall took up part of the open area in the back. There was an open air shower off to the side and a straw covered cabana, perfect for an afternoon nap. Comfortable beach chairs surrounded the pool, some out in the open for sunbathing, some in the shade of colorful bushes and palm trees. Upon entering the house, there was a large dining room off to the left with a long wooden table in the middle

184

of it. Ten high-backed chairs surrounded it. This opened up, without any walls between, into an open-air living room. This again had the tile roof extending over it. Comfortable wicker chairs and a wicker table filled this room.

A large wide screen television stood in a corner of the living room. Ingrid could not believe her eyes – a television set out in the open with only a roof over it. From here it was only a few steps to the pool. On entering the house, there was a bar on the right and behind this, the kitchen. From there, the building curved into one side of the horseshoe shape. Three beautifully appointed guestrooms, each with its own spacious bathroom, canopied bed and wonderful marble floors were located in this area. The other side contained a small apartment – this is where Ernesto lived – and a large storage space. The entire front of the second floor consisted of the master bedroom, with two huge walk-in closets and an emperor-sized bathroom with a Jacuzzi big enough for four people. Off to one side was an all glass-enclosed shower, and on the other side, looking like a small wooden cabin, was a Swedish sauna. The left wing housed a second bedroom and a game room, in the center of which stood a full sized billiard table covered with blue felt. The right wing contained the library, which was also the music room with a magnificent grand piano. Behind this was a spacious office.

Ingrid could not believe her eyes as she wandered from room to room. She had never been in a private residence that was so large or so beautifully decorated.

"Well, what do you think of my little house in the country?" Roberto asked her after she had surveyed the rooms and admired a piece of furniture or an especially interesting painting on a wall or a beautifully crafted vase strategically placed in a cabinet.

"I can't believe it," Ingrid answered, as she held both of her hands against her cheeks. Her eyes kept wandering around the room.

"And you know what the best thing is?" he continued. "The best thing is that it is ours, and that I have you here to share my favorite place with me."

She took a few steps up to him and threw her arms around his neck and squeezed, hugged and kissed him so passionately that he had to catch his breath once she let go of him.

"I had hoped you would like it here," Roberto said as he hugged her back, "and obviously you do."

Once they were downstairs by the pool, Roberto turned to her and said, "There is one important task that I am handing over to you as of right now." Ingrid looked at him expectantly. "Now, don't worry," he continued, "I think you might enjoy it. Every evening before he leaves for the day, Mario asks me what I want to eat the next day. In the mornings, I only have fruit. Lunch is served at noon, and dinner at seven o'clock. I hope that is all right with you. Quite honestly, I don't always know what to tell Mario, but he has such wonderful ideas that I usually just agree with whatever he suggests. I would really appreciate it if you sat down with him and planned the menu for the whole week, but not for Sundays. That is when the entire staff is gone. I then eat breakfast at the club and have my dinner at a restaurant. Have him cook whatever you like. Go and buy some of the ingredients yourself, if you want to. I tell you, Mario is a magician. You'll be amazed at what he can cook." Roberto looked at Ingrid slyly and said with a grin on his face, "But don't forget where you are. The fruits and vegetables are phenomenal, the meat is so-so, and please, forget about sauerkraut."

The next day, Roberto showed Ingrid around the Casa de Campo complex. They went to the clubhouse with its restaurants and bars. He then drove her, in his golf cart, along one of the three immaculately maintained golf courses, out to the polo grounds and the equestrian complex.

"Have you ever been on a horse?" Roberto asked her. Ingrid shook her head. "Well, then you are in for a wonderful experience. I love horses. As a matter of fact, I have three of them stabled here. The rest I keep at my place in Argentina."

He then drove her down to Las Minitas Beach, where they slipped off their sandals and walked hand-in-hand in the warm waters of the Caribbean Sea.

The next day after breakfast, Roberto asked Mario to come to the dining room and had him sit down opposite Ingrid. He explained to him that from now on she would plan the menus. A smile came across the cook's face as he looked at Ingrid, who sat slightly red-faced across the huge table.

"You see how happy he is?" Roberto pointed out to her. "I have truly wasted his talents here. Please challenge him. Give him something to sink his teeth into. Bring out the culinary genius that lies hidden within him. And don't worry, Mario," he continued, "my wife speaks perfect Spanish. You'll understand everything." He looked back and forth between the two. "Well, start planning," Roberto said jovially, as he threw up his arms in mock tribulation.

Both of them had watched him with amusement, and both of them answered almost in unison, "Si, Señor."

They slept in on Sunday. After a stroll through the Teeth of the Dog Golf Course, always along the sea, they came to the Casa de Campo Club House. Here, they enjoyed a leisurely buffet breakfast, all in the thatch-roofed building, which came right up to the golf course. There were flowers everywhere, and the colors were so bright and beautiful that Ingrid could not get enough of them.

"Do you think you can survive here?" Roberto asked her as he held her hand across the table.

"Anyone who cannot survive here," she answered as her eyes surveyed the magnificent scenery before her, "is either dead or should be shot."

Roberto laughed out loud. No one before had ever expressed his enchantment with this place in such terms.

Later that afternoon, Roberto took Ingrid out to the equestrian center and introduced her to Caesar, his big black stallion; Luna, a beautiful brown mare; and Estrellita, a small brown and white checked horse, who continuously nudged Roberto with her nose as if to say, "Where have you been all this time?"

Roberto really did introduce Ingrid because he said to each of the three horses, "Now listen carefully. This is my wife Ingrid. I want you to be good to her. I want you to be gentle with her. She comes from a strange, cold place with many cars and where the people eat pea soup with sausages and drink red and green beer. So be patient with her and love her as much as I do." And as Ingrid looked at them and stroked their smooth necks, it almost seemed to her as if they had understood every word Roberto had spoken to them.

In the evening they drove to La Marina, a Porto Fino-like bay shaped arrangement of restaurants with sherbet colored town houses and chic European shops. As they sat under the open sky and ate their meal, Ingrid looked out into the harbor, where a great number of sleek sailboats were moored, and along the pier, where huge multimillion-dollar yachts were anchored, one next to the other. She lifted her glass of red wine toward Roberto; he lifted his and held it out toward her, and with her face more beautiful and radiant than he had ever seen it before, she said to him, "I think I am in paradise."

Although the pace of life here was slower and more relaxed, Ingrid felt that the days flew by so fast that she never knew where all the hours had gone. In the mornings, she would check in with Roberto in his office to see if he needed her services, but usually, he would just get up from behind his desk, hold her in his arms, give her a big good morning kiss and tell her that she should just run along and do whatever she pleased. He would be along in a short while. He had explained to her that he had made it clear to all his top people that here he was not to be disturbed unless absolutely necessary. Since he was an early riser, he was usually in his office by seven and would finish well before noon. Once in a while, he did have something in German or Russian for her to translate, but she did not consider these tasks to be work at all. Ingrid was happy that she could be helpful in some way.

Many times, when Roberto was done with his work, he would sneak up behind her, while she was reading a book by the pool, or while arranging the new pots with flowers which she had bought in La Romana, and he would listen to her sing. She sang in a clear soprano voice, out loud, for all to hear. He did not always understand all of the words, since most of her songs were in German or Russian, but she also sang in perfect Spanish that beautiful song about the "Paloma", and "La Golondrina." Sometimes, she sang in English – songs with words like "start spreading the news," and "I want to hold your hand" and "your teddy bear." He

189

would then tip toe up behind her and kiss her gently on the neck. When she turned around, not at all surprised by his presence, she would continue her song until she had finished singing it. He would call her his little songbird, his lark, and then, with his arms around her waist, he would twirl her until she squealed and giggled like a happy little girl.

Lunch and dinner had now become a gastronomical experience for Roberto. During the day, he would watch with amusement at how Ingrid huddled with Mario and Juanita. He watched how Mario took copious notes and how all three of them then left in the Range Rover, only to return hours later with bags and bags full of groceries. Many times, Ingrid would be in the kitchen and help Mario and Juanita, always asking questions about this ingredient or why that vegetable was prepared in this particular manner. Later, she would be so happy when Roberto praised the meal that the three had prepared, although Ingrid was modest enough to give the credit to Mario and his assistant, Juanita.

At other times, Roberto would see Ingrid walking with Pedro, pointing to a bush or a tree. He saw how she carefully listened as the old gardener answered all of her questions. Once in a while, she would be by his side with a spade in her hands, and he would show her how to dig the right hole for the bush she had bought, how to carefully cover it again with soil and then fertilize and water it.

Ingrid would sometimes sit and speak with Ernesto, the manager who ran the estate. He had placed a little table outside his rooms so that he could work in the shade of the thatch roof canopy and enjoy the gentle breezes from the Caribbean Sea. Whenever he saw her coming his way, he would put down his pencil and close up his books to make it clear to her that she was not interrupting him in his work. She enjoyed speaking with him. He spoke beautiful, precise

190

Spanish, and she asked him if he would not mind it if she would occasionally ask him about Spanish words or grammatical constructions or idioms that gave her a particularly hard time. He consented most willingly because this contact with her made his somewhat boring job quite a bit more interesting. He would ask her about Germany, Berlin and New York. When she spoke, he would very gently point out minor mistakes and explain, giving numerous examples, why a particular phrase had to be constructed in this way, but not in that way, because then it became confusing and misleading. Sometimes, he would ask her how certain words or phrases were expressed in German, and soon, he took great delight in greeting her every day by saying "Guten Tag." And usually, when she walked away, he would say "Danke schön," or "Auf Wiedersehen."

On some days, Ingrid would go skeet shooting with Roberto, who was an excellent shot. Later, they would stop for drinks at the club. She was quite aware of the pride he showed when he introduced her to his many friends. On other days, they would go horseback riding, and she was touched by the way he personally saddled little Estrellita and told her once again to be careful with his dear wife. At first, he led the horse by the halter and walked around the polo field while she got the feel of the saddle and the horse's movement. Then, he ran with the horse, still holding on to it, but very soon, Ingrid asked him to let go and managed quite well on her own.

Once in a while, they went sailing. Roberto would rent a little sailboat, and then, they went out way beyond the breakwater. He would ask her over and over again whether she felt all right and if she wasn't scared when the boat tilted precariously to one side. She only laughed and brushed the hair out of her face. She had complete confidence in him.

The only time Ingrid was ever alone was when Roberto went golfing. This was one activity she could not share with him. She herself could not explain why, but for some reason, she simply had no interest in it. She was glad that Roberto was sensitive enough not to make an issue out of it. During those hours, she would walk down to the beach. She would have one of the attendants put a beach chair in the shade of a palm tree, and then, she would read. She never read for very long, however. Soon, she would put the book aside and look out over the blue sea and watch the big ocean cruisers come and go. She wondered where they might be coming from and where they were going. She would lean back with her hands folded behind her head and look at the green of the trees above her and the blue patches of sky beyond the white, billowing clouds that drifted off into the distance. Her mind would often wander to back home, where now it was rainy and cold. She thought about her brother, to whom she had just sent five thousand dollars, on Roberto's insistence, so that he could live in a decent place while he pursued his studies. She thought about Erika and the little flat they had shared, and about Mrs. Lemke, who kept her husband's grave so beautiful and tended to the graves of Ingrid's parents. She thought of her office and Herr Winkler, her boss, who was a little disoriented at times, but otherwise a truly decent fellow. She thought of strolling down the wide avenues in Berlin and dancing in the discos until the early morning hours – all of this seemed so very long ago. For twenty-four years, her life had been that of just about any other girl who grew up under the same circumstances, and then, in just a few days, her life had taken off into a direction that she would have never dreamed of. Here she was, lying on an exclusive beach on a Caribbean island. She lived in a villa with her every wish fulfilled by well-trained servants. She went horseback riding in the afternoons when everyone else she knew was busy at work. She could have just about anything she wanted. She smiled. All of this was not so terribly important. What really mattered was that she was loved, and she did not doubt Roberto's love for her for one second.

Life for Ingrid on the beautiful island was one long dream. Every morning, she had to remind herself where she was and what had happened that had brought her here.

Christmas, to be sure, was something very different. Although her family had not been very religious, as was the case with most people who had lived under the communist regime, they always had a small beautifully decorated Christmas tree in their tiny apartment. She remembered how the four of them had sung "Stille Nacht" on Christmas Eve, and how there was something so festive and special about this night that it was indelibly etched into her memory. Roberto had presented her with an absolutely stunning diamond necklace. She had secretly taken his riding boots from his closet, and during one of her trips to Santo Domingo with Ernesto driving her, had a new pair made exactly the same size, which deeply touched Roberto when he opened the package with the words on it, "for the man who has everything."

They returned to New York at the end of March, and life became a little more hectic again. Ingrid helped out at the office when she was needed, but Roberto made sure that she was not overworked. "Remember," he told her, "we are on a mission. You are to be the most beautiful mother in the world, while I will be the proudest father you have ever seen."

Ingrid went back to Berlin for two weeks in May. She took time to visit her brother, her friends, and especially Mrs. Lemke. Together, they walked to the cemetery, Ingrid holding the elderly lady by the arm. She hugged her and wiped her eyes when she saw how lovingly her old neighbor had cared for the graves. She spent the rest of the day reminiscing in her tiny apartment, nibbling freshly baked cookies and enjoying the tea that she made every afternoon. They held each other for a long time when Ingrid said good-bye, with a promise to come back the following year. It was only when the old woman cleared away the dishes that she was saw the envelope left by Ingrid under her saucer. It contained ten crisp one hundred dollar bills and a handwritten thank you note for all she had done for her.

This summer Roberto fulfilled a promise that he had made to Ingrid the year before. They drove to the Adirondack Mountains, and Ingrid found it funny that there would be a city named Potsdam in upstate New York. They went on to Montreal and Quebec City and then traveled leisurely down the east coast, all the way from New Brunswick through Maine and Boston to Martha's Vineyard and back to New York.

On another trip, they flew to New Orleans, and Ingrid could not get enough of the colors, the history and the music of the vibrant and noise-filled French Quarter. Roberto took only one three-day business trip to London, and Ingrid decided not to go along. He certainly did not need her language services, and she did not feel like wandering alone around the city while he sat in lengthy business meetings.

The summer passed by quickly, and Roberto asked Ingrid whether she was looking forward to returning to their "country house."

"Oh, yes," she replied, "and this time I have all kinds of plans. I really think we should redo the bedroom and the living room, if you don't mind. I think the landscaping could do with some freshening up. I've seen some very beautiful gardens, with more flowers and blooming bushes. Maybe we can install a fountain – the splashing water would be so soothing. The gravel driveway has to go. It should be done in inlaid stones. I think a red tiled canopy in front of the main entrance would add a touch of class."

Roberto looked at her and shook his head, "You never cease to amaze me. I've been thinking about doing something with the outside too, but I would have just hired an architect and a landscaper to do it for me. You do whatever you have in mind. As a matter of fact, I will introduce you to the best architect on the island. He is from Switzerland, and I'm sure you'll come up with something absolutely stunning. There is only one thing I ask. Please, don't touch my office and my library."

It was on a Wednesday afternoon, a week after they returned to the island, when Linda knocked on the library door. Ingrid was in her favorite chair reading a book. Linda told her that Roberto asked for her to come downstairs; there was someone he wanted her to meet. She found Roberto sitting in the living room with a gray-haired gentleman. He wore a blue blazer and tie, despite the warm temperature and high humidity. Both men rose as she entered, and Roberto introduced Heinz Bertl, the Swiss architect who now worked exclusively in the Dominican Republic designing opulent villas for some of the richest people in the world. They shook hands, and Mr. Bertl addressed Ingrid in German. She immediately felt comfortable and knew she would enjoy working with him. They walked around the front of the house, and Ingrid explained what she had in mind for the house itself and also laid out in broad terms how she envisioned the garden in front of the house.

When she had finished, Mr. Bertl took Roberto aside and said, "You told me your wife was an interpreter, but I

195

tell you something, my dear friend, her ideas about the house and garden are not bad, not bad at all. I will come back in a few days and bring you some drawings of how I see the front of the house. I will bring with me Mrs. Gonzalez, my favorite partner when it comes to landscape architecture. I'm sure she will come up with something that both of you will like."

"If my lovely wife likes it," Roberto answered gallantly, "then I will absolutely adore it."

That afternoon, while Ingrid sat by the pool leafing through a few interior design magazines and quietly humming a few bars of an aria, Roberto came and sat down beside her. He looked across the pool where Ernesto had just gathered his writing materials and gone into his rooms.

"There is something I would like to talk to you about," Roberto said, and his voice sounded more serious than usual. Ingrid listened, wondering whether she had done anything that had given her husband cause for concern. "It's about Ernesto," he began. "I've noticed that you sometimes spend a few minutes with him." Ingrid felt a slight tension growing within her, but she simply looked at him waiting for what else he had to say. "There's something I need to tell you about him, which I should have done long ago. You see, his father was my father's chief caretaker. That means, he paid all the bills, hired and fired the household staff and made sure that the ground keepers kept everything perfect on our rather large estate outside of Buenos Aires. He made sure that everything, from the food to the guest rooms, was absolutely perfect, whether we were alone or whether we had guests. You see, my father was a perfectionist, and since he considered himself to be a self-made man, it was very important to him what others in high society thought of him. Ernesto's father did his work outstandingly, and my father was very fond of him. When Ernesto's mother died giving birth to him, my father assured him that Ernesto would always have a place in our home. The father died when Ernesto was twelve years old. My father had him live in our house and provided for his education. When I came home occasionally from one of my many jobs, it seemed like I had a little brother living there, and I always tried to be like a big brother to him. Although he had the opportunity to study anything he wanted, he said that he would like nothing more than to do the work that his father had done. I think my father was a little disappointed that he did not have higher ambitions, but I know that he was secretly pleased that this bright young man wanted to stay in the service of our family. At first, he shared the duties with another one of our employees, but then, shortly before my mother died, she and I agreed that he should be put totally in charge."

Ingrid looked at Roberto, then across the pool, and then back to her husband. "That is very interesting and also sad," she said, "but where do I come in all of this?"

"Let me finish," Roberto went on. "You can see, can't you, that he is not a very happy man. I try to make his life as interesting as possible by letting him work back home when we're not here, but I'm not sure whether he has any friends there either. You must have noticed that I've tried to include him in some of the things that we do here, but he always finds a reason to decline, and that is why I don't ask him anymore. Don't get me wrong. He does his work excellently and we get along fine, but we do seem to be in two different worlds, and I wish there was something that I could do to help him." He reached across the table and held her hand in his. "Please do me a favor," he continued, "include him more in the activities around here. Let him drive you when you go into town. Ask him if he wants to go to the beach when you go. I've seen him there. He never goes in the water, just sits in the sand and looks out across the sea. With you there, he'll have someone to talk to, and given his age, he'll probably find it much easier to talk to you than to me."

"How old is he?" asked Ingrid.

"He's twenty-eight, and for a man of that age, he is much too melancholy, don't you think?" Roberto looked questioningly at Ingrid.

"I'll try my best," Ingrid answered, "but it's impossible to look inside a person. Who knows what's really troubling him?"

"I know," Roberto replied, "but promise me you'll try. Will you, please?"

A few days later, Mr. Bertl returned with Mrs. Gonzalez, a tall, stout woman with jet-black hair, wrapped tightly in a bun. She wore bright red lipstick and huge sunglasses, which she never took off. The Swiss architect spread out several large drawings, and everyone studied them closely. They were all wonderfully conceived and matched the house perfectly. After weighing the pros and cons of the various designs, Roberto and Ingrid agreed on Plan II, the one that had the red tiled canopy supported by three classically styled pillars. This proportion seemed best to them, and Mr. Bertl agreed that this was his favorite plan also. They then walked around the front yard, and Mrs. Gonzalez took notes and made quick sketches in her notebook. Once back at the house, she quickly outlined her plan on a large sheet of paper, indicating the new driveway and portico, and what should be done to give the entire front of the property a look of understated elegance. She told them that she would work out all of the details in her office and bring back the completed plans in a few days.

198

Ingrid went to town the next day to pick out new curtains for the master bedroom and the three guest rooms. She knew exactly what she wanted for the master bedroom, but she wanted to do something unique, something very creative with the three guest rooms. Each room was to be different; it was to have its own theme that would be reflected in everything inside the room. This was the challenge she had set for herself. She wanted this to be a big surprise for Roberto. He had made it quite clear that she should do whatever she wanted as far as decorating was concerned. She asked Ernesto to drive her because there might also be some things that they needed to bring back to the house. At first, Ernesto seemed a little reluctant, but when Ingrid told him that Roberto wanted him to assist her, he agreed and seemed quite happy to leave the house for a while.

On the ride to the city, Ingrid asked Ernesto to tell her something about himself. He spoke quite willingly about his childhood on the Delgado estate. He told her that he had never known his mother and that he truly loved his father, who had been very kind and loving to him, but who did not have very much time for him because of his many duties. He had nothing but praise for Roberto's father and mother, who had treated him like their own son.

"I truly love Roberto," he continued with Latin honesty, which Ingrid found most endearing. "I am very grateful to him for everything he has done for me and still does for me. I am very happy that now he is so happy. You know, he is a completely changed man since you have entered his life."

Ingrid blushed slightly. "It seems to me that he was a happy man before he met me," she ventured.

"Yes, he was jovial and friendly with everyone, but I could tell that something was missing in his life, and you have filled that gap," Ernesto replied.

Ingrid shared with Ernesto her plans for redoing the three guest bedrooms in three different themes. One room was to be done in a Polynesian style - bamboo canopy over the bed with bamboo furniture. The tiles in the bathroom, the curtains and the towels were all to reflect a South Sea island setting. Another room was to be done in the style of Louis XIV: all in yellow with blue fleur-de-lis. The bed would have blue canopy curtains hanging down from it; the furniture would be in period style, and on the largest wall, there was to be a heavy gold framed painting of the monarch standing in his ermine robe, heavy sword on his side, looking very much the regal ruler who had been called the "Sun King." She had seen such a painting in New York and would have it sent to them.

"These two rooms I definitely want," she told Ernesto, "but I'm not sure what I should do with the third room. I want each room to be as contrasting as possible with the other two rooms. What do you think, Ernesto?"

"I think it's a fabulous idea," Ernesto answered enthusiastically. "Just think, if a guest should ever come back a second or even third time, you could put him in a different room and the person would feel as if he's experiencing his stay for the first time. Now as far as the third room is concerned, I have an idea." He stopped for a second.

"Well, what is it? Out with it," Ingrid asked with a giggle.

"You might think this is a little far out, but all of the great European palaces had at least one room like this."

200

"Come on already, don't keep me in suspense," Ingrid pressed him with childlike impatience.

"I think a Chinese room would really be cool," he said in voice that sounded like a teenage boy talking about a motorcycle he had always wanted. "Chinese," he continued, "you know, all in lacquered red and black and green. Just think what you could do with the decorations: vases, statues, a little pagoda." He took his eyes off the road for just a second and looked at her. She looked at him and winked at him.

"That's it," she shouted, as she clapped her hands together, "that's what was missing. Ernesto, you're a genius," and she slapped his right knee in an unpremeditated outburst of youthful enthusiasm.

The days now flew by with planning and buying and getting everything organized. Mr. Bertl had brought in his team to construct the portico and the new driveway. Mrs. Gonzalez had come past again, and Roberto and Ingrid approved her plans for the landscaping. Ingrid herself was busy in getting the three guest rooms done. Roberto had to promise not enter any of the three rooms until she was done with them. Ingrid decided to leave the floors in each room as they were because an appropriate carpet would cover anything unsuitable. This would save a great deal of time and money.

The first finished room was the Polynesian one. Ingrid chose several shades of green, yellow and brown for the walls. The wallpaper depicted various kinds of tropical foliage. Real bamboo poles were affixed to the walls to create a three-dimensional feeling. The bed was difficult to find, but finally, she and Ernesto found just the right piece in a second hand shop in Santo Domingo. Prints depicting life in a Polynesian village were hung on the walls, and pots with exotic shrubs and bushes were strategically placed throughout the room. Yellow silk sheets hung from three sides of the bamboo reed covered bed. Ingrid was in her element. Everyone in the household was called into action, except Roberto. He followed his usual daily routine and only shook his head when he saw his beautiful wife, often totally drenched in sweat, help the servants or delivery people carry in a heavy cabinet or mirror or some other strange object which she had found God knows where.

It was around nine in the morning on a late October day when Roberto went back to the bedroom after Ingrid had failed to wish him a good morning. Although he always got up earlier than she did, she had never missed coming to his study to greet him with a big good morning kiss. He found her curled up in bed, her head half covered by a pillow. He sat down on the edge of the bed and stroked her blond disheveled hair.

"Are you feeling all right?" he asked, and his voice showed genuine concern.

"I don't know," she answered sleepily. "The same thing happened yesterday, but I thought it might have been something I ate. But this morning, I had to vomit again, and my stomach feels so queasy. I'm not sure, Roberto, but I think this is what we have been waiting for." She turned her head slightly, looked at him and through her agony, she managed to produce just a hint of a smile.

Roberto did not comprehend for just a second. Then, he took her head in his arms and squeezed her so tightly against himself that she could hardly breathe. He gently rocked her from side to side, whispering, "Oh my God, oh my God. Yes, it has to be. It just has to be. I love you. I love you. I love you! This is wonderful. This is it. We've done it!" He now held her at arms length and looked at her tired face,

202

which was trying hard to look cheerful. He kissed her on both cheeks. Then, he slid off the bed and knelt beside her, their faces now at the same level. "I will call Dr. Barthelme," he said, as he gently stroked her cheeks. "He has to come here immediately and check you out. Can I get you anything?" She shook her head. Roberto held her hand for just a few more seconds and then hurried to his office to call the doctor.

Dr. Barthelme did not come to the house. He explained to Roberto that the only way to be sure that Ingrid was indeed pregnant was to do a urine and blood test. A few hours later, they were in the clinic, and in a short while, Dr. Barthelme confirmed what they wanted to hear. Ingrid was pregnant. Roberto could not stop talking on the drive home. He went on and on about how happy he was, how happy they were, how they would have the most beautiful baby in the world, and how they would be the world's greatest parents.

That evening, they celebrated. Roberto invited the entire staff to come to dinner with them at La Marina. Linda and Rudolfo, Mario and Juanita wore their Sunday finery, and Ernesto and Pedro, the gardener, had dressed up, too. The wine flowed freely, and Roberto could not stop urging everyone on to order something else on top of what they had already eaten. They all simply had to try this fruit dessert or that chocolate concoction. Everyone had to get into the spirit, and Ingrid, too, who still was not feeling all that well, tried to do her best to join in the festivities.

In the weeks that followed, Roberto seemed like a new person. He was more active than ever before – in the mornings, he did his work; then, he would look in on Ingrid. Next, he was seen in the kitchen conferring with the cook. Now, he was watching the progress on the building construction and in the garden. He was everywhere –

always smiling, singing, laughing, slapping someone on the back here or poking someone on the arm there. And always, he kept on checking in on Ingrid, stroking her belly, although there was really nothing to be stroked yet.

Dr. Barthelme told them that he expected the baby to be born somewhere in the middle of May. This suited both of them just fine, because that meant the child would be born in New York, and Roberto definitely wanted his child to be born in an American hospital and be an American citizen.

Sometimes, they would leaf through magazines and look for ideas of how to decorate the baby's room, what kind of baby carriage would be best for strolls in Central Park, what kind of diaper service they would order. They would kick around the hundreds of little details that were involved in bringing a baby into the house. Ingrid was absolutely touched and fascinated by the patience and involvement that Roberto displayed in dealing with the preparations for the little bundle of joy that was due to arrive in May.

One day, Roberto sat down beside her and said, "You know, we haven't talked about a name for our little one. What do you think, should we just pick a boy's name and a girl's name that we like, or should that name be in honor of someone we love?"

"I don't know," Ingrid answered. "I was quite willing to leave the naming of the child up to you. After all, you come from a family with a famous name. Everyone knows the Delgado's from Argentina. There must be someone that you want to honor by naming our child after him or her."

Roberto sat quietly for some time looking down at the floor. Then, he turned to her and said gently, "The only people that I wish to honor are your father and mother. They are the ones who gave me the greatest gift that I have ever received. Through you, they have made my life complete. If you don't mind, if it's a boy, I would like to name him Karl, after your father. If it's a girl, then your mother will live on in our little Anna."

He looked at Ingrid and saw the tears well up in her eyes. He then held her in his arms until she stopped sobbing and her breathing was calm again. Slowly, she freed herself from his embrace and he could barely hear her whisper, "Thank you."

When Ingrid felt better, Roberto asked her if she wanted to go and see their farm, or "hacienda" as he called it, on the northern part of the island near Rio San Juan. He explained that tomorrow he would have to spend all day at the club for a business meeting with an investor from Los Angeles and that he had to promise this man at least eighteen holes of golf on the Teeth of the Dog golf course. But Ernesto would go on his weekly trip there to handle all of the bookkeeping. It might be good for her, Roberto explained, to get away from here for a day, and it would be good for Ernesto to have someone to talk to during the three hour car ride. And anyway, soon she would not be able to take these kinds of trips, and he definitely wanted her to go and see the farm.

They set out early the next morning, and by the way Ernesto drove, it was clear that he had driven this route many times before. Along the way, he pointed out the little villages along the road and usually had something to say about its history, or about what was grown in this region, or about some famous person who had lived here. Ingrid noticed that there was a very different side to this quiet and somewhat melancholy seeming Ernesto; he became quite animated and peppered his little stories with humorous anecdotes and such colorful descriptions that it was an absolute joy to listen to him.

The farm turned out to be a lot more than Ingrid had imagined. To her, a farm consisted of a little farmhouse with a few acres of land around it where the farmer would raise his crops. Maybe he would also have a few pigs and cows and chickens. This was the kind of farm that she knew.

The house itself was quite impressive, and as they walked through the spacious rooms, Ingrid felt that it was sad that nobody lived here except the old caretaker and his wife, who had greeted them as if they were royalty and now walked ahead of them opening the doors to the various rooms to show them that everything was in the best of order. Then, Ernesto showed her around the farm itself. There were rows and rows of banana trees, but also, arranged in perfect order, there were endless beds of cabbages, tomatoes, onions, radishes and garlic. In another area, there were groves of pineapples, oranges, mangos and even apples. Everywhere they went, workers greeted them, and it was very apparent to Ingrid that Ernesto was very much liked by everyone at the farm. He asked one man about his little daughter and whether her broken leg was better again. He asked another whether the baby had already come. Everywhere, he had something kind to say to the workers, and those farther away waved to him and shouted something that Ingrid did not understand.

After lunch, which the old lady had prepared, Ernesto settled down to handle the paperwork, and Ingrid drove to the beautiful beach, the Playa Grande. She sat in the warm white sand and realized that she was looking straight to the north, toward New York, and that there, in the very near future, the child, once born, would change their family and add one more piece to that complex puzzle which makes up American society. Here would be a new American, with an Argentine father and a German mother, and this new American would speak English, Spanish, German, and if she could help it, also Russian. Wouldn't he or she be the perfect American?

On the drive back home, Ernesto explained that Roberto had at one time considered selling the farm because he really did not want to deal with it, but the old man, the caretaker, had persuaded him to keep it and to donate all of the profits from it to local charities. He had explained that this farm provided a living for about fifty families and that the money generated from the sale of the crops could do a lot of good for the poor people on the island. Roberto agreed, and now the farm supported not only the workers and their families, but also provided funds for a hospital, an orphanage and a trade school. "And you know what is really wonderful about all of this?" Ernesto went on, "Roberto never takes any credit for this. His name does not appear anywhere. Most people there do not even know who he is. As a matter of fact, most of them think that I am somehow behind all of this, and they thank me for helping them."

Ingrid listened with great interest. Wasn't that just like Roberto? And was that perhaps the reason why he had never brought her here himself? It was just like him not to be in the forefront but to let others receive the praise. She pulled herself out of her thoughts and turned to Ernesto. "Tell me," she said, "What were some of the people saying to you? I mean, especially some of the women asked you something about a woman or wife?"

Ernesto smiled, "They asked me whether you were my wife. You heard them say "bonita," did you not? I think most of them feel that I should be married by now."

"And why aren't you," Ingrid asked coyly.

Ernesto looked straight ahead. "I don't know." He paused. Then, he continued, "But tell me, who would want to marry me? Look at my existence. I live half the year in Argentina, the other half here in La Romana. I really don't do anything. I don't think any woman would be happy with such a life."

Ingrid did not say anything and looked at the curving road ahead.

After a while, Ernesto continued, "How could I expect any woman to live with me? I really don't have anything of my own. Don't get me wrong. Roberto pays me well, but all I do is manage things for others. And, to be honest with you, I don't think I would be a very good husband. I actually like the way I live. I don't have too much to do and that leaves me all the time I need to do what I really enjoy doing."

He paused and waited for her to ask him what that might possibly be. Ingrid, however, kept looking straight at the road ahead.

Ernesto went on, "You have probably noticed that I like to daydream. I like to look out over the ocean and let my mind wander, or I like to look at a flower for some time and contemplate why it has such a strong effect on me. And as I drive through villages such as these, I like to imagine what joy and grief occurs here in these peoples' lives, and then I make stories out of all of this. Stories that probably don't make any sense to anyone else because they come from so deep within me that I cannot imagine that anyone else would even try to understand them. They are so subjective, so tainted with my own interpretation of things, that I am sure I would be laughed at by anyone who was a serious student of literature."

After a while, Ingrid said to him, still looking straight ahead, "I knew that you lived in a world of your own, and that your world had to be a beautiful world, because everything that is truly beautiful is in some way also sad. It cannot be any other way." She paused and took a deep breath. "Has anyone ever read what you write?"

"Never!" he answered rather vehemently, and then he went on more gently, "no one has ever read that nonsense that I write, and I don't think anyone ever will. All of that is really just for me."

"How much have you already written?" Ingrid asked.

Ernesto thought for a while. "If you count the poetry, the little plays, short stories and one full length novel, I think you could possibly make four nice sized books out of all of that. At the moment, however, all I have is stacks and stacks of notebooks taking up space in the drawers of my writing desk in Buenos Aires."

"How old were you when you began writing?" Ingrid continued.

"I must have been about twelve when I began to write things down that had made some impression on me, and soon, I knew what I wanted to do. I knew that I disappointed Roberto's father by not taking my studies seriously, but I just could not have become a lawyer or doctor or teacher or businessman, like Roberto. That would have drained me too much and would have left no room for my daydreams. And so you see, Señora Delgado, I am not the right man for any woman. I think that this was just meant to be this way." After a short pause, he added, "But please, don't tell Roberto about any of this."

The rest of this year's stay in the Caribbean went by quickly. Roberto attended to his business, played golf and stayed involved in the rebuilding of the façade of the house and the reworking of the garden. Ingrid worked harder than ever on the renovation of the Polynesian room, and Ernesto helped her whenever possible. By January, her tummy began to show that soon a happy event would be celebrated. Roberto insisted that Ingrid slow down her activities, and since the Polynesian room was already completed, she did slow down her pace considerably. She would spend more time again with the cook in the kitchen, or she would just sit on the beach and look across the deep blue sea. Sometimes, Ernesto would come by, and they would talk for a while or just watch the endless waves of the sea roll ashore. At other times, Ingrid would stop by when he was writing outside his rooms, but whenever he saw her coming, he would hide whatever he was working on under the ledger and the various correspondences that he had laid out before him. One time, Ingrid asked him if she would ever get to see any of his writings, but he only looked up to her with his sad smile and said, "Who knows? Maybe someday."

Roberto, Ingrid and the little treasure inside her left for New York in March, and Karl was born on May 18th. He was a healthy, pudgy boy – eight pounds, six ounces – and his cries were so loud that Roberto jokingly observed that surely here they had created a future great tenor, perhaps another Luciano Pavarotti or Placido Domingo. Everything now revolved around little Karl. It was touching to see how Roberto, usually so businesslike and correct, now crawled on his hands and knees up to the beautiful cradle, looked inside, made gurgling noises and rolled his eyes and then gently touched the little nose or round cheeks as if to make sure that they were made of flesh and blood, and that this beautiful little thing, so peaceful while sleeping, was not just a pretty lifelike, but lifeless, doll bought in one of the many shops that specialized in such things.

Soon, the proud parents were seen pushing the baby carriage through Central Park, and everyone who looked inside and saw the baby complimented them on how

210

beautiful their child was. Ingrid would often sing to little Karl, and Roberto enjoyed nothing more than to stand off to the side and watch his lovely wife nurse their precious boy while she hummed a tune so sweet and gentle that his eyes became moist and he could not imagine how he could be any happier.

October came, and the three of them arrived in Casa de Campo, and now life here changed for everyone. The entire staff simply could not get enough of the little one, and everyone tried to spoil him as much as possible. Mario and Juanita asked over and over again whether there wasn't something special that they could cook for him; Linda and Rudolfo volunteered to push the baby carriage whenever they could get away from their duties. Pedro carved a little bird from a bamboo branch, and Ingrid hung it down in front of the child, who never tired of watching it turn and twist above his eyes. Ernesto would often come by and look in on the child. As he gently rocked the baby carriage, he would say, "Oh, you lucky child, be happy, be happy."

Ingrid and Ernesto continued working on the Louis XIV room. They traveled to Santo Domingo to find just the right bed and curtains. The carpet and chandelier were found in an antique shop in La Romana. The crowning piece, the huge painting of the monarch, was ordered from a store in New York.

The days flew by, and all of their lives were so filled with activities that one could hardly speak of the normal leisurely pace of life in the Caribbean.

As soon as Ingrid and Ernesto had done all that they could do in the French room, they began remodeling the third guest room, the Chinese room. They painted the headboard wall a deep red and the other three walls in a bright, creamy yellow. They had found a black poster bed, and from its canopy, they hung red silk see-through curtains, which swayed ever so gently with the slightest movement of air. In one corner, they placed a jade tree in a magnificent pot that was decorated with marvelous Chinese symbols and dragons and flowers. In another corner, they positioned a four-foot tall vase, all in black and red and yellow. They found a black dresser with an ornamental mirror over it in a second hand shop in Santa Domingo and placed it along one wall. And then they made the find, which they thought made the room complete. In the Colonial Quarter of Santo Domingo, they found an antique shop which had two standing lamps, each on a green marble pedestal about five feet tall, and topped with a most colorful round paper lantern, and this came along with a matching round paper lantern which could be placed over the ceiling light. When these lights were turned on at night, the room was bathed in a mysterious, exotic and seductive red light. The two of them congratulated each other when they saw the finished room for the first time in this mesmerizing, almost eerie glow.

As they stood there and looked at the room, Ingrid felt that there was still something missing on the left wall. Ernesto agreed; the space needed something. Suddenly, Ingrid exclaimed, "I've got it. Yes, that's it. That's what we're going to do."

"What is it? Please enlighten me," begged Ernesto.

"You'll see," answered Ingrid. "Tomorrow we'll go to town and get it. I saw it in a store, and it will be just perfect. I hope it's still there."

Ernesto made a few more attempts to find out what she was so enthusiastic about, but Ingrid put him off by simply saying, "You'll see. It will be perfect."

They went back the next day to the dilapidated looking store on Calle Conde. Ingrid went straight to the back wall and immediately found the item she sought. She looked expectantly at Ernesto as she pointed to the magnificent Samurai sword hung among all kinds of things. Ernesto gave her a puzzling look, but Ingrid was not to be stopped.

"Look at the beautiful artwork on the scabbard," she said, "and the elegance of the handle and the curvature, so graceful but yet so powerful. You'll see, it will provide the perfect contrast to the otherwise rather feminine décor. We need something strong and masculine in there."

Once they brought it home, Ingrid explained how she wanted it mounted on the wall. "You see," she said, "this wonderful blade must not be hidden. That is why we will hang the sword higher, gently sloping downward, and then, parallel beneath it, we will hang the scabbard. The parallel line, so simple, is so effective, don't you agree? And then, the shining strong blade, with the dark and hollow sheath underneath, are so masculine and feminine, so yin and yang. I think we have just created something magical."

At last, the time had come to let Roberto see what the two of them had created. Ingrid led him by the hand to the door of the Louis XIV room. Here he had to step inside while keeping his eyes tightly shut. All of the lights were turned off. Then, in the darkness of the room, Ingrid said, "Now." Ernesto switched on the lights, and Roberto opened his eyes. At first, he stood there in absolute amazement. Then, he began to walk around and inspect every corner. He looked at the carpet and stood a long time in front of the golden-framed picture of the Sun King. Then, he lay down on the bed and flaying his arms about, he laughed, "I feel like a king. I am the king of this island, the world and the universe." He then jumped out of the bed, hugged his wife and slapped Ernesto on the back. "You two," he said, while he had his arms draped around each of their shoulders, "are quite a team. This is absolutely magnificent. Come on, show me the rest."

The same thing happened in the Polynesian room. Again, Roberto inspected every nook and cranny. He touched the wallpaper in one corner of the room and let his hands run over the smooth cloth, which billowed down from the canopy. He checked if a plant by the bed was real or fake. He even got on his hands and knees and investigated the texture of the thick carpet, which replicated the soft sand one would find around a hut in a Polynesian village. And again, he lay down on the bed, spread out his arms and as he looked up to the sky blue canopy above him said, "Who needs the South Sea islands? Who needs the Caribbean? I think I'll just stay in here for the rest of my life and never go outside again."

Roberto's biggest surprise, however, came when he stood inside the Chinese room. After Ingrid had told him to open his eyes and Ernesto had simultaneously switched on the lights, Roberto could not believe what he saw. The paper lantern lights gave off a soft reddish glow that bathed the entire room in a mysterious and sensuous hue. In one corner, he saw a sleek jade tiger and on the other side a magnificent black screen painted with the most exquisite flowers. The floor had been left in the original greenish-gray marble, and the one red wall and the other yellowish walls contrasted perfectly with it. Everywhere, there were interesting little art objects. After Roberto had investigated it all, he opened up the curtains to the bed and looked inside. "This," he said, "is not just fit for a king, but for an emperor, and I shall be the emperor before whom all shall bow and tremble in fear." He laughed, and Ingrid and Ernesto bowed down deeply before him. He then walked over to the wall where the Samurai sword was hung. He looked at it for

214

quite some time and then took it off the wall and held the shining blade in both hands. "This is so beautiful and yet so deadly," he said gravely. He held it by the handle and stepping around the room, he made the sharp blade swoosh through the air in circular, figure eight and x shape motions. Finally, breathing a little heavy, he stopped in front of Ingrid and Ernesto, who had watched in amusement, and raising the sword straight up toward the ceiling, he bellowed in the harshest voice he could muster, "Beware of the wrath of the great Khan, beware all ye evildoers of the world, for vengeance is mine!" He then lowered the sword and almost doubled over with laughter because of the little show he had just put on.

The winter went by quickly once again. Little Karl grew beautifully and was the pride and joy of the entire household. Roberto would conduct his business in the morning, then play a round of golf or go to the polo grounds. Sometimes, he would accompany Ingrid and Linda to the beach, and he would proudly push the light baby carriage right up to the sand. He would sit and watch Karl sleep in the shade while Ingrid splashed about in the water. When Karl was awake, he would hold him in his arms and walk with him along the beach in the shade of the tall trees that lined the water's edge. He would usually stay with the women and Karl for about an hour. After that, he would hurry back to the house because there still was work to be done, or he went to the club for a drink with one of his friends, or he rode his horses. He was always back for dinner, which was served promptly at seven.

Ingrid and Ernesto would occasionally drive into town to do some shopping. Ernesto would then sit in the front and drive and Ingrid, with little Karl in a baby seat, sat behind him. When they arrived at their destination, Ernesto would fling the door open, hold out his hand to Ingrid, bow deeply, and say, "Your majesty." Then, he would reach inside and take Karl and would say to him, "Here comes the little prince, the ruler of North and South America." They would sit him in the stroller and walk down the streets of the town, looking very much like a handsome young couple with their beautiful baby boy.

One evening in early March, as the four of them sat in one of the outdoor restaurants at La Marina, Roberto suddenly put down his knife and fork, and looking out to the boats docked along the pier, he said, "I have an idea. A wonderful, no, a super idea." He looked at Ernesto and then at Ingrid. "I don't know why I haven't thought of this before," he continued, "but the time is now better, much better. What do you say, Ernesto, why don't you come and visit us in New York this summer? You've never been there, and believe me, it's a great city. There is so much to see. Get away from this lethargic life down here. Get into the hustle and bustle of a real city. Wouldn't that be great, my dear?" He had placed his hand on Ingrid's forearm. He looked back at Ernesto, "What do you say? This would be so good for you, for all of us. Right, dear?" He looked at her again, and she could tell that he wanted her to share his enthusiasm.

"Of course," she said, "that's a great idea. I know Karl would be very happy to see him again, wouldn't you, my angel?" and she tickled Karl under his chin until he let go with a bright squeal of delight.

"Well, it's settled then," Roberto continued, "I want you there. Ingrid wants you there, and Karl wants you there. There is nothing to discuss. I would suggest the middle of July. That's when business is the slowest, and I would have more time to spend with all of you."

Ernesto raised his glass, and Roberto and Ingrid did the same. "To New York, to friendship, and to a long and happy life," he said, and then the three of them clinked their glasses together carefully, not to shatter the beautiful, but oh so fragile, Bohemian crystal.

July came, and so did Ernesto. He was very happy to see that little Karl still recognized him. The boy was now crawling about everywhere, and quite often he would hold on to something, stand up and take a few very shaky steps before he fell back with a soft thud on his diapered behind. Then, he would look around at everyone in the room and throw his arms up and down wildly as if he were saying, "Come on, applause, please." And everyone did applaud, most of all the proud father.

Roberto kept his word. He took off from work as much as he could, and the four of them explored the city almost every day. The Statue of Liberty fascinated Ernesto especially, and they spent almost an entire day at Liberty and Ellis Island. They drove up to Martha's Vineyard and as far south as Savannah. Ernesto found everything most exciting and was very much interested in the history of every place they visited. Often, he would stop while they were walking, pull out a little notebook from his back pocket, and jot down a few notes. When Roberto asked him what he was doing, he simply answered, "This will help me to keep everything fresh in mind."

Roberto nodded and turning to Ingrid, he said, "Isn't that just like our Ernesto? Everything neatly stored away in its proper place to be at hand when needed." And with that he threw his arms around Ernesto's shoulder, and said, "You know I love you, little brother. What would I ever do without you?"

The three weeks of Ernesto's stay were soon over, but their parting was not a sad one, because in just a little over two months, they would see each other again, under the warm Caribbean sun.

It was two weeks before their departure to Casa de Campo that during dinner, Roberto turned to Ingrid and said, "I hope you won't be mad about this, but today I called Ernesto, who is now down in Argentina, and asked him to send me my six favorite polo horses to the island. I've been thinking about this for some time. You know, I'm not getting any younger, and you know how much I love the sport. A few of the fellows at the club have asked me when I would join them. I hope you don't mind, but I am going to join the polo team, because if I don't do it now, I never will."

He looked at Ingrid, and the expression on his face showed that for once he was not quite sure what her reaction would be. She reached across the table and patted his hand and said in a very serious tone, "Don't ever do that to me again."

"What?" he asked, slightly taken aback.

"Scare me like that," she now answered with a smile. "Of course I don't mind. You should do whatever you enjoy doing. Haven't I told you often enough not to work so much? For heaven's sake, don't worry about Karl and me. I have so much to do down there. I want to do much more work with Pedro – you know, he is amazing with plants – and Mario can still teach me so much. I also want to spend more time at Altos de Chavón and watch the artists at work. Who knows, I've always wanted to paint. Maybe I can get a start there."

Roberto smiled back at her, "Thank you, my love," he said tenderly and looked into her eyes.

"And there is one more thing," she went on. Roberto looked at her questioningly. "A long time ago, you told me that golf was one of your few great passions in life. But you hardly ever go and play. Not here or at Casa de Campo. I read in a brochure that the golf courses there are among the best in the world. Go out and play more. Enjoy yourself. If there is anyone who deserves it more, it's you. And don't worry about Karl and me. We'll be just fine, won't we?" She looked over at their son in his high chair who was busy putting one pea after another into his little mouth.

At the beginning of October, the little family was back at their favorite place, their "house in the country," in the Dominican Republic. Ernesto was there, too, and he could not wait to show Roberto the horses that had just arrived a week earlier. A few days later, Roberto surprised Ingrid early in the morning as she was just getting up. He stood in the doorway to the bedroom, fully dressed in his polo player's outfit. He cut quite a dashing figure in his brand new riding boots into which the white jodhpurs were tucked. Over this, he wore a shirt with blue and white vertical stripes, and on his head he wore a riding helmet, with the strap pulled tight under his chin.

"My, oh my," Ingrid exclaimed, as she sat up in the bed, and he now walked back and forth before her like a mannequin showing off the latest Parisian fashion. "Don't you look dashing! I don't know if you will be the best player out there, but you will surely be the handsomest. So make sure you keep your eyes on the ball and not on the ladies watching you."

He stopped and knelt before her, "You are such a silly little goose," he said, as he pinched her cheeks, "don't you know that anyone who knows the game fully understands that the only beautiful things out there on the field are the horses?"

And life at Casa de Campo now went on much as it did before. Ingrid and Linda would go to the beach with Karl almost every day until lunchtime. Then, there would be an hour or two of naptime, depending on how long Karl slept. The afternoon was spent shopping, or going to Altos de Chavón, where Ingrid did watch the artists at work while Linda strolled about with Karl. Sometimes, Ingrid would spend the morning gardening with Pedro, or she would spend some time in the kitchen with Mario and Juanita. One day, she drove out to the hacienda with Ernesto, Linda and Karl, and the workers at the farm, especially the women, could not stop in their admiration of the darling little boy who toddled among them.

It was at the beginning of December when Ingrid came out into the courtyard and slowly walked toward Ernesto, who, seeing her approach, put the notebook that he was writing in under the thick logbook where he kept various records.

"What are you hiding from me now?" she asked, half jokingly and half seriously.

"Oh, it's nothing," he replied, "Just a little story I'm working on."

"And does this story have a title?" she continued to question him.

"Yes, it does," he answered, looking up at her.

Ingrid pulled a chair from the table that was next to him and placed it facing him. She sat down. "Would you mind telling me the title of the story?" she went on.

"The story is called, 'The Nightingale,' he answered, and he kept his eyes fixed on hers.

"So," she continued, "is this a story about a real nightingale, the bird, or is it about something else?"

"It's about everything," he answered. "It's about a bird that flies south when it gets cold where it is, and that flies north when it gets too warm in that place. It is about songs and music. You see, the nightingale is said to be the best singer of all the birds, and this nightingale sings even more beautifully than the others. This nightingale is young and beautiful and wants to experience everything – and so she flutters back and forth and sticks her little beak here and there and sings so wonderfully that everyone is simply enchanted with her."

"That's very nice," she said, looking at him seriously. "But how does the story end? She can't just fly around all the time and be happy. Even nightingales get old, don't they?"

Ernesto looked down, "I don't know," he said softly. "Maybe I can make her into a magical nightingale who just plays and sings forever and through this brings happiness into the life of all of those who hear her. But I don't know. I haven't really thought this story out to the end yet. That's the beauty of it. Anything can happen."

The days went by quickly. Roberto did spend a great deal of time at the polo grounds and on the golf course. Sometimes, Ingrid would take Karl and Linda, and they would drive out to the polo grounds and watch him practice with the other players. When he saw them, he would wave to them as he flew by on his speedy, powerful polo horse. After practice, he would ride over to them and lift little Karl into the saddle of the sweat-drenched horse. Karl loved this and would look down from his high perch as if this were the most natural place for him to be.

"You see," Roberto would beam, "here is a true horseman, a caballero of the highest order. Just see how he feels at home here in the saddle. My son, I am proud of you!" And then he would lift him down and with his hand under the boy's chest and legs, he would, making airplane engine sounds, twirl him around until he felt himself getting dizzy. Ingrid had never seen him as happy as he was now.

It was at the end of February when at lunch Roberto asked Ingrid what she planned to do that afternoon. Ingrid told him that she and Linda and Karl would first go to the beach after Karl's nap and that later she wanted to drive to the shops at La Marina, where she had just seen the most gorgeous new sandals. Roberto kissed her and Karl goodbye. He was off to the polo grounds, not to play, but to look after one of his horses, which may have sprained an ankle during yesterday's practice. They agreed to meet for dinner at seven.

Roberto went to the stables and saw after the horse. The groom assured him that the mare was not seriously injured, and he led her back and forth before Roberto, who watched every step most carefully. He had to agree with the trainer that the horse was walking quite normally again and that in a few days she would once more be able to be ridden. Then, he went to the club where he had a drink with a few of his friends while they discussed the big polo tournament that was coming up in two weeks.

After an hour and a few drinks, the little group dispersed, and Roberto decided that today might be a good day to go to La Romana, to his favorite stationary store, and buy a new fountain pen. The old one had become leaky. He still insisted on writing all of his personal notes with a real fountain pen, with real ink. His purchase made – he had found his favorite MontBlanc pen – he walked slowly along Calle Duarte toward where he had parked his car. He came past a store which had the daily newspapers laid out in front among fruits and vegetables and ice-filled tubs containing various soft drinks. The headline of the sports page caught his attention – Argentina favorite to win World Cup. Roberto picked up the paper, went inside and paid for it. He loved soccer, but living in the United States and in the Dominican Republic had taken him away from the sport. He continued walking down the street with the paper under his arm, until he came to the Bolivar Café, a small place with a few tables along the sidewalk that were shaded by colorful umbrellas. Roberto sat down and began reading the paper. A waiter appeared, and Roberto ordered an iced coffee. He read the paper, but once in a while he would glance over to the Franco Hotel, almost straight across the street. On both sides of the main entrance, there was a terrace, and a few people sat drinking coffee or eating ice cream. Roberto was just about to put the paper down, which he had held up before his face, when he did a double take. Wasn't that Ernesto coming out of the hotel? He quickly raised the paper again, but peered from its side across the street. Coming quickly down the steps, without looking left or right, was Ernesto. When he reached the sidewalk, he turned left and walked away at a quick pace. Roberto had to think. Ernesto had told him earlier that he was going to drive to Santo Domingo, where he was to meet a friend and spend the night. But now, he was here. Perhaps he had changed his mind, or maybe his friend had called him and canceled. Whatever it was, it was none of his business, he thought. He was sure that Ernesto would tell him all about it.

Roberto was just about to fold the paper and go to his car when his eyes looked across the street. He quickly raised the newspaper again. His heart raced. It couldn't be. He carefully peered past the side of his paper. Yes, he had seen right. Walking quickly down the steps, wearing the white Capri pants and yellow top with green flowers that where his favorite, head covered with a large straw hat, came Ingrid, head down, oblivious to everything around her. At the bottom of the steps, she turned right, and after a few more steps, at the corner, she turned right again. She disappeared from his sight.

Roberto laid down the newspaper with trembling hands. He looked up and took a deep breath. His face was drenched with sweat. He sat like this, motionless, for a few minutes longer, only his heaving chest showed that there was a live person sitting in the chair. He then got up awkwardly, like an old man, and walked slowly away, leaving the open newspaper on the little round table.

Later, at dinner, Roberto asked Ingrid whether she had a nice day. She told him she, Linda and Karl had been at the beach for some time, but then she had remembered the sandals that she wanted to buy. She had left Linda and Karl at the beach and had driven to La Romana, and not La Marina, as she had originally intended, because the store in La Romana had a much better selection, and she wasn't so sure anymore about the sandals that she had seen in the store in La Marina. Ingrid called Linda and asked her to bring the sandals that she had bought today. In a few minutes, Linda brought the sandals and Ingrid held them

224

up to Roberto and asked, "Aren't these the most stylish sandals you have ever seen? And they're so comfortable." In just a few seconds, she had them on her feet and paraded around the table with them, as she looked questioningly at Roberto.

"Yes, very nice, my dear," Roberto said dryly, as he took another sip of red wine. "Very nice," he continued, "I'm glad they have what you like in La Romana."

At nine-fifteen the next morning, when Ingrid came into Roberto's office to give him his usual good morning kiss, Roberto asked her to sit – he wanted to talk to her. Ingrid sat straight across his desk from him and looked at his serious face and waited for him to say something. Roberto sat forward against the desk with his elbows resting on the smooth surface - his forearms pointing straight up. His chin rested on his hands, which he had cupped one above the other. Finally, he sat back in his chair and looked into Ingrid's eyes. "I have something to tell you," he began, "which might upset you." He kept looking right into her eyes. Although she did not flinch, he could see the tension rising within her.

"I have called Ernesto on his cell phone and told him that he should report immediately to our estate in Argentina. A buyer from France will arrive shortly to look at some of my best horses, and I want Ernesto there to supervise the whole thing." Roberto saw how Ingrid breathed a sigh of relief.

"Okay," she ventured timidly, "what's the problem with that? You've sent Ernesto on these kinds of missions before."

"Yes," Roberto said gravely, "but this time he will not be coming back, at least not for some time."

Now, he saw the shock quite clearly on Ingrid's face. She sat quietly and only after a while did she ask with a trembling voice, "Why? What happened? Has he done something wrong?"

"He lied to me," Roberto answered firmly, his eyes still fixed on hers. "He lied to me. He told me that he would spend yesterday and today with a friend in Santo Domingo. Yesterday afternoon I saw him in La Romana, coming out of the Franco hotel. When I called him this morning, he told me that everything was fine in Santo Domingo. He and his friend went looking at cars because his friend's old one had broken down. In the evening, they went to the movies. But obviously he was not looking at cars in Santo Domingo yesterday afternoon. He was right here in La Romana. Why would he lie to me?" Roberto's voice had become quite agitated. Now, he sat back in his chair, breathing heavily, his eyes still fixed on Ingrid.

"Well," she said, after a while, "he is your friend, and this is something that you have to work out with him."

Roberto rocked back and forth in his seat, still always looking at her. Suddenly, he looked at his wristwatch and jumped out of his chair. "I'm supposed to meet the other team members at the club in half an hour. I'll have lunch with them. I'll see you back at home for dinner." He gave her a quick peck on the cheek and hurried out of the room. She sat motionless, staring at the empty chair in front of her. When she heard the car being started and when the sound of the engine faded in the distance, she rose slowly from her chair and walked down to the swimming pool, where Linda was playing with Karl. Without saying a word, she picked him up and walked with him into the garden, where she stood motionless, holding the child clasped in her arms until she had to put him down so that she could wipe away the tears that were streaming down her face.

The summer in New York was uneventful. Roberto worked more than usual and went on two business trips – four days to England and five days to Hungary. Each time, he came back with wonderful presents for Karl and Ingrid. He would take a few days off, and they would spend the whole day in the city, strolling through the parks and eating pizza in the garden of a quaint pizzeria that only the locals knew about. Once, they drove out to Coney Island and Karl enjoyed playing in the sand; he did not play in the water very much, for as soon as he had put his little feet in the water, he noticed that it was much colder than the warm water he was used to in the Caribbean.

It was in the middle of August when Roberto came home early one day from work and immediately went to Ingrid as soon as he had entered the apartment. She was watering the African violets that grew in colorful pots, which she had lined up in front of the east windows. He took her gently by the arm and led her to the sofa. He sat down on the armchair facing her.

"I just received a phone call," he began, and Ingrid could tell by the tone in his voice that he was quite upset. She did not say anything and looked him straight in the eyes. "It was Ernesto," he said softly, his eyes wandering over to the windows. "He told me that he is leaving my employ. He has to do something different. He said that I was right, that his life was lethargic, that he had to move on. When I asked him what he was going to do, he said he really didn't know. He had always wanted to go to Europe, and now he was going to do it. I asked him if he wanted more money, but he said that I had been more than generous to him, that he was set for quite a few years. But most of all, he wanted to do something – get involved, start living and stop dreaming."

Roberto looked over at Ingrid, who had listened to him with her eyes lowered to the floor. Now, she looked up at him.

"I asked him," Roberto continued, "whether I or anyone had in some way offended him, but he assured me that he loved all of us. I think he was crying, and I was close to tears myself. He closed our conversation almost abruptly. He said goodbye and wished all of us a happy and healthy life. Before I could tell him to stay in touch with us, he had hung up. I immediately called back at the estate, but I was told that Ernesto had left two days ago and no one knew where he was."

Ingrid looked past him at the paintings on the wall. Finally she asked, "So, what are you going to do?"

Roberto looked aimlessly around the room. He looked at her, and in his eyes she saw more pain and love than she had ever seen before. Almost inaudibly he whispered, "All we can do, my love, is wait."

When they returned to Casa de Campo in October, Karl was able to walk quite well on his pudgy little legs. He would run so quickly that everyone had a hard time keeping up with him. Ingrid had gone to Altos de Chavón several times, but she could not decide what she wanted to do - should she try her hand at painting, sculpting or pottery? In the end, she decided not to do any of these things; she would only make herself look foolish, she thought. Once in a while, she would look in on Mario and Juanita in the kitchen, but on the whole, she let them decide what to prepare – Mario always had such good ideas anyway. She did spend a little more time with Pedro, the gardener, but when he explained to her how a row of orchids along the rear boundary of the property would add

228

a wonderful touch of color to that part of the garden, she told him almost apologetically that he should do whatever he pleased. Anything would be all right with her. She felt badly when she saw him walk away with his back bent and his head down. It was obvious that he had been looking forward to working with her and getting all kinds of beautification projects going in their spacious garden.

Roberto involved himself more than ever in his business, his polo team and golf. This year, he explained to Ingrid, his team had a real chance of winning the Central America Cup. He asked her to be patient. He also played more golf, and it seemed to Ingrid that more and more business associates were coming to Casa de Campo to play golf with him.

Ingrid did not mind all of this. She was happy that Roberto kept himself occupied and that he was finally doing all of the things he had always wanted to do.

Shortly before Christmas, she received a telephone call from her brother, who told her that at the end of January, he would complete his studies and that he already had a job offer from a major architectural firm in Frankfurt. He was bubbling over with enthusiasm, and Ingrid was happy for him. She wrote Christmas cards to all of her friends, and in the card for Mrs. Lemke, she included a generous check.

Ingrid's life went on much as it had done before. She would take Karl to watch daddy play polo, and they would cheer him on from the sidelines. They would go shopping at La Marina or in La Romana, and sometimes would even drive to Santo Domingo with Rudolfo and Linda.

It was right after lunch on a day in late January when Roberto had gone to the polo grounds and Karl was taking his nap that Linda gently knocked on the bedroom door.

Ingrid opened the door, but Linda motioned her to step into the corridor.

"A few days ago, I received a little package," she began, "and it contained this note." She handed a little piece of paper to Ingrid and then walked away quickly. Ingrid looked at the note. She felt her hands trembling. The handwriting was clearly Ernesto's. She read, "Dear Rudolfo and Linda. Please take this picture and hang it above the sword in the Chinese guest room. Thank you, your friend, Ernesto."

Ingrid hurried down the stairs, across the courtyard and past the swimming pool, but a few steps before the door to the Chinese room, she slowed down, and her hand trembled as she slowly turned the knob. What could he possibly have sent? She opened the door almost cautiously, and as soon as she stepped inside, she turned on the light. She immediately looked at the space above the sword. She had no idea what to expect. If she had not decorated the room herself, she would have never noticed that anything had changed inside the room, but she saw it right away. There, in that previously empty space above the center of the sword, hung a picture; a small picture in a simple black wooden frame. She stepped closer to see what the picture was. Finally, when she was only a few steps away, she realized that the picture depicted a bird. It was a very plain picture, probably cut out of a magazine, but as she stepped even closer, she noticed a very light print under the bird's feet. She took the picture off the wall and held it close to her, and now she read "The Nightingale." Her hands shook and her eyes were filled with tears, but she stood there and stared at the simple picture of the bird for a long, long time. Then, she looked at the backside of the picture to see if there was some kind of note attached, perhaps a short message.

230

But all she saw through her tears was the plain brown paper backing.

The remaining time on the island was spent as usual. Roberto worked in the mornings. After lunch, he would go to the club and either play a round of golf or check on the horses. Sometimes, he would come to the beach and sit with Ingrid, Karl and Linda in the sand for a while and watch the waves roll gently onto the beach. Occasionally, he would play a few minutes in the water with Karl, but then he would leave.

Ingrid slept later in the mornings. She would rarely go into the kitchen, and Pedro did not see her very often either. Sometimes, she would drive to Altos de Chavón and look at sculptures and paintings, but she never bought anything. In the past, she would have a manicure once a week, a pedicure every other week, and her hair cut and styled once a month. She now no longer kept her previous schedule – it must have been over three weeks that she had her nails done, and her last haircut was some months ago. She spent much more time at the beach, with a book beside her in the sun, looking across the never changing movement of the sea. At other times, she would sit for hours in her favorite café in La Marina, drinking one mocha after another, while Linda walked back and forth with little Karl along the pier with its magnificent yachts.

Back in New York, she and Roberto would take Karl outside when the weather was nice. They held his hands from both sides, and on the count of three would lift him in the air and walk several steps with him seemingly flying over the sidewalk. He would laugh and scream with delight, and his parents would have to do it over and over again.

At times, Roberto would stand silently behind his wife, who had been reading to little Karl, who was now sound asleep on her lap, and he would listen to her sing softly. Sometimes he would catch her humming a tune while she wrote a letter or watered her plants. In moments like these, a melancholy smile would settle on Roberto's face for as he listened, it seemed to him that all her songs and melodies were sad, so very, very sad.

****

I had just entered our church hall and was about to greet Mrs. Miller, a fellow singer in our choir, when I heard a loud voice from across the room boom out, "Well, well, well, if it isn't our author."

Henry came towards me with big steps, shook my hand and slapped me on the shoulder. "Good job," he said, loud enough for everyone to hear. "Yes, yes, a very good job, especially for a first effort. Finished it last night, enjoyed it very much."

He took a deep breath, just long enough for me to say, "Thanks, that's very kind of you."

"No, no, not at all," he went on, "great stories, made me think. Definitely very good."

He paused, but I felt he wasn't done yet.

"But," he continued in a much softer voice while he took my arm and led me a few steps to the side, "why did you end that last story, you know, the one about the nightingale, why did you end it the way you did?"

Before I could say anything, he continued, "I don't like it when stories end that open endedly – what happens to those

232

people? How do their lives turn out? And in this story especially, the main characters are still quite young, except for Roberto, and he is what, in his early fifties? That's not old. And why end that story, the entire book, in such a melancholy way? It just leaves you so depressed."

I stood there speechless. I had been quite willing to accept any criticism of my book; after all, I am not a professional writer. Poor character development, weak descriptions, monotonous sentence structure, tedious plot development – I was willing to accept all of that, and learn from my mistakes in case I should ever try my hand at writing again.

"The ending is not meant to leave you depressed," I answered. "It's just that life isn't always one big happy Leave it to Beaver show. Even for the best of people things don't always work out so great. And there is not always someone to blame. It just happens, and people go on with their lives and do the best they can. I think if there were some way that we could check it, we would find that there are more tears and sighs in the people around us than we could have ever imagined."

Henry listened and nodded. "You may be right," he finally said softly. "You may be quite right. But that's exactly my point. With so many problems all around us, do we need another sad story? Don't we see enough of that on television and in the papers?"

We stood alongside a wall facing each other, and Henry must have noticed the disappointment on my face.

"Don't get me wrong," he said gently, as he padded my arm again, "I definitely like the stories; I like the entire book. And for heaven's sake, keep on writing. I think you really do have something to say, but next time, maybe a little more cheerful, a little happier?"

That was seven years ago. I thought that the ending to the story was most appropriate for the last of the three stories that made up my book, Trio in D minor. Every music lover knows that the minor keys are the more subjective and more melancholy ones – the ones that put you in a somber mood and perhaps even leave you with a lump in your throat once the piece of music has ended. A poet once said that everything that is truly beautiful is also sad in a way. I always felt that there was a profound truth in this.

And yet, Henry's words stayed in my mind. Did the story have to end like this? Was there any way in which this story could have a happy end? How many times had I not listened to a beautiful sad piece of music in a minor key, where the composer, at the end of the piece after a long hovering chord, finally resolved into one uplifting, glorious chord in the major? What joy! What a tremendously satisfying feeling – a relief; yes, a release. One could breathe freely again. The world looked bright and cheerful once again!

As time went on, I had to agree more and more with what Henry had told me that Sunday morning in our church hall. There certainly was enough sadness and pain around us – the evening news and the newspapers reinforced that depressing fact on a daily basis. And yes, the characters in the story were for the most part still quite young. Maybe I should try to give that story a major key ending. (I always thought of the three stories as three movements in a musical composition). And didn't Mozart himself, perhaps the greatest composer of all time, who had suffered so much and who died such a sad death still before his thirty-sixth birthday – didn't he write all but two of his forty-one glorious symphonies, and also all but two of his twenty-seven magnificent piano concertos, in bright, uplifting, life-affirming major keys?

And if the aging, ill and deaf Beethoven could open the crowning glory of his works with the words, "Oh friends, not these tones! Let us raise our voices in more pleasing and more joyful sounds" – what reasons could I possibly have to not join in on that great chorus of life-affirming joy?

Seven years have also passed since Roberto listened to Ingrid's sad songs while tiny Karl slept soundly on her lap. The little family lived their lives fairly much as they had done before. Roberto was forever busy with his duties as the head of his ever-growing and very prosperous business empire. Ingrid spent most of her time with Karl, who was tutored at home from the age of four. Then, when he was enrolled at Stafford, an exclusive private school not far from their penthouse apartment, she participated in the charitable work in which many of the other parents were involved.

The little family always spent their winter vacation at their villa in La Romana. Karl loved to go swimming in their pool and the sunny beach. He swam like a fish, climbed the trees on their property like a monkey and quite often scared the daylights out of his mother when he called out to her from high up in the branches of the tallest trees.

During the summer months, they would usually travel to Europe to see the wonders of Paris, Rome and ancient Greece. Before returning to New York, they would sometimes spend a few days in Berlin, so that Karl could see where his mother came from. And they would always visit the small country cemetery where the now quite old Mrs. Lemke lovingly tended the graves of Ingrid's parents. Ingrid also enjoyed paying surprise visits to her friends, who would never get enough of her intelligent and handsome boy who had always grown and matured so much between each visit.

Karl was the single greatest joy in Ingrid and Roberto's lives. He was highly intelligent, got only the best grades, and his teachers simply could not praise him enough when Ingrid went to the semi-annual parent conferences. He spoke fluent English, Spanish and German. His parents had devised a system in which all three of them would practice their language skills. At the dinner table, or on one of their outings, each of them could only speak the assigned language of the day. It was delightful to hear one of them ask a question in Spanish, receive an answer in German and have the third person continue in English. This worked out very well, but there were quite a few funny moments when Roberto, trying his very best with confusing sentence structures and those unpronounceable words, consented to be the "German" for the day.

At the age of four, Karl had become fascinated with the Steinway concert grand piano that stood in the bay window of their penthouse living room. At first, he simply pounded on the keys, but Ingrid showed him that when two keys were pressed down simultaneously, not playing the one in the middle, one could create a pleasing harmony. Soon, Karl sat on the piano bench for hours at a time and ran his little fingers up and down the keyboard at amazing speed. Mrs. Balkovsky, the leading piano teacher for children, was hired to give Karl piano lessons twice a week. Karl, contrary to so many other children, enjoyed these lessons and made tremendous progress. At a third grade talent show, he played so beautifully that everyone was amazed.

Much to his father's joy, Karl also learned to be an outstanding horseman. Whenever Roberto went to polo practice or to one of his tournaments, Karl would come along. A beautiful horse, especially selected for him by his father, was always waiting for him to ride.

And so the years went by. The family spent as much time together as possible, but Roberto sometimes missed a birthday, an anniversary, or an important event at Karl's school. He would return home with beautiful presents for his wife and his boy. Ingrid and Karl knew that they could not expect the kind of life with him as most working class families enjoyed. Roberto's world was too big. His input was needed everywhere. He had to travel to Spain with the polo team, or else the team simply wasn't complete. His presence was needed in China, or the partnership with the motorcycle company could not have been finalized. He had to return to Argentina, or the Delgado Empire could wind up with serious legal problems. His life was one long schedule, and he tried his best to fulfill it.

It was a cold February afternoon in New York when Ingrid received a call from Florida. She knew immediately that something terrible had happened, even before the voice at the other end identified herself as Head Nurse Irma Sanchez of the Miami Sisters of Mercy Hospital. Her husband, she was told, had had an accident at a polo match. It was very serious. Would she please come down immediately?

Ingrid had her maid call corporate headquarters to arrange for a private jet while she hurried to the Stafford school to pick up Karl. Less than an hour later, they sat alone in the cabin of a corporate jet as it sped down the runway for the agonizing flight to Miami.

Dr. Hansen, chief administrator of the hospital, met them at the reception desk. He shook their hands and asked them to follow him. In an empty waiting area, he stopped and asked them to sit down. His eyes moved from one to the other, and then he looked down. Finally, he raised his eyes again and said softly, "I'm sorry, very sorry, but there was nothing more we could do." He looked toward the windows. It was obvious that he was trying to find the right words. Again, his eyes moved from one to the other, "The injuries were just too severe. I'm sorry."

Ingrid was about to say something, but Dr. Hansen cut her off saying, "Mrs. Delgado, please come with me, and you, young man, please stay here for just a moment. We'll be right back."

He led Ingrid a few doors further down the corridor. He stopped in front of Room 117 and turned to Ingrid, who had walked a few steps behind him.

"Mrs. Delgado," he began once again, with his back toward the door, as if to block it from her, "the accident was so unusual and unfortunate – the injuries were so severe – I didn't want to say this in front of the boy. When your husband was thrown from the horse, he fell in such a way that his neck was broken, and that would have paralyzed him for life. But then we discovered that a horse had stepped on his midsection – the internal injuries were massive. I'm sorry, but there was nothing we could do. I had him brought up here, a regular room, so that you and the boy didn't have to see him down in the morgue. I'm sorry, but..."

"Thank you, Doctor," Ingrid interrupted him, as she lifted her eyes up to meet his, with a clear indication that she wanted him to step aside.

"Of course," Dr. Hansen said, as he stepped away from the door. "I'll wait with the boy."

Ingrid opened the door slowly and entered the room. She was afraid to look at the bed in which Roberto lay, covered with a white sheet up to his neck. She advanced cautiously, still not looking at his face, until she stood by the side of the bed. Finally, she dared to lift her eyes, and when she looked at him, it did seem as if he was simply asleep. He looked as handsome as ever – only the pallor of his skin betrayed that life had been drained from him.

She stood beside his bed for quite some time, and she herself was surprised that she did not cry. She then stepped closer and kissed him ever so tenderly on his forehead and gently touched the cover on his chest. Then, she turned and walked resolutely toward the door.

Dr. Hansen sat in one of the waiting room chairs while Karl looked out the window. Ingrid walked up to him and put her hand on his shoulder. He turned toward her and made no attempt to hide the tears that were streaming down his young face. Ingrid took him into her arms, and they stood in this close embrace until she felt his trembling subside. She then reached into her purse and handed him a tissue. Karl wiped his face with his head lowered, but then, after blowing his nose one more time, he looked up, nodded toward the corridor and said, "Let's go."

Ingrid followed her son into the room, closed the door and remained standing a few steps into the room while her son walked to the side of the bed. After he had stood there, with his hands folded in front of him, Ingrid came and stood by his side. She put her arm around his shoulder, and so they stood there, neither one saying anything.

Finally, Ingrid cleared her throat, "Your father was the best, most kindest man I've ever met, and he was the most wonderful father any boy could possibly wish for."

She waited a little while, but Karl did not say anything. Ingrid knew that his was perfectly all right, because any words would have been superfluous. The bond between them had been so strong that Ingrid had at times felt just a little bit of an outsider. But that was all right, too; it was her son's happiness that mattered most of all.

Three days after the funeral, Ingrid received a call from a Mr. Wilmington, of Wilmington, Strauss and Brewster. He told her that he had something to give her and that he would like to stop by the next day. That is all the information he volunteered.

Mr. Wilmington arrived promptly at ten, the agreed upon time, and Ingrid met him in the living room. He politely declined the offer of tea or coffee. When they were comfortably seated, facing each other, Mr. Wilmington reached inside his jacket pocket and took out a small envelope. He took a deep breath and finally said in his low sonorous voice, "Mrs. Delgado, your husband gave me this envelope about two years ago with the instructions that I should give it to you just in case anything should ever happen to him. This is why I am here now." He handed her the envelope, stood up and said, "If you don't mind, I will wait in the next room in case you should have any instructions for me. I'm sorry." He bowed awkwardly and left the room.

Ingrid held the envelope in her hand and just looked at it. She did not rip it open. After a short while, she got up and walked to the adjoining study. She sat down at her writing desk, took the shiny letter opener and slowly and carefully opened the envelope. She took out a piece of plain white paper and immediately recognized Roberto's handwriting, in ink, of course. She read:

My Dearest,

When you read this letter, I will no longer be with you, and so I want to say to you what I should have told you so much more often. I have loved you from the first day I saw you, and my love has grown greater still. You and Karl have fulfilled my life to a degree that I would have never found possible – you two have brought me happiness far beyond what I deserve. Always remember that and have no regrets about anything. I could not possibly love you more.

Some time ago, I transferred some funds into Ernesto's account. I want him to be able to pursue his artistic ambitions without having to worry about his livelihood. You know that I have always looked at him as my little brother, and I want him to be happy – I want all of you to be happy.

Juan Perez will take over all of my corporate responsibilities, and Roger Wilmington will handle all legal matters. These are people you can trust.

Everything, my dear, is yours. Karl will receive his inheritance when he is twenty-five. Mr. Wilmington will explain it all to you.

My dearest Ingrid, I thank you once more for everything you have given me, and I beg your forgiveness if I have ever wronged or disappointed you in any way. Be as happy as you have made me. Be happy!

With all my love,

Roberto

Ingrid's hand trembled as she laid the letter on the desk. Slowly, her eyes began to fill with tears. Sitting there, motionless, as the tears streamed down her face, she looked straight ahead, seeing nothing.

She suddenly remembered Mr. Wilmington. She wiped here eyes, got up and went to the washroom to wash her tear-streaked face with cold water. She quickly reapplied her make-up. Then, she went out to Mr. Wilmington, thanked him and told him that he should do whatever needed to be done.

A week before the beginning of summer vacation, Ingrid asked Karl what he wanted to do. The final decision, however, was to be his. Ingrid suggested going to their villa in the Dominican Republic; a summer camp for Karl in upstate New York, with swimming and canoeing and hiking with kids his own age; a horseback riding vacation – out West; or a road trip through the entire United States, just the two of them, going wherever their whim would take them.

Karl thought about it for almost a minute, then he said, looking sheepishly at his mother, "I'll do the road trip with you under one condition." He grinned mischievously.

"And what would that be?" Ingrid asked with unmistakable amusement in her voice.

"We'll go on this road trip if you," he hesitated and winked his eye at her, "if you let me choose the car."

Ingrid looked at him questioningly, "Okay," she finally conceded, "as long as it's not a Hummer."

"Oh no, don't worry," Karl replied, "it's as much the opposite as you can imagine. Guess."

"A Lincoln Town car?" she asked.

"Definitely not!"

"A Ferrari?"

""Getting closer."

"A Mercedes sports car?"

"Very close."

"Okay, I give up," Ingrid moaned, in fake exasperation, as she threw her hands up in the air.

Karl grinned, "I'll go with you, and we'll have a great time, if we get a Chevy Corvette!" He looked at her with his eyebrows raised. "Convertible," he added for emphasis.

"Done," she said enthusiastically, as they slapped each other a high-five.

Two weeks later, they sat in a sleek red and white Chevy Corvette convertible. First they headed north and stopped at Hyde Park to see FDR's home and the Vanderbilt mansion. Karl had just learned about this president, and he found everything most interesting. From there, they continued on to Niagara Falls, where they were both awed by the power and the grandeur of this natural wonder.

They continued driving leisurely through southern Canada, crossing into Michigan, where they spent a day in the lovingly recreated Bavarian city of Frankenmuth. They crossed the state to see the Great Sleeping Bear Park and sand dunes. They were amazed that so far into the interior of the country four hundred feet tall sandy white dunes could be found. Crossing the impressive Mackinac Bridge and continuing on to North Dakota and Montana, they turned south to visit Yellowstone National Park.

Ingrid drove the sports car expertly. Most of the time, they drove with the top down, Ingrid's blond hair blowing in the wind while Karl had his racing cap tight on his head. They laughed and sang along with the radio, and sometimes, one of them would point off into the distance to some noteworthy spot, and the other would nod. They did not hesitate to turn off the main road to see some sight or visit a town that had been advertised for mile after mile along the roadside, only to turn out to be a rundown place that had seen its better days many years ago.

They saw the Grand Canyon and were awed by its natural splendor. The Great Sand Dunes National Park turned out to be a pleasant surprise – such great mountains of sand and no water in sight. After traveling across the northern part of Texas, through Oklahoma and Arkansas, they reached Memphis. A quick visit to a famous mansion and a peanut butter and banana sandwich for lunch was in order. They now turned southeast reaching the Atlantic Ocean at Savannah, and from here traveled at a leisurely pace north along the Atlantic seaboard all the way back to New York. They had agreed to see the West Coast and the Midwest on another road trip.

Although they did not speak about it, they both sensed that this time together was something that both of them needed. They had an absolutely wonderful time together. Only at times when Karl would say something like, "I wish Dad could see these horses, especially that black one back there. I know he would just love it," or when Ingrid would say, "I wish your Dad was here. We should have done a trip like this, the three of us," they would fall silent for a while, and neither interrupted the other one's thoughts. Occasionally, Ingrid would take Karl's hand and hold it for a few minutes, finding comfort in the gesture. Both of them knew that nothing needed to be said.

After Karl had returned to school, Ingrid had gone to the company headquarters a few times. As she walked through the long corridors, she was well aware that all eyes were on her, the young, beautiful and wealthy owner of ISI. Lea Greenfield had greeted her most affectionately, and Mr. Perez had done his best to explain the current state of the company to her. He assured her that everything was going well, that the company was in great shape and that he would do everything in his power to keep it that way. But Ingrid did not go back any longer because on every one of her visits, when she had seen Roberto's office, the door open, and no one behind the desk, it had shaken her to the core, and she had to leave the building as quickly as possible.

She also met with Mr. Wilmington at the law offices of Wilmington, Strauss and Brewster. Mr. Wilmington had volunteered to come to her house, but she did not want to talk about legal matters in her private residence. Roberto had, she was told, left everything to her; she was the head of his corporate empire. Karl was to receive twenty-five million dollars on his twenty-fifth birthday, and he would become the head of the corporation at that time, if he so desired. Mr. Wilmington also disclosed that a man by the name of Ernesto Soledad had been given five million dollars. Mr. Wilmington asked Ingrid if she knew this man and she answered, "Yes, he was a friend of ours."

As long as the weather was nice, Ingrid would walk with Karl to school in the morning. Then, she would walk to her favorite café, right off the park, and drink her favorite coffee latté while she read the morning papers. When the weather was exceptionally beautiful, she would take a book along, get her coffee to go and then read sitting on a park bench. For some reason, she had picked the bench closest to a group of tall maple trees. Here, she would read the paper or her book, leisurely sip at her coffee and then leave after about an hour to begin to do all the things she had scheduled for the day.

It was on a gorgeous Tuesday morning in early October when the weather was still wonderfully mild with just a hint of fall crispness in the air that Ingrid sat once again on her favorite park bench leafing through the newspaper. Suddenly, a boy on a bicycle rode up to where she was sitting, came to a screeching halt, which totally startled her, and handed her a small envelope and said to her with a smirk on his face, "For you." Before she could say anything, he was back on his bike, and within seconds, he turned off the path and was out of her sight before she could shout after him.

She sat there stunned. There was nothing written on the envelope, the kind in which one would place a "Thank you" card, nothing on either side. She looked down the winding path in both directions, but there was no one in sight.

She opened the backside carefully as if not to destroy anything important that could be inside. She pulled out a small, folded card on which stood, written in a hand she recognized immediately, one word – NIGHTINGALE.

She held the envelope and the card in her trembling hands as she looked straight ahead. She saw nothing, she heard nothing – she had suddenly lost all sense of space and time. She did not think of anything. Only gradually did she lower her eyes to her hands on her lap, which held the envelope and the card. She put the envelope next to her and slowly opened the card. The message, in the same fluent handwriting was short. She read,

The story is not finished –

Walk to the right and you decide.

Walk to the left and it ends sadly.

There was no signature.

She read the lines over and over again as if she did not understand the words. Her head was spinning, but even in this confusion, she understood one thing – he was here in New York, perhaps a few steps from her. Again, she looked to her left and then to her right, but saw no one. She told herself to stay calm, but could feel her heart pounding in her chest, her lips dry. Through all these years, she had tried not to think of him; that was all in the past. She had her own life to live with her son and her husband. There was no need to reminisce, to think about what might have been. She had a wonderful child and a loving husband. Materialistically, she had more than she could have possibly ever imagined, and she had deliberately tried to keep their life as simple and uncomplicated as possible, given the circumstances. Since Roberto's death, Ingrid had not thought about having another man in her life – que sera, sera – she had thought, and Karl's life did not need to be complicated by the presence of another man.

And now this!

She slowly placed the card back into the envelope and put it in her purse, picked up the newspaper, put it under her arm, stood up and turned to the right.

Ingrid walked slowly and did not feel her feet touch the ground. It seemed to her as if she were floating down the asphalt path, and yet, she was conscious enough to throw the newspaper into a waste container on the side of the path. Now she began to think – what should she say? What would he say? Were they still the same people? Should the past remain the past? And again, she thought – que sera, sera.

Her face lightened up, and she began to walk faster, looking eagerly for him. Then, unexpectedly, after a sharp turn in the path, she saw him sitting at a picnic table under the branches of a huge chestnut tree. He waved to her and she waved back. He did not get up as she hurried toward the table. When she was just steps away, he motioned to the bench opposite him, and without finding this gesture strange, she sat down, facing him. He placed his hands palms up on the table, and she nestled her hands in his. They sat like this, motionless, her hands in his as they looked into each other's faces.

Ernesto looked older. He had let his hair grow longer. His slightly fuller face was now framed by a carefully trimmed beard, which suited him very well. There was something very learned and cultured about him. His hands were soft and betrayed a man who was involved in intellectual pursuits. His full head of hair was still pitch black. His eyes, his beautiful dark eyes, had not lost the unmistakable sparkle that reflected his character and wit.

As Ernesto looked into Ingrid's face, he still saw the beautiful woman he had known years ago, but she was not quite the same either. To be sure, her hair, her eyes, her facial features were the same, but she no longer had that girlishly innocent young look that everyone had loved way back then. Here, in front of him, with her delicate hands in his, sat a mature woman, who, with added years and experiences, had only gown more beautiful.

"I'm glad you decided to come," he began, as he looked into her eyes. He waited.

248

"And I'm glad you decided to come," she answered softly.

There was silence all around them as they looked into each other's faces.

"You knew I would come, didn't you?" he continued, still looking intently at her.

She lowered her eyes and did not say anything. Ernesto kept his eyes on her, but he did not press the matter. He knew she needed time to work through all of this.

Then, without looking up, she whispered, "I didn't know what to think. I didn't want to think." She paused. "And what was I supposed to think about? I, who had been given everything, I …" She lowered her head until her forehead touched her hands, and he felt the hot tears on his hands, as he saw her body shake gently as she cried her heart out.

He pulled his right hand out from under hers and tenderly stroked her hair over and over again. Finally, her sobbing subsided. She pulled her other hand out from under his, sat back and reached for her purse beside her. Taking out a few tissues, without looking at him, she handed one to him across the table and said, "Here, I think you might need this, sorry." She wiped her eyes, straightened herself up and looked right into his face. "Oh, where were we?" she said almost cheerfully, and he saw how she struggled to put on a brave front.

Ernesto waited a little and then said, "I am here," and he pointed to his chest, "and you are there," he pointed to her. "And we can be wherever you want us to be." He looked at her expectantly, but she just kept looking at him.

A smile flickered across her face and in a voice that made it clear that she wanted to change the subject, she replied, "So what have you been up to lately?"

Ernesto was sensitive enough to pick up the hint. He looked to the side and then back to her, and in his thoughtful way of speaking, he replied, "I've been everywhere, and I've been nowhere. At first, well, at first, I just had to get away. I traveled all over the world – Africa, Asia, Europe. I spent days in Berlin, walking the streets, wondering if these were the streets you walked on. I traveled all over the United States; there is so much to see..."

"Where you ever in New York?" she interrupted.

"No," he replied as he again looked off to the side, "No, not in New York. I thought about it often, but I couldn't, I just couldn't."

She looked down.

"And so I traveled from one place to another, like a man without a home. And that was true; I didn't have a home. After a few years, my funds had been nearly exhausted, and then something miraculous happened." He looked at Ingrid to see if she would ask him what that was. But she just continued to look at him. "What happened is this," Ernesto continued. "My bank notified me that a deposit had been made into my account, a substantial deposit, and that there was a letter waiting for me at the bank, too." He looked at her and again there was no reaction. "Well, you won't believe this," he went on, "the letter was from Roberto."

Ingrid interrupted, "And he left you five million dollars!"

Ernesto froze. "You know about this?" he finally asked in absolute amazement.

"Yes, he wrote me a letter, too. He told me about that," she answered him, her voice now firmer. "If you don't mind, please tell me about the letter."

"Of course, I don't mind," answered Ernesto. "In the letter he told me that he had always loved me like a brother. He asked me to forgive him, if he had ever wronged me in any way, and not to have any regrets. Can you imagine, he asked me to forgive him. He also wrote, 'I want all of you to be happy.' Do you have any idea what he could have meant by that line?"

Ingrid took out another tissue and covered her face. It was a long time before she wiped her eyes and began to speak. "Yes, I know what he meant by that. You see, I was given a letter from him too after he died. It said that he loved me, that I should have no regrets also, and that I should forgive him if he had wronged me, too, and that I should also be happy, and he emphasized, 'I want all of you to be happy.' Do you understand now who 'all of you' really is?" She looked at him and clearly saw the shock on his face. "Yes, that's right," she continued. "I had hoped that this is what he meant, and I was right. He didn't say you, or you and Karl, or both of you; he said, 'all of you.' And he said the same thing to you. 'All of you.' How great must his love have been for us both!"

Ernesto looked away. It was obvious that he was deeply touched. Then, he held his hands out across the table again, and she put her hands in his. They looked deeply into each other's eyes. They sat there, silently, totally oblivious of the world around them.

Finally, Ernesto pulled his hands out from under hers and said, "You know the story about the nightingale that I worked on so many years ago. Well, it still isn't finished. But it's your story, and do you remember how I told you that anything can happen, yes, that the beauty of it is that anything can happen? You must write the ending to this story. Only then will the story end the way it should end."

He stood up and came to her side of the table. He opened his arms wide. She stood up and entered his embrace, her soft hair resting on his shoulder. He held her tight and whispered, "I love you. I love you more than anything in this world." And he held her even tighter. He kissed her gently on both cheeks. He now held her by her shoulders at arms length, looked deeply into her eyes and said, "The ending to this story must be carefully worked out, and it must be the best ending for everyone involved. I repeat; it must be the ending you want." They kept on looking into each other's eyes. Ernesto took one step back from her and said, "This is my suggestion." He paused and kept his eyes fixed on her beautiful face. She did not say anything, but waited for him to continue. "I suggest that we give each other a little time." Ingrid kept her eyes fixed on his, and then nodded barely noticeably. He looked at his watch and said, "Today is the sixteenth of October, and it is ten o'clock in the morning. I suggest we meet right here, at this table, under this tree, at exactly ten o'clock on," he thought a second, "on the sixteenth of April of next year, rain or shine."

He looked into her eyes, and she could clearly see that he wanted nothing more than to see her again – sooner or later did not really matter. She thought about it for just a moment. Six months – a long time, but the right time.

"Yes," she answered, and there was a hint of a smile on her lips, "April sixteenth, ten in the morning, right here."

He took her into his arms once more, and this time she put her arms around him, too, and they held each other as tightly as it was possible to do out there by the picnic table in a park in the middle of New York.

Winter came early, and Ingrid and Karl were happy when the winter break started and they were able to escape to La Romana. Karl was as active as ever enjoying the ocean, the beach and the sun. Ingrid, however, saw this place, her initial island paradise, in a completely new light. She spent hours walking along the beach looking out onto the wide sea in the direction of her home in New York and in Berlin. She thought of how much her life had changed in such a short time – the first meeting with Roberto, coming to New York, coming to his place, the birth of Karl and meeting Ernesto. All that seemed so long ago, and yet it was just over ten years when all of this was set in motion on that fateful morning in the Bellevue Hotel in Berlin. No matter how much she thought, she could not see how things could have been any different, this was her fate, but now she felt for the first time that it was up to her, that she was in charge and that she would have no one to blame but herself if she made the wrong decision.

She thought of Roberto, that wonderful man who had given her everything a woman could possibly ask for. He had been so kind, so gentle, and so considerate. Anything she wanted would have been hers if she had asked for it, but she hardly ever asked for anything.

Ingrid spent hours in the gardens and looked at the plants that she and Pedro had planted. They had matured so beautifully. Linda and Rudolfo still worked in the villa and were happy to see Ingrid and Karl again. A new cook had been hired to prepare the meals during their holiday stay, but the meals, although expertly prepared, were not the same. Somehow, there was something wrong with just the two of them sitting at the long dining room table.

On the last day of their stay, Ingrid went to see the three guest bedrooms that she and Ernesto had so lovingly decorated. Although the three rooms were kept meticulously clean like the rest of the villa, nothing at all had been changed in them. The Louis XIV looked as regal as ever. The wallpaper was brilliant with its fleur-de-lis and the huge bed surely was fit for even the greatest king.

She paused inside the Polynesian room. The cleverly installed lights made everything appear so bright and sunny. There were lush plants everywhere, and even Ingrid could not tell which one's were real and which ones were not.

Finally, she entered the Chinese room. This room had been Ernesto's idea, and as far as she was concerned, it was the most beautiful of all the rooms. The paper lanterns once again bathed the room in mysterious shades of red. There was something seductive about the entire space – one simply felt drawn into a world of enchantment and illusion. And on the wall there still hung that shiny, deadly sword, with its magnificent scabbard beneath it. "The sword of justice," Ingrid thought. But right above the center of the sword, there still hung that small picture in a plain wooden frame. Although she knew quite well what that picture was, she stepped closer and looked at it for a long time. After the tears had dried that had moistened her eyes, she stepped up to it, took it down from the thin nail that held it, and put it gently in her pocket.

Fall came and then the winter, but Ingrid hardly noticed the change of seasons. Yes, as long as it was still warm, she spent an hour or so every morning in the park, reading a

254

newspaper or a book. She did not, however, venture to the tall chestnut tree. It was as though something was directing her away from that spot, although in her mind she saw the picnic table, the tree, the curving path so clearly as if she were standing just a few steps away from the scene. Even at night, when she closed her eyes, she saw the tree with its gnarled bark and saw the two figures standing there in a tight embrace.

Then, when it got colder, she involved herself more than ever in volunteer work at the school and at charity events. Everywhere she went, she was a welcome guest, and everyone noticed that something was happening with her. There was a serenity about her – a serenity that was obviously grounded in happiness and harmony. She was always kind and helpful and never as high strung and temperamental as some of the other rich women who were active in the social scene – and many of them were not anywhere near as rich as she was.

And then the winter broke. The last snow had melted, and there was something in the air that clearly announced that spring had arrived. Crocuses and daffodils graced the fronts of the elegant mansions and hotels that stood along the exclusive boulevard that ran along the park. Bicycles appeared again and baby carriages, too, pushed by well-dressed maids or the proud mothers themselves. Life had come full circle – everything bloomed and blossomed. Busy workers brought out tables and chairs to set up the ever more popular outdoor cafés that would soon be filled with people who wanted to enjoy the sunshine and the hustle and bustle of outdoor life after having spent so much time indoors.

The sixteenth of April was a magnificent spring day. Ingrid had walked with Karl to school – not that he needed to be walked to school, he was much too old for that – but it was also the way to the café and the park. She had bought a newspaper and a latté to go and at nine-thirty she was seated on her favorite park bench. She looked around. There was perfect stillness all around her except for the chirping of a few birds in nearby trees. She leafed through the newspaper, tried to read a few articles that would normally be of interest to her, but after a while, she gave up. She folded the newspaper and laid it next to her. She closed her eyes and let the sun shine its warmth on her upturned face. She thought about nothing – all her thinking had been done, that was now behind her. Anyone who could have seen her sun-bathed face would know that here sat a woman who had followed and now had found her bliss.

Ingrid stood up, straightened out her skirt and began to walk to the right on the curving asphalt path. She began to walk faster and came to an abrupt stop at the sudden curve in the path that opened up her view to the tree in the distance. She saw the tree – but there was no picnic table, just the tree. She stood frozen. Then, she saw a figure step from the side of the tree into the open light. She threw her hands against her face and gave out a shriek – and then she ran as fast as she could on her elegant high-heeled shoes.

He did not come toward her. As she came closer, she did not see how beautiful the chestnut tree looked with its white blossoms so that the whole tree looked like a magnificently lit chandelier – she only saw him and how he slowly opened his arms wider and wider until she flung herself against his chest and her arms draped around his

256

neck. He wrapped his arms around her waist and twirled her around and around, and when he finally stopped, he kissed her long and passionately. Then, when they stood in a close embrace and the world had stopped spinning around them, she heard the birds singing in the trees. And she knew, yes, she was absolutely sure, that somewhere high up in the branches, there was a nightingale that sang more beautifully, joyfully and happily, than she had ever sung before.

The End

Author

$\mathcal{H}\!elmut$ $\mathcal{S}\!tefan$ is a retired

Chicago public school teacher who loves to read and to

travel. Both of these passions have inspired him to write his stories, which always have an international flair.

In 1998 he was awarded a National Endowment for the Humanities Fellowship to study "Mozart, the Man, his Music and his Vienna". This experience led him to write Trio in D minor, which was

published in 2005.

He and his wife Ingrid and their grown children live in the Chicago area.

Other books by Helmut Stefan: *Trio in D minor* - Helmut Stefan (2005); 3 short stories; ISBN: 0-595-34317-1; Paperback, 6x9, 163 pp, $13.95; iUniverse.

258

www.ingramcontent.com/pod-product-compliance
Lightning Source LLC
Chambersburg PA
CBHW071133260626
47162CB00003B/767